Slough

BOROUGH COUNCIL

...ity Services Department

R..., ARTS & INFORMATION

KT-427-048

Paul Doherty was ...
history at Liverpool ...
obtained a doctorate ... ...esis on
Edward II and Queen Is... ...s now Headmaster
of a school in North-East London.

Acclaim for Sir Roger Shallot's Journals.

'Lively historical whodunnit… Shallot himself is a splendid braggard, a Tudor Flashman' *The Times*

'A rich stew of conspiracy, horror, sexual treachery and dry humour' *The Tablet*

'Set in a fascinating period of English history… Sir Roger Shallot [is] a colourful and likeable rogue… plenty of swashbuckling and intrigue' *Liverpool Daily Post*

'Cleverly twisting tale of murder and mayhem' *Brighton Evening Argos*

'Brother Cadfael had better look to his laurels' *Kent Today*

'Definately another gem from one of the best historical mystery writers around' *CADS*

Slough Borough Council

38 0674 1241 3061

The Gallows Murders

Being the fifth journal of Sir Roger Shallot
concerning certain wicked conspiracies
and horrible murders perpetrated
in the reign of King Henry VIII

Paul Doherty

SLOUGH LIBRARIES
AND INFORMATION

HEADLINE

Copyright © 1995 Paul Doherty

The right of Paul Doherty to be identified as the Author of
the Work has been asserted by him in accordance with the
Copyright, Designs and Patents Act 1988.

First published in Great Britain in 1995
by HEADLINE BOOK PUBLISHING

First published in paperback 1996
by HEADLINE BOOK PUBLISHING

10 9 8 7 6 5 4 3

All rights reserved. No part of this publication may be
reproduced, stored in a retrieval system, or transmitted,
in any form or by any means without the prior written
permission of the publisher, nor be otherwise circulated
in any form of binding or cover other than that in which
it is published and without a similar condition being
imposed on the subsequent purchaser.

All characters in this publication are fictitious
and any resemblance to real persons, living or dead,
is purely coincidental.

ISBN 0 7472 4928 8

Printed and bound in Great Britain by
Mackays of Chatham PLC, Chatham, Kent

HEADLINE BOOK PUBLISHING
A division of Hodder Headline PLC
338 Euston Road
London NW1 3BH

www.headline.co.uk
www.hodderheadline.co.uk

To the memory of Bridge and Billy Clynes,
my grandparents.

Some Historical Personages Mentioned In This Text

EDWARD IV: Yorkist King of England (1471–1483).

ELIZABETH WOODVILLE: his Queen.

EDWARD and RICHARD: Children of the above (the Princes in the Tower).

RICHARD OF GLOUCESTER (later RICHARD III): Edward IV's brother. He usurped the throne in 1483 from his nephews.

ROBERT BRACKENBURY: constable of the Tower under Richard III.

SIR JAMES TYRRELL: one of Richard III's henchmen.

DIGHTON and GREENE: two shadowy characters, charged with the responsibility of the young Princes.

HENRY VIII, King of England, the 'Great Beast'.

CARDINAL THOMAS WOLSEY: Archbishop and Chancellor; Henry's minister.

SIR THOMAS MORE: lawyer, humanist, Chancellor under Henry VIII, author of a book on the reign of Richard III.

SIR FRANCIS LOVELL: henchman of Richard III.

Prologue

Black-hearted, red-eyed murder! Like the mist which hangs above the marshes of Burpham Manor then spreads its tendrils out around the oak, sycamore and ash which fringe the far side of the lawn, so murder seeps up from my past. It plagues my sleep and jolts the enjoyment of my waking days. I lie in bed at night (between the lovely Phoebe and Margot) and stare up at the ceiling. Always the past! It's ever around me!

Two weeks ago, just before midsummer, the great Elizabeth came to Burpham as my guest. She sat and giggled in my private chamber. In that room there are no gaps between wainscoting and wall. No peepholes, no squints for any spy or eavesdropper like my little chaplain. Yes, that horrid little man, that viper vile, my sweet little tittle-brain is not above listening at keyholes. Oh, the little, noddle-pated fool, that greasy tallow-catch should be more careful of our Queen. Elizabeth once threw her slipper at old Walsingham, her master spy, and scarred him for life. On another occasion she wrote such a fierce letter to the Earl of Essex that he fainted, his body becoming so swollen that all the buttons on his doublet popped off as if cut away by a dagger.

Anyway, on this latest occasion, Elizabeth and I sat in my damask-draped chamber eating comfits and drinking sweet wine. The Queen looked magnificent, even though she's well past her sixty-fifth year. Her nose is a little

1

more hooked, her teeth all black, her hair is false and she still insists on wearing very high-heeled shoes to make her appear more majestic. Not that she needs it. Her face is oblong and fair and those small eyes, dark pools of nothingness, still arouse in me a pleasant smile. We giggled as we talked, remembering this and recalling that. Abruptly Elizabeth put her glass down, the smile fading from her face. Only a small smile! You see her face is covered by so much white paint it cracks if her lips gape too widely.

'Before I leave, Roger,' she'd declared on a previous visit, 'I'll need your fairest mirror and, for every crack I see in my face-paint, I'll fine you ten pounds sterling. In gold!' she added, rolling her tongue round her carmine-painted lips.

Of course I paid. That's one thing about Elizabeth, never mind about 'fair heart in a woman's breast'. She's as hard as flint when it comes to money! Mind you, a great girl! Lovely lass! My Queen, my lord, my monarch, my mistress, and mother of our dear bastard son. God knows where that rogue is! Last time I heard he was in Spain trying to sell that noddle-pate, the Spanish King, a map of Eldorado, the silver city of the Aztecs.

Ah well, back to the story. On her last visit, Elizabeth looked in the mirror counting the cracks. She stared at me standing behind her.

'You owe me more this time, Roger!' she exclaimed. 'However, promise to bring me the other mirror and I'll cancel the debt.'

I just shook my head. 'Madam, I do not know what you mean.'

Elizabeth turned, those eyes, black pebbles in her white, snowy face. She seized my wrist and pinched the skin most cruelly. 'You know what I mean, Roger!' she hissed.

I'd just smile back and shake my head. She may well be my mistress, the daughter of Anne Boleyn, the greatest Queen in all the world, but I will not show her that mirror! That's kept in my secret storeroom in a coffer secured by seven locks. A terrible mirror! The one Catherine de'Medici used in her Chamber of the Black Arts at Blois. Nostradamus gave it to her. You know, the man who could prophesy the future and see terrible, burning things falling from the sky. Once in Blois, pursued by an insane assassin, I fled to that chamber. I killed the assassin and stole the mirror. I saw the real power of that mirror. I shall not tell you what I glimpsed there. Those sinister secrets which swam out of a black mist, dreadful scenes from the future!

I dashed the candle to the ground and drove the warlock from my manor, screaming that if I saw him again I'd hang him from the highest branch. I never showed Elizabeth that mirror, but somehow she knew I had it. Anyway, I digress . . . On that day Elizabeth just smiled and turned in her chair. I could tell from her eyes she'd leave the magic mirror to another day.

'If not the future, Roger,' she whispered, 'do you remember the past? What you once told me about the Tower? Well, I have been there again!'

At the time I just looked askance. I did not know what she meant but, when she left and I lay on my great four-poster bed, I suddenly remembered. Now listen, I am well past my ninety-third year. I have lived a life full of mischief. I have met murder in the silken boudoirs of courtesans, the sewers of Rome, the perfume-filled gardens of Istanbul. I have been pursued through icy forests and fought for my life in the ruins of burning cities; but I never forgot the Tower! That narrow, bloody palace of secrets with its stone-walled chambers, secret passageways and hidden rooms! The execution ground of the Great Beast, the mouldwarp, that imp of Satan, His most diabolical Majesty, King Henry VIII of England!

Oh yes, I remember the Tower and how, so many years

3

ago, in the summer of 1523, I and my master Benjamin Daunbey, gentle, dark-haired, serene-faced Benjamin, nephew to the great Cardinal Wolsey, probed its secrets. Oh, that dreadful hot summer when the sweating sickness raged in London and the most cunning of murderers was on the loose! Now I sit here, at the centre of my maze, squeezing the tits of Margot and Phoebe, sipping the finest claret as I prepare to dictate my memoirs. My chaplain is impatient to begin. He always hates these diversions. Oh yes he does, the little tickle-bum! I also know he is sitting there trying to pluck up enough courage to ask me permission to name his marriage day. Oh, I have met his betrothed: face like an angel she has. Eyes as round as saucers, they suit her nature! I wager she has been in more laps than a napkin. Or, to misquote the good book, 'She has been tried and found wanton'. No, no, I tease him. I have seen him walking her through the trees.

'Why do you do that?' I asked. 'Is she a flower which grows wild in the woods?'

'You can never tell about a woman,' my chaplain quips back.

'In her case,' I retort, 'it's charitable not to.'

Oh, I tease. I am sure she's a delightful maid and I have fixed the marriage date for Michaelmas. See how excited he grows! His little bottom twitching! His shoulders shaking! The little bugger had better not be laughing at me. He stares innocently over his shoulder but I know him for what he is. Any man who has two chins must have two faces! No, no, I am cruel to my little chaplain. If he left me, I'd miss him, particularly his sermons on Sunday.

Now, I'll be honest, I don't belong to the Reformed Faith. I am still a Catholic and hear Mass secretly in my private chamber. There I hide the statue that I rescued from Walsingham, carved in ancient wood, the Mother of God holding her child. I make sure candles

4

burn constantly before it. Anyway, as the law says, I have to attend Sunday morning service in the manor church, so I trot along. I sit in my pew in front of the pulpit and spend most of my time smiling at any pretty face. I'm always armed with a catapult and try to take care of the rats which, every so often, try to scurry across the sanctuary floor. You see, the little bastards live in the church, feasting on the candlewax. Now my theory is that usually they hide, but my chaplain is such a windbag and his sermons so long that the rats give up all hope that he'll ever shut up, and so take their chances out in the open against my catapult. As soon as one pops out, a small black pebble goes whirling through the air. The congregation love it. My chaplain never notices.

Indeed, I have tried everything. Once I fired my pistol and the silly bugger still droned on, so I tried a different ruse. Now, some of these prating parsons begin their sermons with a text or a sermon: my chaplain's no different. I thought I should indulge in a little audience participation. You know, the same sort of thing we do at the Globe, when Will Shakespeare's Macbeth appears, the lean-faced villain. I love going to see him and take all the rotten fruit I can, then, with the rest of the audience, throw it at the murderous rogue. Marvellous occasions! Last time I did it, Macbeth picked up the fruit and threw it back! Journeying home afterwards, I had a sweet thought: my chaplain's sermons are no shorter than any of Will Shakespeare's plays, so why shouldn't the audience be allowed to join in?

The next Sunday, up he gets, straight as a pole in the pulpit. 'Why?' he began lugubriously, 'do people call me a Christian?'

'Because they know sweet bugger-all about you!' I shouted back.

It made little difference, so I sat in my pew, arms crossed, glaring at him. An hour must have passed. I slept for a while, drank a little of the wine I always take with me, and suddenly saw a fresh opportunity.

'Dear Brethren,' my chaplain intoned, 'I ask you solemnly: reflect on the Gospels and ask yourselves, would you be in the light with five wise virgins, or in the dark with five foolish virgins?'

'Ask a daft question,' I bawled back, 'and you'll get a daft answer!'

The congregation collapsed in laughter. Oh, my lovely, lovely chaplain. I hope he knows what he is doing by getting married. I once asked for forgiveness from one of my wives as she lay dying. I murmured, 'You must have thought many a time, of asking for a divorce?'

The sweet woman turned to me and smiled. She weakly grasped my hand and whispered something to herself.

'What's that?' I asked.

She turned her face towards me. 'Roger, in all the time I have been married to you, divorce has never crossed my mind. Murder has, but never divorce.'

Ah well, the poor woman died. A happy relief. She was always ill with this complaint or that. You can see her tombstone in the church: her name, her age, her virtue. Underneath, I wrote her epitaph: 'I told you I was ill.'

My chaplain is now glaring at me, though I can see the laughter bubbling within him. He knows I lie. I loved all my wives more dearly than life itself. Old Roger can only deal with tragedy by turning it into a joke; that's how I survive, that's how I sleep when all those ghosts swarm round my bed. Henry, the Great Beast, glaring at me with his red, mad, piggy eyes. Beside him Wolsey with his olive, Italianate face. The men I have killed; the murderers I have trapped. I always close my eyes and summon up a face that's never there: long and dark, gentle-eyed and merry-mouthed, my eternal friend, Benjamin Daunbey. So, I go back, searching for his soul down the long, dusty corridors of the years when Henry

6

the Great Beast terrorised England and Wolsey ruled both Church and State. When London was all a-bubble with sickness, and murder, in all its horror, made its bloody hand felt.

Chapter 1

The year of 1523 was sharp and cruel. A violent, snarling time when princes dreamed of war; all of Europe teetered on the brink of a great precipice, ready to tear itself apart over divisions in religion. In Denmark, Christian II had been deposed for cruelty. In Switzerland, Zwingli attacked the Pope and called him the Antichrist, whilst in Brussels, two of Martin Luther's adherents were burnt alive in roaring flames. Across the Narrow Seas, Francis II dreamed of being another Charlemagne, whilst long-jawed Charles V, the Hapsburg Emperor, planned on finding rivers of gold in the distant Americas.

In England, however, little had changed . . . thus far. Henry VIII, the fat bastard, the mouldwarp of Merlin's prophecies, still clung to sanity. So far he had not shown, except to me, that cruel streak of venomous temper which would drench his kingdom in rivers of blood: that was still a few years off. Henry was more concerned about his pleasures. He wanted to be a great wrestler, the keenest of archers, the best dancer, the most ferocious jouster. Henry believed he was a fairy-tale prince, and those who danced with him little suspected that the nightmare would soon begin. By 1523, the worms were eating their way into the marrow of his soul. Henry's wife – plump, sallow-faced Catherine of Aragon – had not produced a living male heir, and the gossips were beginning to titter and chatter behind their hands. Some said Henry's seed was rotten (they were probably right). Others uttered darker words, that Henry was a Tudor: his father might have been a Welsh prince but his grandfather was a Welsh farmer, so what right did he have to the Crown and Empire of England? Henry heard them and, worst of all, Henry was growing old. I suppose Bacon was right when he wrote, 'Golden boys and golden girls must, in their turn, turn to dust.' Henry's body was beginning to betray him. An open ulcer on his leg, a belly like a beer-barrel. Phlegm stuck in his throat and nose, so thick and hard it turned him deaf. Henry himself was growing concerned. Oh, he had a daughter, pale-faced Spanish Mary, as well as the bastard offspring of golden-haired Bessie Blount. Nevertheless, in his bed at night (or so the Beast later told me), Henry began to wonder if God had turned his hand against him.

Nobody in the palaces of Whitehall, Windsor, Hampton Court or Sheen could guess what was coming. It was like one of those masques, so beloved of Will Shakespeare nowadays, when all the players gather on the stage. (Like his most recent one, *Othello*, about the blackamoor general hired by Venice.) Everything is colour and light. Beautiful people sweeping backwards and forwards, glorious speeches about fame, honour, glory and love. Nonetheless, the audience holds its breath and waits for black-hearted Iago to slip amongst them and bring it all crashing down with rape and horrible murder.

Henry's Iago had yet to appear: Anne Boleyn, more bewitching than beautiful; petite Anne with her long dark hair and fiery eyes. Trained at the court of France, a consummate lover, she would ensnare Henry's heart. Of course, poor Anne did not survive long. One daughter (the great Elizabeth), three miscarriages, and one stillborn son and she was finished. They accused her of having three teats (and she did have). Men cursed Anne

10

but I found her dark, fiery eyes irresistible. Do you know, when Anne was executed she refused to be blindfolded? The executioner found her eyes so disarming that he got someone to distract her whilst he took off his shoes and stole up behind her to cut off her head. I was there. He did a good job! Anne asked me to be present to make sure he did. She had hired an executioner specially from Calais and, on her last night in the Tower, asked me one favour.

'Roger, make sure the sword is sharp!'

Oh yes, the Tower. I will come to that by and by, and the horrid scenes enacted there, long before Anne Boleyn took her final morning walk to the execution block.

Now, as I said, old Tom Wolsey, Cardinal Archbishop and Chancellor of England, ruled the kingdom. Everything in the garden was still rosy. Henry played Robin Hood, or King Arthur of the Round Table, whilst the real power lay in Wolsey's hands. The Cardinal's cronies whispered how Wolsey controlled the King through a witch Mathilda Brigge: they claimed Wolsey had hired her and, in return for gold, Brigge fasted from all food and drink for three days a week and summoned up demons to do her will.

Now there was little in life Wolsey really loved, except for his beloved nephew Benjamin Daunbey. However, in the summer of 1523, the Cardinal left us alone to enjoy our golden youth in the manor he had given us at Ipswich. Our youth might have been golden; we were not. Benjamin was tall, rather swarthy, a good-looking young man with a wise face and the heart of a lamb. And old Shallot? Well, I suppose I was comely enough: black, tousled hair, sunburnt skin, generous-mouthed (or so the ladies told me). Oh and a slight squint in one eye. You have probably seen my portrait. I am quite proud of it. I've heard others whisper they've seen better faces in the death-cart going to Tyburn. But who gives a toss about them? They have all gone and I am now

Sir Roger Shallot, Lord of Burpham Manor, Knight of the Garter, Knight of the Bath, Lord of the Golden Fleece, etc, etc.

Well, nonny no, back in the summer of 1523, we had just returned from Florence, where Benjamin and I had trapped the cruellest of murderers. Richly rewarded by the Cardinal, we had gone home to Ipswich. Benjamin once more became involved in his good works, particularly his school at our manor for those little imps of hell from the village. Now Benjamin, God bless his kind heart, tried to persuade me to participate in this.

'Roger, you have a gift for words,' he declared. 'A sense of the dramatic. The children love you, you make them laugh.'

I wouldn't be flattered. 'They laugh at me, Master,' I replied. 'And a teacher should be serious. After five minutes with their horn books, I'd have them out in the fields and meadows.'

'Yes, yes.' Benjamin glanced away.

He was tactful enough not to refer to the time I'd taken the children out to re-enact the fall of Troy. Well, how was I to know that, when I told them how the Greek soldiers massacred the men and raped the women of Troy, poltroon Simpkins Threebottle would take my words literally and launch himself upon poor Maude Rossingham!

'I don't want to be a teacher,' I answered defiantly.

'Well, you should,' Benjamin replied, but chose not to pursue the matter any further.

So I was left to my own devices, wandering hither and thither pursuing one wench after another. My wits grew idle and, of course, I turned to mischief. Now, as you know from my former journals, I have always cursed doctors. I don't call them liars. I only wish I had their money. Have you noticed how everyone is deeply interested in their own health? My last wife was a good example. She called in a physician, when all she really wanted was an audience. My dear little chaplain not only complains of diseases for which there are no cures, but of some for which there are no names. At the same time, you can't heap all the blame on physicians. They come with their zodiac charts and urine bottles, boxes of pills and powders. They scratch their heads and know they won't be able to leave, or charge their patients, until they have pronounced sentence and produced a cure. Anything, be it the balls of boiled dogs or the juice of the acorn. So you can appreciate my deep interest in medicine. Why should I be a teacher? (What I didn't tell Benjamin is that I never forgot the ruffian who taught me when I was a boy. On a winter morning, the bastard would whip us for no other reason but to warm himself up. On another occasion he would beat us for swearing and, as he did so, swore the most horrible oaths.)

Benjamin however, knew of my interest in physic and tried to advise me. 'Remember Vicar Doggerell? You gave him a cow-pat to cure his baldness.'

'Yes, but I didn't tell the silly bastard to smear it on his head on Sunday morning and stink the church out,' I retorted.

Benjamin smiled and shook his head.

My ambition to make a fortune in the world of medicine received further encouragement when I received a letter from my old friend Dr Quicksilver: a true charlatan who pretended to be the greatest physician on earth but who lived his life in the slums around Whitefriars. He wanted more elixirs, and who was I to refuse him? So I went back to my games. Oh no, nothing dangerous: the mixing of thyme, camomile and hyssop as an aid to rheumatism. (It actually worked!) Or the skull of a hare and the grease of a fox, crushed and warmed, to be rubbed in the ear to cure deafness. I loved distilling these concoctions. One day Benjamin called me into his private chamber. He sat behind his desk which was piled high with horn books.

13

'Roger, my dear friend.'

'Yes, Master?' I asked innocently.

'If you must involve yourself in physic . . .' Benjamin hitched his furred gown further up his shoulders. The lattice window was open and the morning breeze rather chilling. '. . . If you must have your physic then, I beseech you, do not work in your chamber and make the house stink like a stableyard. I shall provide a special room for your experiments.'

Well, I took to it like a duck to water and, for the next few weeks, locked myself in a secret room high in the manor house, shrouding myself in a cloud of strange smells. I filled jars with the dried corpses of frogs and newts. I even managed to buy the skin of a donkey and concocted a sneezing powder to clear the head. I sent some to Quicksilver. Then, heigh nonny no, I packed all my medicines on a sumpter pony and trotted off to Ipswich market. I put the donkey in a stable and became a huckster. I bought a tray and created my own stall. Of course, I had to move, and did so briskly, when officials of the pie-and-powder court, those tyrants who man the tribunal which governs market affairs, came looking for me. Oh, but I enjoyed it: the shouting, the bargaining, the bartering, the recitation of the most incredible stories whilst keeping my face straight. No, I wasn't a trickster but a trader. None of my potions were dangerous, indeed many of them were quite helpful. No bailiff ever came looking for me with a warrant in his hand. However, as they teach in geometry, like is attracted to like, and I was soon on first-name terms with every rogue in Suffolk.

Once the day's business was done, I'd head straight for some boozing den, my bun full of money, rubbing shoulders with the priggers, the prancers, the dummerers, the riflers and rufflers, the foists, the naps, the morts, strumpets and whores. All lovely people! Most of them would have sold their mother's knuckle-bones

14

for dice. They lived on a knife-edge, fearful of the chatts, their slang term for the gallows, yet ever ready for a free peck or meal, their fingers itching to cut a purse or rob a shop. I laughed, drank and gambled with the best of them. They conned me, I conned them. One little foist, who cheated me at cards, I treated free, giving him live spiders to eat, covered in butter to help his cough. Another who boasted about ill-treating a poor widow, was told to mix blood from a black cat's tail with cream from a slaughtered cow and drink it to cure the pox. (The stupid bugger did, but still scratched his private parts.) To honest folk I tried to be honest. The taverner who gave me a free drink was told that, to gather the fleas of a chamber into one place, he should put a staff on the floor covered with the grease of a fox or hedgehog, and all the fleas would gather on it. And, if that didn't work, to fill a dish with goat's blood, put it by the bed, and every flea in the tavern would drink and drown itself there. (By the way, this worked, you should try it!)

When the day's work and enjoyment were done, I travelled back to the manor and supped with Benjamin in our dark oak-panelled hall, decorated with banners and tapestries, and with large wooden shields bearing the devices of Daunbey and Shallot which had been devised and painted by me. Of course, I'd always return a little fearful. After all, here we were enjoying the idylls of life, but London was not very far away and Wolsey never forgot us. When the Cardinal turned and snapped his fingers for us to come running, he'd always send that strange creature – black-garbed, sinister Dr Agrippa – to collect us.

I have mentioned Agrippa before. He was Wolsey's familiar. A magus, a warlock, a man who never grew old or died. No, no, my wits aren't wandering. Agrippa, with his cherubic face and soulless eyes, lived and lurked in the shadow of Wolsey; yet I have met those who will swear on oath that Agrippa was with Richard III at

15

Bosworth Field. According to these old men, Agrippa advised that cruel prince to make the dreadful charge which ensnared him in a marsh, and so Richard lost his life, his crown and the kingdom. And there are others, even as I am now past my ninetieth year, who have made their way to Burpham Manor to tell me how they met Agrippa in the dark green woods of Virginia outside Jamestown, in the sun-scorched streets of Constantinople, or even in the snowy, icy wastes outside Moscow. They always tell the same tale: dressed in black, Agrippa hadn't grown a day older than when I knew him in those blood-drenched days of Henry VIII.

Agrippa would come, but on those evenings when I found the stables empty and my master waiting alone for me in the hall, I'd heave a sigh of relief. Tonight, at least, I'd sleep the sleep of the just. We would sup and I would listen to Benjamin chatter about his school, though keeping one eye on a young, buxom chambermaid who, when she served my meal, dipped her generous bosom to show both her glories.

Oh, I confess, our life at our manor was a veritable Eden, but every paradise has its serpent. Eventually ours appeared in the shape of a plump, well-fed matron, Isabella Poppleton. Goodwoman Poppleton and her sneering sons lived on the other side of the valley and deeply resented my master's good fortune. The sons were bloated bags of wind, but Isabella was a veritable viper in petticoats. If she had bitten an adder it would have died of poisoning. She had a tongue which would clip a hedge and could shovel dirt faster than a gravedigger. Her tongue was a sharpened sword and she made sure it never went rusty. I called her, the 'Great Mouth'.

Trouble first appeared one Sunday morning as Benjamin and I left Mass. We were out of the porch, walking towards the lychgate, when I saw Goodwoman Poppleton standing amongst the gravestones with a gaggle of gossips who hung on her every word. As we passed they fell silent, but Isabella's eyes, bleak and

16

hateful, bored into my master. I quietly made an obscene gesture with my middle finger. However, the bitch hadn't been to Italy, so she didn't know what it meant, though she must have understood the spirit in which it was intended. Now such hate worried me. I tried to talk to my master. He just shook his head and refused to listen, so I wandered down to the White Hart tavern in the village where, after Mass, all the gossips gathered to tear their neighbours to pieces. When I entered the taproom, a group of young bloods sitting in the corner looked up, sniggering behind their hands. I recognised one of them as Edmund Poppleton, the elder of the Great Mouth's sons.

'What's the joke?' I asked.

The landlord, a goodly man who served me a tankard of ale and a beef stew pie, glanced sadly at me and shook his head. The gigglers returned to their whispering, so I drank my ale, broke my fast and returned to the manor.

The next morning, Benjamin came into my chamber where I was concocting a new remedy to cure catarrh: powdered goose bones mixed with garlic and salt. It was making me cough and sneeze so I judged it to be a good cure of the rheums. Benjamin sat down on a stool on the other side of the table. I babbled away about what I was doing. He remained silent but, when I looked up, his eyes were sad, pricked with tears.

'What's the matter, Master?'

'This morning young Tom the miller's son told me about the rumours going around the village,' he replied. He swallowed hard. 'That I only started the school because I like young boys.'

I dropped the knife I was holding.

'You, Master, an apple-squire? A bum-boy? And did Tom believe it?'

Benjamin shook his head. 'He was very angry. He claimed the Poppletons were behind such dreadful rumours.'

I cursed the Great Mouth with every filthy word I

17

could muster. Benjamin shook his head and got up but, even as he left, I glimpsed the tears trickling down his face. The first time I had ever seen him cry! I'd often accompanied him along the Thames to Syon where Johanna, his betrothed, who had lost her wits after being evilly seduced by a nobleman, was cared for by the good nuns. Never once did I see him weep. Now he sobbed; I felt like killing the Poppletons.

Later the same day, I sought my master out to reassure him, but he smiled wanly and I went cold with rage. Now I am not an evil man, nor vindictive: my chaplain will tell you that. Even when he steals my claret I only tell him off and shake my cane. I've never really beaten him. At least, not yet! Ah well, 'Vengeance is mine; I will repay, saith the Lord.' Yet, it's also written, 'The gods help them that help themselves.' And since revenge is a dish best served cold, so I bided my time and plotted, even as the rumours grew as thick and fast as weeds in a dunghill.

At last, I, Roger Shallot, made my power felt. I won't bore you with the details. First I disguised myself and secured entry to the Poppleton household as a labourer. Now people like the Poppletons never even deign to look at a servant. I was employed to clean the cesspits and latrines, which gave me every right to wander down the galleries and passageways of the house. In their large dining room, or hall as the Great Mouth liked to call it, the Poppletons had a tun of wine: a small cask with a bung in it which the steward would remove whenever the Great Mouth and her family dined. Now, that's one thing servants will not steal. Everything else they can lay their hands on, but never the master's wine, at least not from a barrel which has been broached. So, one fine morning when everyone was elsewhere, I tipped the cask on its side and removed the bung. I then poured a specially prepared powder containing the most powerful of purgatives and a few secret ingredients of my own. I replaced the bung, dropped the bucket of shit I was carrying, and fled like the wind.

The next day I travelled to Castle Acre and called at the Willow, a dingy tavern where my good friend Dr Quicksilver, whom I had summoned from London, had taken chambers. Now Quicksilver was villainy incarnate. A consummate actor, a born liar, a cunning man who knew every trick of the fair. Thin as a beanpole, with long, straggling grey hair, Quicksilver had the face of an ascetic and a skill even the great physicians of Salerno would have envied. His eyes were innocent, the soft skin of his face freshly shaven, and his lips always twisted into a most benevolent smile. You know the sort, often seen on the faces of vicars and chaplains, especially when they're giving unctuous advice to one of their underlings. Quicksilver also dressed the part. He wore a jacket with a round neck, edged with precious fur, the sleeves gathered at the shoulders into thick pads which made him look broader. Underneath was a waist-length doublet, tight and padded; on his spindly legs were hose of the same colour. On his head he wore a broad-brimmed hat which further increased his air of respectability and grandeur. One thing I noticed: his hands and wrists were always hidden under ornate cuffs.

He met me in the Willow taproom.

'Roger, my dearest, dearest, dearest boy.'

Quicksilver grasped my hand and shook it warmly. I smiled and told the bastard to give me the ring he had just taken off my finger. The charlatan smiled and passed it back.

'And keep your hands well away from my purse,' I growled. 'And none of your games, Quicksilver. Don't start running up bills to send for me to pay.' I placed two gold coins before him. 'These are for now, and three more when you've finished.'

The coins disappeared in a blink of an eye: hence the fellow's name.

19

He sat down, hailing the landlord, and grandly ordered the best the house could offer. Although thin and scrawny, and at least sixty years of age, Quicksilver ate like a horse and all the time asked me questions. Why had I summoned him? Did I have new medicines? What was he to do?

I told him all about the Great Mouth and the Poppletons. Quicksilver listened intently, then sat back, rocking with laughter. 'Lord above, Shallot, they'll spend all their time on the jakes. And you put aniseed powder in as well? Their skins will be peppered with pustules.'

'How do you know that?' I retorted. 'You are a quack.'

Quicksilver's face suddenly went stern. For a brief moment I saw another man behind those eyes. Do you know, I suddenly realised I knew nothing about Quicksilver: who he really was or where he came from.

'Roger, Roger.' He waggled a finger at me. 'I have never insulted you. I am not what I appear to be.'

'Most men aren't,' I quipped. I glimpsed the anger in his eyes. 'I am sorry,' I apologised, and gave him my most winning smile. 'I truly am and, when you have finished, most learned of physicians, there will be four, not three coins.'

I must have stirred memories in Quicksilver's soul: he leaned forward and hissed, 'I have heard of you, Shallot, and your doings at court for the great Wolsey.' He gave an icy smile. 'I, too, once worked in the shadows of the great ones: summoned at the dead of night to the Tower; taken to secret rooms to sit by the beds of princes to hear their confessions.' He drew back, as if he had said too much. 'But,' he shrugged, 'that's in the past.'

I never questioned him further. If you live in the shadowy world, as I do, you never ask questions. Take poor Kit Marlowe, killed over a meal. Kit, with his angelic face, mocking mouth and merry eyes. He'd never tell you who he really was. He's twenty years in his grave and already the debate has begun. Was Marlowe a spy? An assassin? Was he an atheist, a Lutheran or a Papist? God knows. The same is true of Will Shakespeare: he's dabbled in enough secrets to provide matter for a thousand plays.

Old Quicksilver's manner had now changed. Eager for mischief, he waited for my orders. After I whispered to him the plot, he crowed with laughter, clapped his hands and solemnly promised that, by tomorrow, he'd be taking chambers at the White Hart.

The next day, just before sunset, I walked into our village tavern. I looked around but there was no sign of Quicksilver. I cursed and hoped the thieving bugger hadn't taken my gold and hopped back to London as fast as he could. I sat by the inglenook with my pot of ale, then in comes the Great Mouth's steward, eyes round as saucers, hands all a-tremble. He grasped his tankard, digs his face into it, and then declares for all to here:

'Good sirs, pray for Mistress Poppleton and her family.' His voice sank to one of those dramatic whispers so beloved of playwrights like Jonson. 'All the farting,' he exclaimed. 'Running like greyhounds for the jakes, their skins covered in pustules and blisters.'

'The plague?' one yokel asked. 'They say there's a terrible sickness in London!'

The steward, an inveterate gossip who deeply relished his moment of glory, just shook his head.

(Oh, my little chaplain's asked a question: why wasn't I recognised? The noddle-pate! When I worked for the Poppletons, I'd been disguised.)

'No one else has caught it,' the steward trumpeted, 'Lord save us. The house stinks like a kennel.'

'You say pimples and pustules?' A voice rang out from the doorway leading to the stairs. Quicksilver stood there in his best fur-trimmed robe, a pair of spectacles upon his nose. His hand tapped the seal (counterfeit, of course), which proclaimed him to be a member of the Guild of Physicians in London. 'Pimples and pustules?'

he repeated, sweeping into the taproom. 'And bowels just like water?'

'Yes, sir,' the steward replied, tugging at his forelock and glancing at the landlord.

'This is Dr Mirabilis,' the landlord declared in a hushed voice. 'A physician of London, patronised by the great Cardinal himself. On his way to see relatives in Norwich.'

Oh Lord. I fought to keep my face straight and stuck my face into my tankard. Quicksilver, of course, acted the part, and old Marlowe would have given his left hand to have seen it. The tavern's best chair was pushed up, and he sat down on it like a king on his throne, looking severely over his spectacles at the steward.

'Pimples and loose bowels,' he repeated.

'Yes, my lord.'

Quicksilver pulled a face and clicked his fingers. 'An undoubted case of Rotterus Arsicus,' he declared grandly.

'Is it contagious?' the steward asked.

'Don't be stupid!' Quicksilver replied. 'But it's a savage ailment. I have treated it before in Montpellier and Salerno.'

'Is it fatal?' the landlord asked hopefully.

'How long have the victims been suffering?' Quicksilver demanded gravely.

'About three days. Yes, my lord, this is the third day.'

'It takes a week,' Quicksilver declared pompously, 'before the real rottenness sets in and death ensues.'

The steward nearly dropped his tankard, and had to be helped to a stool. I don't think he was really bothered about the Poppletons, but the prospect of losing his sinecure made him weak at the knees.

'Oh, good sir,' he gasped, mopping his brow, 'can you help?'

'Of course!'

'And how much will it cost?' The steward screwed his face up into what he thought was a shrewd look.

'Cost! Cost! You dare to talk to me about cost? Me, Dr Mirabilis!'

Quicksilver half rose out of his chair, but the steward threw himself on his knees. 'My lord, come with me, please!' he begged.

The good physician finally agreed and, without even a glance at me, stepped out of the tavern, the steward trotting ahead of him. I waited till they had gone, then fled the place to laugh myself witless in a ditch. Well, the bait was down, the lure was out. Later that night I stole back and met Quicksilver under the moonlight by the gibbet near the crossroads. The rogue was laughing fit to burst.

'There's no wine left in that cask,' he declared. 'Even when they were sick they insisted on drinking it. To fortify,' he gravely mimicked the Great Mouth's tone, 'our poor bodies.'

'And you recommended?'

Quicksilver shrugged. 'I followed your instructions. I gave them no medicine, but told them not to eat or drink anything except sugared water, and that I would return tomorrow evening.'

'And?' I asked hopefully.

'Then I'll strike. I'll continue the medication but develop the seeds I sowed today. How Rotterus Arsicus is really a mysterious disease, more the product of the humours of the mind than anything else. They must have done great ill, maligned someone: this has infected the soul, turned the humours morbid, which expresses itself in horrid pustules and looseness of the bowels.' Quicksilver smiled and arranged his cloak, easing the cramp from his limbs as he sat on a stile.

'The gulls will bite,' he said softly. 'I'll be well paid. You'll have your revenge and its heigh ho back to London.' He pointed to the skeleton which swung in its iron gibbet from the scaffold. 'Do you think we'll end up like that, Roger? A pile of musty bones? The plaything of some evening breeze at a lonely crossroads?'

I stared at the scaffold, bathed in the light of a summer moon, and a shiver ran down my spine. It wasn't usual for Quicksilver to be so melancholic. I jumped down from the fence and clapped my companion on the shoulder.

'He wasn't a rogue,' I declared. 'Don't you know your anatomy, Dr Mirabilis? That poor fellow suffered from Rotterus Arsicus and, in a fit of rage, went out and killed someone.'

Quicksilver burst out laughing. I shook his hand and told him that, if all went well, I'd deliver the rest of the coins, and set off back to the manor.

In the end, all did go well. Every night I went back to the White Hart, where Quicksilver loudly reported how the Poppletons were progressing. The steward sat beside him, nodding solemnly, opening his mouth in one glorious hymn of praise for old Quicksilver's skills. So the trap was closed. On Saturday night I could tell from the charlatan's face that all was going as planned: he designed to notice me in the inglenook corner, brought me a cup of claret and raised his own in a toast, his eyes full of devilment.

The next morning, my master and I went down to church for morning Mass. Benjamin was still subdued. Indeed, I had hardly seen him or talked to him. I could tell the insults had rankled deep.

Accordingly, you can imagine my glow of triumph when Vicar Doggerell stood on the altar steps, hands extended, his fat, foolish face wreathed in smiles. He beamed at the Poppletons, now returned to rude health, sitting in one pew, and then at my master.

'This week,' the old fool declared, 'the parish has seen a great victory. One of our noblest families snatched from the jaws of death.'

He turned and, clasping his hands, bowed towards where Quicksilver sat beside a pillar. Good Lord, the rogue looked so saintly, for a few seconds he even deceived me.

Vicar Doggerell continued. 'Now this miracle is not only the result of a physician's skill, but also of a deep-thinking woman realising she may have offended, albeit unknowingly, against a fellow Christian. Mistress Poppleton now wishes to make amends.'

Well, up gets the Great Mouth in her dark brown dress and a ridiculous flurry of veils framing her fat, sullen face. She stood at the mouth of the roodscreen looking as if butter wouldn't melt in that horrible mouth.

'Dear Brothers and Sisters in Christ,' she intoned. 'There is a dreadful rumour running like a sore through this parish that this good man –' she pointed at Benjamin – 'this county's most excellent teacher, is the subject of unnatural lusts.' Her voice rose. 'I, Goodwoman Poppleton, declare such rumours to be an arrant lie. Master Daunbey is the jewel of our parish! A benefactor of the poor! His school's one of the great glories of the shire, to which purpose,' she plucked from the sleeve of her voluminous gown a heavy purse, 'I now donate this silver for the education of poor scholars.'

Well, everyone began to clap. Benjamin smiled: his body, taut as a spring, relaxed. He rose from the bench, strode towards Goodwoman Poppleton and there, in full view of all, exchanged the kiss of peace with her. (I jumped up and grabbed the silver.) Mass was then celebrated in a joyous fashion.

Afterwards, everyone gathered round Benjamin, slapping his back and saying what a fine fellow he was. I then made a terrible mistake. Old Quicksilver was for the off. He had carried out his task and, grinning and winking, sidled up to me, hand half-extended. In any other circumstances I would have cursed the idiot roundly, but Benjamin looked so happy that I slipped Quicksilver the purse of coins and turned away. As I did so, I saw the Great Mouth's elder son was glaring

25

daggers at me. Ah well, in for a penny in for a pound is old Shallot. I smiled beatifically back as Quicksilver ran like a hare towards the lych-gate and the safety of London Town. Nonetheless, on reflection, the incident not only saved my life but that of Benjamin. It also helped us thread our way through a bloody maze of murder to unlock one of England's darkest secrets.

Chapter 2

Within days the axe had fallen. Benjamin summoned me to his chamber. He was sitting like a hanging judge just before sentence is passed.

'Sit down, Roger.'

I did so.

'Roger, what you did was brave and good.' Benjamin smiled across the desk at me.

Well, you know old Shallot. I just stared owlishly back at his eyebrows. It's an old trick – if you do that, people think you're being manly and holding their gaze, open and honest. Actually, some of the biggest rogues I have ever met could stare you in the eye and let the lies trip from their tongue. Oh yes, and a few of them wore skirts . . .

'Master?' I asked innocently.

'The business with the Poppletons, Roger,' Benjamin replied. 'I know what happened. Mistress Poppleton is a wicked woman and, on reflection, I could not understand her speedy conversion to the truth.' He waved a hand. 'Oh, don't worry, she won't recant, but they are now asking questions, Roger. They are searching for a servant whom their steward hired to empty the jakes pots. He dropped one on the floor and mysteriously disappeared. They have also made enquiries about the great Dr Mirabilis. Moreover, the Poppleton steward, to save himself, has suddenly remembered how, when Dr Mirabilis was holding forth

27

in the taproom of the White Hart, you were always present.' Benjamin joined his hands and leaned across the desk. 'To cut a long story short, Roger, the Poppletons are after your blood. They are threatening to lay certain information about you before the justices.'

'I have done nothing wrong,' I retorted. 'And if they wish to make fools of themselves in public . . .'

'Oh, they won't mention "Rotterus Arsicus",' Benjamin replied, trying not to laugh. 'But they will allege you sell potions and physics, that you are a counterfeit man.' He shrugged. 'And you know where that could end? A fine, prison, the stocks or the whipping post.'

'My medicines are good,' I wailed.

'All of them?'

'Well, I do my best. They are no better, and certainly no worse, than what is being sold in London.'

'But they'll say different.'

'You could appeal to "dearest Uncle"?'

As soon as the words were out of my mouth, I knew it was a mistake. If Cardinal Wolsey, old fat Tom, knew I was heading for a beating, he'd just sit back, let it happen, and watch the fun. (Strange, isn't it? Thomas Wolsey, Chancellor and Cardinal! In his prime he didn't give a fig about old Shallot. However, years later, when he was dying and his throat began to rattle and he began to fear hell-fire, whom does he turn to, but old Shallot?)

Benjamin's face told me there would be no comfort there.

'What do you advise?' I sighed.

Benjamin threw a purse of silver across the table.

'Roger, you are to go into hiding. I have a kinsman, a very distant one, more an acquaintance really. He is the Prior of St Dunstan's outside Swaffham. I have sent him a message asking him to protect you. Go and hide there.'

'In a priory?' I yelled. 'Amongst mouldy monks and fornicating friars? No ale, no wine!'

'Aye and no wenches,' Benjamin added. 'Roger, it's the

safest. The Poppletons are wicked people. If the justices have no time for them, they will hire others to do their bidding.'

'I can take care of myself,' I replied, pushing my chest out and pulling back my shoulders. 'I am skilled at dagger and club, and Seigneur Damoral, our fencing master, says there's little more he can teach me.'

'And that will be your defence?' Benjamin replied. 'Against ten rogues on a dark and lonely lane? Or a musket fired behind a hedgerow? Or a crossbow bolt as you sit fishing on the riverbank?'

Benjamin was a very wise man. I am not a coward. I just run very fast. I am also not a fool. It's all right for you young men who read stories about idiots leading charges, but I am of a different mould. 'He who fights and runs away may get out of fighting on another day', is one of Shallot's favourite maxims. Three hours later I left the manor. I'd washed, shaved and changed. Benjamin's silver was in my purse. My swordbelt on, my horse the best we had, and all of my worldly possessions (including my medicine chest) strapped to a sumpter pony. I shook my master's hand. I stared at his eyebrows and solemnly promised I would be the best monk in Swaffham.

I reached the priory late that night. I didn't even say who I really was. I pretended to be Dr Mirabilis journeying between York and London.

'Now, that's really strange,' the grizzled, old guest-master declared, fingering his lips. 'Only recently we had another Dr Mirabilis pass this way. He treated some boils on Brother Ralph's backside.'

'Oh?' I asked.

'Oh yes. He gave him a potion.'

'And the boils went?' I asked hopefully.

'Oh yes, but Brother Ralph is now weak on his feet.'

'Oh, that Dr Mirabilis.' I drew my brows together. 'He's a distant kinsman of mine.' I pushed open the door leading to the warm, clean-swept guest-chamber. 'That's one of the reasons I am going to London,' I declared in hushed tones. 'His Excellency the Cardinal has asked me to follow this Dr Mirabilis round the country and expose him for the charlatan he is.'

Oh, heigh nonny no: the monk accepted every word I said. I spent a very comfortable night at the priory. I ate a hearty breakfast and left a bottle of my elixir for weak legs in lieu of payment.

'Oh,' I added as I mounted my horse in the courtyard, 'tell Father Prior that I bear messages from Master Benjamin Daunbey. Roger Shallot will not be coming here. The poor man has had a sudden conversion and decided to join the Cistercians at Mount Grace in Yorkshire.'

I shook the guest-master's hand and galloped out of the priory, heading like an arrow straight for the fleshpots of London. I arrived there two days later and took chambers in a tavern, the Mitre and Pig, which stands between two brothels in Southwark, overlooking the Thames. I ate heartily, bedded one of the wenches, and plotted what I should do. Naturally I spent a great deal of the time in the taproom searching out the lie of the land, but the news I heard there chilled my blood. A terrible sickness was sweeping through the city. Sudden and violent, it gave people the cramps followed by sweating and vomiting. Buboes appeared in the armpits and groin and, once this happened, death followed in a matter of days.

'Oh yes,' an old tinker assured me, 'they be dropping like flies across the river. The King, the great Cardinal, and all the Court have gone to Windsor.' He lowered his voice, whispering through where his teeth had once been. 'The city is going to die. Satan has risen from Hell to collect his own. People say this is a curse from God. A plague sent to punish their sins.'

I let the old fool prattle on. To me London was not the

mouth of Hell but a veritable paradise: the streets were packed with morris dancers, hobby horses, minstrels, men in armour and trumpeters. Nevertheless, next morning when I crossed London Bridge, through the gatehouse and past the chapel of St Thomas à Becket, I noticed a difference. There were not so many carts. Nor the crowds who stand and gape on either end of the bridge at the severed heads and quartered, pickled limbs of traitors.

As I walked deeper into the city I realised the old tinker was not a fool but a prophet. Entire streets had been closed, sealed off with bars, wooden railings and chains: dark, gloomy tunnels where the refuse had not been collected but simply burnt and left to smoulder. An occasional flicker of flame showed through the heavy pall of smoke which hung there, trapped by the overhanging houses.

In Cheapside the markets and stalls were empty; not even the whores touted for business. A whining beggar on the corner of an alleyway in the Poultry told me how the rich and powerful had fled the city, following the King and Court for the fresh air of the countryside. I could scarcely believe it. I wandered back down towards the river, but the cranes and wharves were empty. The fine shops and houses of the merchants were locked and barred, their windows shuttered. So I went to the area around Newgate, always a busy place, the justices and their bailiffs forever carrying out sentence. In the Great Beast's London you could be hanged for stealing a hawk's egg, letting out a pond, or buggery (though that was rare, you had to catch them red-handed). Or for cutting a purse, as well as conjuring, sorcery, witchcraft and all those other roguish hobbies. The great yard in front of the prison doors, however, was deserted. I found the same at Smithfield. London had become an eerie city, where smoke from burning fires wafted like ghosts amongst the houses. I called into a tavern. The landlord stood far off and inspected me most carefully.

'Are you hale and well?' he asked.

'As merry-legged as you are!' I retorted.

'Well, there's nothing the kitchen can offer you!' he snapped.

I told him not to be surly, and demanded a cup of wine and half a loaf of stale bread whilst I sat and plotted. Now I had left Southwark speedily, so I bartered with the landlord to stable my horses. I also hired a chamber with a heavy chest fortified by three locks to keep my possessions in. I came downstairs and walked back into the taproom. Near the window a fellow was sitting, some bardmonger cheerily humming. I ordered another cup of wine and sat and watched him: he kept mopping his face and running a finger round the neck of his shirt. The day was warm but, on close inspection, I noticed the sweat running like water down his face. The landlord, too, became alarmed.

'You were hale and hearty when you came in,' he shouted from behind the beer-barrels, as if these great vats were a bulwark against infection.

The man got up. 'I feel ill,' he stammered. 'I . . .' He staggered a few paces, gave a groan and collapsed on the floor.

The landlord screamed and ran into the scullery, slamming the door behind him. I felt like following, but the man moaned, arching his back as if in dire agony. I walked over and knelt down beside him. His face was pallid, his clothes damp with sweat.

'For Jesus' sake, help me!' he gasped.

Well, what could I do? I couldn't let the poor bugger die there. So, putting my hands beneath his armpits, I dragged him out into the stableyard. I swung him across my pony and made my way up the deserted streets to St Bartholomew's Hospital in Smithfield. The great market area before the abbey church was deserted. No quacks, no gingerbread stalls, no hucksters. I hammered

32

on the door of the hospital, screaming at the top of my voice. A small postern-gate opened. An anxious-faced lay Brother popped his head out.

'Go away!' He yelled, glancing fearfully at the man whom I had lashed to the saddle.

'For the love of Christ!' I snarled back. 'This is a hospital and this man is ill!'

The lay Brother sighed and, holding a vinegar-soaked cloth to his mouth and nose, stepped out. He walked over to my patient, mumbled something at me and fled back into the hospital. I went back myself: my hand brushed that of the victim. He was ice-cold. I crouched down and looked up into his face: his jaw sagged, his eyes were open.

God have mercy, the poor creature had died during that short journey from the tavern to St Bartholomew's. That was the sweating sickness, sudden and violent. I cut the body loose and lay it in the door of the church; if they didn't help the living, at least they could bury the dead! I walked back towards my tavern. It was now early afternoon. A few more people were about, but so were the death-carts. Huge, monstrous affairs, these trundled about, their drivers dressed completely in black, like shadows shot up from hell. They'd stop by a house, knock on the door, and corpses in their shifts, sometimes sewn into black canvas sheets, were thrown out like heaps of refuse. The carters, laughing and talking amongst themselves, would pick up the corpses, toss them into the cart, and trundle on. These men loved their job. They adorned themselves with black plumes and feathers and decorated their grisly carts with white-painted skeletons or the figure of death. Their bell-boys were similarly garbed: these would go in front of the carts, tolling a handbell and shouting, 'Bring out your dead! Bring out your dead!' Those houses where the infection had struck were boarded up and a great red cross daubed on them.

In some streets, looting and pillaging had begun. The riflers and cut-throats were breaking into empty houses and, with all the cheek of the devil, heaping their booty up in the carts. No one dared stop them. Oh, there were soldiers and city watchmen, but they were more frightened than helpful. They were wary of the infection and kept well away from any house bearing a red cross. The only time I saw them act was at a house just off the Shambles in Newgate. A family, fearful of an infected relative, were trying to flee, only to be forced back by the soldiers.

I returned to the tavern but the door was now closed and barred. I went round to the stableyard. My sumpter pony was standing forlornly there and, beneath the window, the iron-bound chest which contained my possessions lay smashed against the cobbles. For a while I stood and cursed, screaming at the landlord to open up. At last he replied, flinging open a window and spilling out the dirty contents of a nightjar which narrowly escaped me.

'Be gone!' he cursed. 'You're infected yourself. You'll find all your possessions there!'

I called him Satan's spawn and every other filthy name I could muster. At last, exhausted, I opened the chest. I took out my saddlebags and headed for the reeking alleyways and runnels of Whitefriars to seek out Dr Quicksilver.

I found him in his shabby tenement on the corner of Stinking Lane. He was just sitting down to sup. He greeted me as if I was the prodigal son and he the loving father.

'Roger, Roger, come and dine with me.' He took my saddlebags from my shoulder, weighing them carefully in his hands. 'More medicines, Roger, for the great Dr Mirabilis?'

'It's because of Dr Mirabilis,' I snapped back, 'that I'm in London! The Great Mouth found me out: I need lodgings.'

Quicksilver put my saddlebags down and spread his hands. 'Roger, this is your home. All that I have is thine.'

'Aye,' I replied, 'and all I have is mine!'

Quicksilver smiled. 'Come, come, Roger.' He peered at me. 'Why lodgings here?'

'The city is rotting,' I replied.

'Ah yes, the sweating sickness.'

Quicksilver's eyes wandered back to my saddlebags. He broke a piece of chicken he was eating and pushed it across the table. He then gave me a battered cup from a shelf, filled it with wine and insisted we finish our meal. I told him about the Poppletons, my journey to Swaffham, then the sights I had seen travelling around London.

'The whole world has gone mad,' Quicksilver retorted. 'Our elixirs and potions have no effect on the sweating sickness. All we can do, Roger, is eat, drink and be merry.'

I studied that seamed, cunning face, those wisps of hair, those eyes reeking of wickedness, the black soiled doublet and cloak. I gazed round the shabby parlour. There were shelves on the walls: one bore pewter cups and plates, the other a row of skulls. Quicksilver followed my gaze.

'They all died at Tyburn,' he declared. 'It gives my little domain a certain aura, an atmosphere.'

I saw a rat peep out from beneath the broken wainscoting and was forced to agree. The rest of the parlour was taken up with tawdry chests, trunks and coffers. A table stood in one corner, covered with scraps of greasy parchment, but there were no tapestries or hangings against the wall. The stone floor was bare and looked as if it had not been cleaned or scrubbed for months.

After the meal, Quicksilver took me on a tour of his domain. Along dank passageways and up rickety, twisting stairs. The place reeked of death and decay. Shabby, dirty rooms, beds covered with filthy coverlets and sheets. I was given a chamber on the second floor; the bolster was dirty, the drapes round the bed tattered, and the blankets moth-eaten and stained. There was no glass in the windows. These were simply covered by cracked boards, though there was a chest for my belongings, a table and stool, a nightjar and a thick yellow tallow candle fixed in an iron spigot. Now I should have been grateful, but instead I became uneasy. A slight jolting of Shallot's stomach, a pricking at the back of the neck. I gazed over my shoulder at Quicksilver standing near the door. His face looked yellow and more skeletal. I abruptly realised he was not one of those jolly rogues, but a man I hardly knew. I recalled the stories about him: whispers that he was a warlock, a lord of the shadows, a wizard who had renounced Christ and dabbled in the black arts. He must have caught my unease. He gave me that death's-head grin and invited me back to the parlour, to share what he called the best flagon of wine out of Bordeaux.

He was right, the wine was delicious, and the more Quicksilver drank, the more loquacious he became: jovial and filling my cup at every opportunity. Oh, how he babbled!

'I have seen the days,' he declared, cradling his cup and staring across the grease-covered table, 'oh yes, Master Roger, I have seen the days.'

'What do you mean?' I slurred.

'In my youth,' His eyes took on a sad look. 'In my youth, Roger, I was a great physician. An apothecary to the high and mighty. Patronised by kings and princes.'

'Such as whom?' I taunted.

'King Edward IV of blessed memory: his brother Clarence and Richard of Gloucester, who later usurped the throne.'

'But that would put you well past your sixtieth year,' I slurred.

'I started young.' He smiled back. 'I was an apothecary

36

by the time I was eighteen, with a shop in St Martin's Lane. Summoned hither and thither by the mighty ones of the land.' He leaned across the table. 'Potions to get rid of an unwanted child. Powders to make a man weak and fade into death. Pills to turn a man into a stallion in bed.' He tapped his narrow nose. 'Oh yes, there was a time when old Quicksilver was wanted for what he was.'

'If you're so bloody clever,' I slurred, 'why not concoct a potion for the sweating sickness?'

He laughed drily. 'I have, but all my patients have died.'

'It's so quick!' I declared, and told him about the victim I had taken to St Bartholomew's.

He heard me out and stared bleakly at me. 'You are a dead man, Roger.'

Good Lord, I'll never forget his face: long, thin and yellow. The flickering candle made his eyes glitter with malice.

'What do you mean?' I asked.

'You've touched someone ill with the contagion: it's passed to you, mixing in the humours and fluids of your body.'

'In which case,' I said, grasping his hand, 'we'll both dance down to Hell together.'

Quicksilver did not withdraw his hand. 'I have had the contagion, Roger, and survived. Once that happens, you are safe. Your body is fortified. But, come, another flagon.'

'When were you ill?' I snapped.

'Thirty-eight years ago,' Quicksilver replied over his shoulder as he stood over a chest, opening a new flagon. 'Thirty-eight years ago, Roger, the same sickness swept through London. I was safe at the Tower.' He came back and refilled my cup. 'But, come, as I have said, let's drink and be merry, for tomorrow you die!'

And so I did. Now it was a foolish act, but you have

37

heard the phrase 'honour amongst thieves'. For all his strangeness, I considered Quicksilver was a friend, an ally. When I woke the next morning, I learnt the truth. Quicksilver had gone, and so had my boots, my purse, my swordbelt and all my possessions. I tore that sinister little house to pieces, but I could find nothing except a miserable note pinned to the door.

'Dear Roger,' it read, 'Within the week you will be dead. I have left a flagon of wine in the scullery. Best wishes in Hell. Quicksilver.'

I tore the note down and stuffed it into my pocket. For the rest of the day I just raved at the sheer perfidy of that black-hearted bastard. There was nothing in the house to eat or drink except the wine. I smashed that. God knows what Quicksilver may have put in it. I have a strong head, yet for two days after my drinking bout, I felt heavy-headed, thick-tongued and lack-lustre. I am sure Quicksilver mixed something with that wine. Nevertheless, I grew better and, as I did, hungrier by the minute. What could I do? Quicksilver had taken my horse and sumpter pony. Every item and possession.

For a day I wandered the streets but the shops were closed, the bakeries empty. No one would bring food into the city. Others, hungrier and more violent than I, were also roaming the streets. For a while I sheltered in Quicksilver's house, desperate at what I should do next. To return to Ipswich was out of the question. I had no boots, never mind a horse to ride. I admit I did try that. I went up Bishopsgate, only to find that the gates were now guarded and sealed. The city fathers, who had fled, were very determined that no one should follow their example and take the infection out into the countryside. I wandered back and sheltered in a derelict house near the Austin Friars just off Broad Street. I thought I was safe, but a gang of riflers attacked me, stripping me of my jerkin. The next morning, cold and sore, I joined the other beggars outside the friary, desperate for a morsel of bread and a pannikin of fresh water.

I continued to wander the city; it was a descent into Hell. The contagion had grown worse. Whole streets were sealed off. Houses daubed with red paint mocked me from every side. Soldiers, armed to the teeth, drove me off with blows when I tried to beg outside a church. The death-carts trundled by. The corpses were stacked high; their legs and arms flailed as the cart rumbled across the cobbles, putting a strange life back into these grey-white cadavers. The mounds of refuse grew higher: fires burned in every street and the city reeked of smoke and sulphur. At night, dark shapes flitted up and down the alleyways, armed with knives and dirks, to fight like wolves over the most paltry possessions. Now and again, those city fathers who had remained tried to impose order. Soldiers were sent into the streets to enforce a curfew, and everything became as quiet as death until they passed.

I went up towards Newgate. The hunger pains were so sharp I even considered committing a crime so that I could be taken and perhaps be given something to eat or drink. Yet justice had also become poor: those who were caught plundering or breaking the law were summarily hanged. The gibbets along the great, stinking city ditch, some of them six- or seven-branched, each bore the corpse of a condemned felon. I managed to get in to Aldersgate, slipping across into Smithfield only to glimpse greater terrors yet to come.

Now, in Henry's day, Smithfield not only had its fair and market, it was also the city's execution ground. Catering not only for hangings and burnings, Smithfield also boasted a strong stone pillar which soared as high as the trees; from the top hung a great black iron cage. This could be raised or lowered by a pulley, and was reserved for poisoners, especially those who had killed their masters. It was very rarely used. However, on that day, as I sidled along Little Britain Alleyway leading into the marketplace, a terrible stench caught my throat and wrung my belly even tighter. It was sharp and acrid, like the foul odour from some stinking cookshop. When I reached the great common I discovered the reason. It was early in the morning but a small crowd had gathered around the execution pillar. The cage had been lowered: it still hung above smouldering embers. Ever curious, I pushed my way to the front and saw the cage contained the blackened corpse of a man, or what was left of him. His skin and his hair had shrivelled, the legs and hands were blackened stumps, the face all burnt away.

'What happened?' I asked a fellow standing next to me, thin and miserable-looking as myself.

'I don't know,' he replied in a sing-song fashion. 'But this morning the cage was found lowered and the fire burning. God knows who he is.'

'It's no execution!' another called.

Two bailiffs shouted for volunteers to bring buckets of water to throw over the cage and cool it off. They offered a small loaf of bread and a pannikin of wine, so I volunteered. I spent the next hour staggering backwards and forwards across the common carrying buckets of water from the great horse-trough to douse the cage and its grisly contents. The smell was so foul, the sight so horrid, that everyone else drew off. Nevertheless, I and the man I had spoken to worked on. We just licked our lips, feeling the juices in our mouths at the prospect of a loaf and a mouthful of wine. Now, being grilled to death is the most macabre of fates. I have only seen it done once since; that was to John de Rous, the Bishop of Rochester's cook: he had tried to kill his master and his entire household by mixing arsenic in the soup. (Oh, by the way, before you ask, my own cooks are hand-picked. The captain of my guard, the jolliest cut-throat you could meet, is always present in the kitchen when my meats are cooked and my bread baked. Half the rulers of Europe want me dead: the Luciferi of France, the Council of Eight in Florence, the Secretissimi of Venice, not to mention that mad bugger in Russia, the Prince of Muscovy! He still sends letters enquiring after my health. My chaplain, the little dropping, is smiling to himself. If he doesn't stop being insolent, I'll make him principal taster. As you know, there's many a slip between cup and lip!)

Ah well, back to that hot summer morning. Eventually we cooled the cage off, opened it, and dragged out what remained of the cadaver. No one would be able to recognise it, but the principal bailiff, a sturdy, open-faced man, came over. Despite all the horror and death around us, he was one of those honest officials who took his job seriously, and still believed in maintaining law and order in the city. He crouched down, studying the blackened remains. My eye caught something glinting where the wrist had been and I pointed it out. The bailiff picked this up: it was an iron bracelet, a chain with a small medal bearing a death's-head. The bailiff scrutinised it then whistled under his breath. He polished it against his cloak and held it up.

'Lord save us!' he whispered.

'What is it?' I asked curiously.

The bailiff tossed the chain up and down in his hand. He gestured at the blackened, smoking remains. 'Believe it or not, that was once Andrew Undershaft, the city executioner. A leading figure in the Guild of Hangmen which meets at the Gallows tavern just near the Tower.'

'Was he convicted of any crime?' I asked.

The bailiff shook his head. 'The courts haven't sat for weeks, and Andrew had committed no crime.' He stared up at the great stone pillar. 'Undershaft was murdered,' he continued quietly. 'Hard to believe but someone brought him down here late last night, put him in that cage, lowered the pulley and lit a fire under him.'

'And no one noticed that? Surely the fellow's screams

41

would have been heard in Windsor?'

The bailiff looked at me closely. 'You speak well for a beggar.'

'That's because I'm not one,' I replied. 'Just another unfortunate down on his luck.'

I was tempted to mention my master. How I once wore the livery of Cardinal Wolsey. But he wouldn't believe me: even when I am shaved, bathed, my hair cut and oiled, I still have the look of a born liar.

'Well, whoever you are,' the bailiff popped the chain into his purse, 'who cares what happens in London now? The city has become a murky antechamber of Hell. Sorcery is celebrated in Cripplegate, wholesale murders in the Vintry. Entire families are dying of starvation in their locked houses. Who'd care about a man screaming to death in a cage over a fire at Smithfield? It's a sign of the times.' He pulled a face. 'If he was alive when he was put in the cage, and I don't think he was, he wouldn't have screamed long.'

'What about my bread and wine?' I asked.

The bailiff rose and clapped me on the shoulder. 'You can break fast with me.'

And he led me and the other helper across to the Bishop's Mitre tavern which overlooked Smithfield. We ate outside, squatting with our backs to the tavern wall because the landlord would not let us in. The bailiff kept his word. We had bread, wine, even some strips of greasy bacon. Now, I have eaten at the banquets and feasts from one end of Europe to another. I have sat beside dark-eyed, black-hearted Catherine de'Medici and supped from golden chalices: I have picked at the best food the French royal kitchens could provide. (Mind you, I was careful. Catherine's main hobby was poisoning.) Nevertheless, I tell you this, nothing equalled that beggar's banquet outside the Bishop's Mitre in Smithfield so many, many years ago.

I thought the bailiff had done with us, but he came

back and threw a waxen seal bearing the arms of the city into each of our hands.

'If you want a job,' he rasped, 'join the death-carts. It doesn't pay much, but at least you won't starve.'

Of course I accepted. I picked myself up and looked across the great common where those horrid blackened remains were being hoisted into a cart. I thought that was the end of the matter. In truth, the murder of Andrew Undershaft was simply a pointer of things to come.

Chapter 3

I became a corpse collector. I worked with the gangs which patrolled the streets day and night, emptying the houses, collecting the cadavers of all those who had died of the sweating sickness. Godforsaken work! It hardened the heart and bit deep into the soul. The people I worked with were the scum of the earth who feared neither God nor man. Even now, years later, I cannot tell you the dreadful things I witnessed. Houses ransacked, corpses plundered. The dreadful death-bells tolling day and night; the great, yawning burial pits to the north of the city outside Charterhouse. The stories that not all the people taken there were dead are true. A living nightmare! A scene from the Apocalypse. My senses became dulled. I swear, where possible, I did good work. One sole thought kept me working: to raise enough money to be able to slip out of the city and go back to Ipswich.

Satan, however, didn't reign supreme in London. The Carthusians at the Charterhouse, God bless them, fulfilled their job as priests. They came out to bless the corpses and, three times a week, I erected an altar, at which a priest in black or purple vestments sang the Mass for the dead. One man in particular impressed me. John Houghton, the Carthusian priest, a thick-set, stubby-featured man. He would stand by the burial pit, keeping an eagle eye as we emptied the corpse carts, even as he chanted the psalms for the dead. He would allow no plundering, no mockery and was not above using a thick ash cudgel to enforce his orders amongst the rabble I worked with.

One morning, when the smoke was thick and curling, Houghton came too close to the edge of the ditch. He slipped, going down on the mud, into the common grave. The corpse collectors leaned on their shovels and laughed as the Prior, restricted by his grey robes, tried to climb back: the side of the bank was drenched with rainwater, so the more he scrambled, the worse it became. I ran across, leaned down and stretched out my hand.

'Take it, Father!' I ordered.

Houghton's light-blue eyes held mine.

'Take it!' I repeated. 'I will not let you go.'

The poor man was suspicious. He thought I was going to push him further down into the pit or, even worse, pull him up and crack his head with the spade. After all, he was in the company of those who feared neither God nor man.

'By the sacrament,' I whispered hoarsely, 'I mean you no harm!'

He grasped my hand. I pulled him out and helped him brush the dirt from his robes.

'What's your name?' he asked.

'Roger Shallot, Father.'

'Thank you, Master Shallot. I shall pray for you.'

And, shaking my hand, he walked round the pit to give my companions the rough edge of his tongue.

Ah well, the days passed. No jests or jokes here. One morning, I woke in old Quicksilver's house. I felt heavy-headed, my limbs sore to move: every step I took seemed to drench me in sweat. I staggered downstairs. I took a stoup of water and went out to join the gang where they gathered near the lych-gate of St Paul's. God knows how I worked that morning. By noon I was vomiting, my belly taut with pain. When I felt beneath my armpit, I touched the swelling buboes. Of course, the others knew: if I hadn't drawn a dirk which I had taken from one of them in a fight, they would have knocked me on the head and tossed me into the pit. They drove me off with curses and blows. I staggered away through the smoke, past the heaps and mounds of lime, and collapsed before the gateway of Charterhouse. I banged with all my might. I remember the door creaking open and Houghton crouching beside me.

'I have the sickness, Father,' I gasped.

He dabbed my brow with a rag soaked in water. 'But, Roger, we can do nothing for you.'

'I don't want to die like a dog,' I gasped, and then fainted.

After that I can remember little. Brothers, their faces kind and concerned, bending over me. I chattered and screamed, slipping in and out of delirium. Scenes from my past plagued my soul: Mother, who should not have died so early, walking towards me, a basket of flowers in her hand. Benjamin behind his desk, wiping his fingers and shaking his head. Dr Agrippa, his face framed by shadows, smiling down at me with those soulless eyes. I could even smell that strange perfume he wore: sometimes fragrant, but at other times coarse, like an empty skillet left over a fire. And there were other dreams: being hunted by wolves in Paris, or being pursued by those dreadful leopards through the maze at the court of Francis I. Wolsey came, dressed from head to toe in purple silk, his saturnine face creased in concern.

'You should have become a priest, Roger,' he taunted.

'Like you, My Lord Cardinal?' I snapped back.

Wolsey's face became angry and he swept away. Of course, there was always the Great Beast, the 'mouldwarp', the Prince of Blood, that devil incarnate: Henry VIII with his massive body, tree-trunk legs, hands on hips, his piggy eyes glaring at me, those fat, sensuous

47

lips pursed into a grimace of disapproval.

'Shallot! Shallot!' he taunted. 'What are you doing here?'

I tossed and turned; then, late one afternoon, the nightmares ceased. I woke up. I felt weak but the fever had gone. John Houghton was staring down at me whilst, behind him, the infirmarians clapped their hands as if they were witnessing a miracle. Houghton sat down on the edge of the bed. He smiled as he ran his fingers down my face.

'You are a most fortunate man, Roger Shallot,' he declared. 'There are not many who are snatched from the jaws of death.'

'Hell spat me back, Father,' I joked.

He smiled and pulled the blankets closer around me. 'You have talked,' he murmured. 'Oh, Roger, how you have talked: about His Grace the King, Cardinal Wolsey, and His Eminence's nephew, Benjamin Daunbey. What on earth were you doing working amongst the corpse collectors of London?'

'You have heard of the prodigal son, Father?'

Houghton smiled and left, after giving strict instructions to the infirmarian to let me rest.

Of course, I have the constitution of an ox, so I rapidly recovered. The good Brothers regarded me as a sign from God and fed me every delicacy their kitchens could provide: succulent chicken, rich strong broths, eggs mixed with milk, as well as potions and powders which would certainly not be found amongst Dr Quicksilver's collection. My strength quickly returned. I was surprised to find that it had been three weeks since that terrible morning I had collapsed outside the priory gate.

'You are most fortunate,' Houghton declared one morning when he came to visit me. 'There are not many who survive the sweating sickness: now you have, you will never suffer again.'

'And the city?' I asked.

'The fever's dying: the King's rule is being enforced. My Lord Cardinal has brought in mercenaries from the garrisons at Dover and Sandwich, whilst the executioners are doing a roaring trade.' He took my hand and patted it, those shrewd, saintly eyes full of merriment. 'It is well you came here, Roger. Yet if half of what you said is true . . .' Houghton shook his head in mock anger. 'You are a veritable rogue, born and bred. For the rest, stay here, be our guest.'

And so I did. (I wish my bloody chaplain would stop sniggering! That was one of the holiest parts of my life!) I joined the good Brothers in their refectory and in their choir-stalls. I chanted the divine office at dawn and heard Mass at midday. I helped in the garden whilst the infirmarian and the Brothers were quite astounded by my knowledge of physic. (No, don't scoff, no one died.) I must admit I was curious that I had survived, but Bruno the infirmarian said it was the age of miracles – or something else.

'Perhaps you didn't want to die?' he grinned. 'Perhaps the will rather than the humours of the body determine one's fate?'

Do you know, I even considered becoming a lay brother! However, one day I was sent out to a small village to the north of Charterhouse to buy some provisions. All the way there I kept my eyes down, chanting a psalm, but on the way back I grew thirsty and called in at a tavern. Well, I met a wench with golden hair and nut-brown skin, lips full and red and eyes full of mischief. Well, you know old Shallot: I can resist anything but temptation. Two cups of canary and I found myself in a hay barn, the young girl giggling beside me. Oh, too true, the spirit is definitely willing but my flesh was extremely weak! I remember that day in particular because, when I arrived back – minus a few items of clothing; I'd left my cowl and hood in the hay barn – Prior Houghton was waiting for me.

'Roger, you have visitors.'

And, grasping me by the arm, he took me out into the garden. Benjamin, flanked by Dr Agrippa, was sitting on a turf seat watching the carp in the stewpond snap at flies. My master fell on my neck, clasped me to him, squeezing me tightly, then he stood back, his eyes full of tears.

'Roger, I thought you were dead! We searched high and low.'

'It's not time for Roger's death,' Agrippa murmured. He took off his black, broad-brimmed hat and gazed up at me, his cherubic face creased into the most benevolent smile. He looked like someone's favourite uncle, except for the black leather he wore from head to toe and those gauntlets which covered the secret red crosses on the palm of each hand.

'Roger will live for a long time,' Agrippa added. 'The Fates will not cut his life too short.' He got up and glanced at Prior Houghton who was watching us curiously. 'The devil takes care of his own, Roger.'

Agrippa grasped my hand: as he did so, the colour of his eyes changed. I don't know whether it was some shadow or trick of the light; suddenly they became like black pebbles and his face became white and drawn. He gripped my hand a little longer than he should have and my heart sank. Agrippa was warning me that we were about to enter the lair of the Great Beast.

Prior John Houghton became uncomfortable. He kept glancing sideways at Agrippa, even as he told Benjamin about my miraculous recovery. After that, the Prior left us, saying he would send out a lay brother with some white wine and pastries. I stayed, telling Benjamin everything that had happened. (Or, at least, what I thought he should know.) I accepted his teasing of my sudden conversion as a member of the Carthusian Order. For a while we just sat and chatted, sipping the wine and enjoying the fragrance of the flowers and the steady hum of the honey-hunting bees. Now and again, the bells of Charterhouse would toll, calling the Brothers to service, and I realised I could not stay there for ever.

'How did you find me?' I asked.

'Well, I went to Swaffham –' Benjamin pulled a face – 'and I guessed the rest. After that, with the good doctor's help, I searched the city. One of the corpse collectors recognised your description so I came here.' His face became sad. 'Roger, I have been searching for you for two weeks. I thought you were dead!'

'I was robbed!' I wailed. 'I had no money, whilst the Poppletons were waiting for me in Ipswich.'

'Roger, Roger.' Benjamin leaned forward. 'The Cardinal has sent a letter to the Sheriff of Norfolk instructing the Poppletons to offer you no harm.' He smiled mirthlessly. 'They're so terrified they are running backwards and forwards to the jakes again!'

'And, if your dearest uncle had intervened,' I answered tartly, 'that means he needs us.'

'Dearest Uncle does need us,' Benjamin declared, putting his cup down. 'We are to go to the Tower, Roger, then on to meet the King at Windsor.'

I stared round that peaceful, perfume-filled garden. 'I can't stay here,' I murmured, 'but I don't want to go to Windsor.'

Benjamin opened his wallet: he drew out a writ, sealed with the Cardinal's own signet. I read it quickly. I had no choice: Benjamin Daunbey, the Cardinal's beloved nephew, and his manservant Roger Shallot, on their allegiance to the King, were to go in all haste to the royal castle of Windsor. I threw the letter back. On reflection the death-cart, the sweating sickness and those terrible burial pits didn't seem so dreadful! If Wolsey wanted me, then I was about to enter the House of Shadows! Murder and treachery would be my guides.

I quickly packed my belongings and bade a fond

51

farewell to Prior Houghton and his kindly brothers. I
never saw Houghton again. Years later, when Fat Henry
broke with Rome over dark-eyed Boleyn, Houghton, true
to his own soul, refused to take the Oath of Supremacy.
I was out of the country at the time, the unwilling guest
of the Spanish Inquisition (splendid gentlemen!). I
returned to learn that Houghton and some of his
Brothers had been hanged over their own gatehouse: I
sat in the darkness and wept. He was a good man. He
deserved a better death . . .

Agrippa, Benjamin and I left, keeping well away from
the city. We walked by Gray's Inn, skirting the Temple
and Whitefriars to a barge waiting to take us up-river
to the Tower. The oarsmen were all the good doctor's
henchmen, a bigger group of flea-bags you never hope
to meet. Cut-throats, rascals, scum of the earth! As usual
they greeted me like a long-lost brother. I was glad of
the rapturous welcome because, as we walked the hot,
musty streets, both Agrippa and Benjamin had become
strangely silent. Even when I told them about
Quicksilver: raving against his perfidy, threatening to
hunt him down, they just shook their heads, lost in their
own thoughts. At first I thought they were frightened
but, as the barge moved mid-stream, Agrippa's rascals
pulling at the oars, the good doctor stirred. He pointed
to each bank.

'How time goes!' he muttered softly. 'You know, Roger,
I remember Claudius's legions trying to ford this river,
when London was nothing more than mud-flats and
wide stretches of moorland.'

I looked at him strangely. Now and again Agrippa
would make these slips and talk about events which had
happened hundreds of years ago as if they had occurred
that morning.

'They paid for it, mind you,' he continued. 'The river
ran red with blood. The mud-banks further down were
piled high with corpses, like faggots in a woodshed.' He

put on his hat again and looked at me from under his brows. 'It will be scarlet once again,' he declared, and pointed to the poles jutting out from London Bridge where the rooks and ravens fought over the severed heads of traitors. 'A time will come when all the horrors will appear.'

'Might it now?' Benjamin observed drily.

'Why, what's the matter?' I asked.

'Show him, Dr Agrippa.'

Agrippa fished in his pouch and drew out a small scroll of white parchment. 'Read that, Roger.'

I undid the scarlet ribbon and stared curiously at the blue-green writing inscribed in an elegant hand. The first words made me laugh.

'To Henry Tudor calling himself King. I, Edward, by the grace of God King of England, Ireland, Scotland and Wales, do denounce thee as a traitor, a usurper and the son of a usurper, who seized my father's Crown and Sceptre.'

I looked up. 'What is this?' I exclaimed.

'Read on.'

'Now we know,' the letter continued, 'and it is a matter of public knowledge how your usurpation has been punished by God. What you possess will not be passed on to a son. We deem this punishment enough. We are content to bide our time and wait for God's intervention. However, until then, our royal estate must be maintained. What you hold, you do as steward for us. I therefore demand that a thousand gold crowns be deposited just within the west door of St Paul's Cathedral. This gold is to be left at the hour of Nones on the feast of St Dominic. If not, a proclamation publicising your shame will be nailed to St Paul's Cross on the feast of St Clare. Heed ye this warning! Given at the Tower under our seal on the feast of St Martha, the twenty-ninth of July 1523.'

I tossed the letter back at Agrippa. 'London is full of

madcaps and such tomfoolery,' I declared.

'Look at the foot of the letter,' Agrippa insisted, passing the parchment back.

I did so and gaped. Now, as you may know, when a letter is signed and sealed by the King, it carries two seals. First his own, the signet, often in green wax; then it is passed to the Chancellor who impresses the Great Seal of the Kingdom in red. This letter was no different, except that the seals were not those of Henry VIII but of Edward V.

'This is impossible,' I whispered. 'They are forgeries.'

Agrippa shook his head. 'No, they are not. The vellum is the most expensive that can be bought in London. The ink is that used in the Royal Chancery, as is the wax. Those seals are no forgeries.'

'But Edward the Fifth died,' I declared. 'He perished in the Tower some forty years ago.'

Benjamin looked across at the river. He stared at a great, low-slung, Venetian galley as it came out from the quayside, its oars dipping and rising as it began to make its way down to the open sea. Around it, bum boats and wherries still bobbed, as the fishermen and poor people of London tried desperately to sell to this stately galley before it left.

'It should be nonsense,' Benjamin declared slowly. 'On April the ninth, 1483, Edward the Fourth died here on the Thames whilst fishing.' He smiled and shrugged. 'Well, at least he collapsed and was taken back to one of his palaces, where he died. Now he left two sons: Edward, eleven years old, and Richard aged seven. The protectorate went to their uncle, Richard, Duke of York but, as you know, Richard usurped the throne and imprisoned his nephews in the Tower, from where they later disappeared. Two years later, in August 1485, Richard the Third was defeated and killed at Market Bosworth by the present King's father. Now all the evidence indicates that the two boy Princes were either poisoned or killed: their bodies were buried in the Tower or tied with sacks, loaded with stones, and dumped into the Thames.' Benjamin tapped the letter with his fingers. 'According to this, however, young Prince Edward survived. He possesses his own seals and is now threatening our King.'

'But it's blackmail,' I said slowly. 'Idle threats to obtain gold.'

'It may well be,' Agrippa replied, 'but listen awhile, Roger.' He leaned forward to emphasise his points. 'First, Edward is supposed to have died forty years ago. True?'

I nodded.

'Secondly, when a king dies – and remember, Richard the Third didn't even allow Edward to be crowned – his seals are collected together and smashed. Richard the Third would certainly make sure those of his imprisoned nephew, the few that were made, would be thrown into a fire. If he didn't, Henry Tudor, our present King's father, certainly would.'

'So, where did these two seals come from?' I asked. 'Couldn't they have been removed from some letter or proclamation?'

Agrippa shook his head. 'No, they are freshly affixed. According to the lettering and insignia they are no forgery.'

'But how are they dangerous?'

Agrippa smiled and shook his head. 'Roger, Roger, examine the letter carefully. Our present King, Henry the Eighth, God bless him, is the son of a usurper. He will not tolerate anyone with Yorkist blood in their veins.'

(Agrippa was right. In his reign, Henry VIII systematically, through a series of judicial executions, wiped out anyone who had Yorkist blood or a better claim to the throne than he. Edmund Stafford, Duke of Buckingham, was one, whilst the de la Pole family, except for Cardinal Reginald who fled abroad, all saw the inside of the Tower. On this matter, Henry was as mad as a March hare.)

Agrippa thrust the seals of the proclamation under my nose. 'Can you imagine, Roger, what happened when Henry saw this? He ranted for days. No one dared go near him. Not even Benjamin's dearest uncle. Henry was like an enraged bull: smashing furniture, issuing threats, cursing and kicking anyone who came near him.'

Oh yes, I thought, that's the Great Beast! He's all sweetness and smiles when he is getting his own way. Yet, once he's threatened and thwarted, he's more dangerous than a madman out of Bedlam. (When he grew older, and the ulcer on his leg began to weep pus, and his great fat, gout-ridden body was wracked by pain, you could find yourself in the shadow of the axe just by sneezing in his presence.)

'But the King didn't believe it?' I asked.

'Oh yes, he did,' Benjamin replied. 'Remember, Roger, Edward and his brother Richard may have disappeared, but no one truly knows what happened to them. Even a hint, a faint suspicion that they might still be alive would send Henry into a paroxysm of rage. Moreover, the writer touched a raw nerve. The King is as superstitious as any country yokel. He really does believe that he has no son because of Divine displeasure.'

'But the people wouldn't believe it,' I retorted.

'Wouldn't they?' Agrippa asked.

He was about to continue, but the oarsmen shouted as they lifted the oars. We were now approaching London Bridge, being swept through the narrow arches by the gushing water. A chilling but exciting experience. I have made that journey many a time. Once the oars go up and the boat is left to the fury of the water, your heart drops and your stomach lurches.

Once we were into calmer waters, Agrippa continued. 'Can you imagine what would happen if such a proclamation was posted in a London now plagued by the sweating sickness? People would begin to wonder and gossip. And the whisper would turn to chatter and, as it does, fable would become fact: the King must be cursed.'

I leaned against the side of the boat and stared into the water. Agrippa spoke the truth. I had seen the sickness in London. I had experienced all the pain and the horror. I'd witnessed the hysteria and knew the anger bubbling beneath the surface. The people would want an answer, and Henry VIII would become their scapegoat.

'Did he send the gold?' I asked.

'Of course not,' Agrippa replied. 'Instead he ringed St Paul's with troops and had the great cross in the churchyard heavily guarded by archers and men-at-arms.'

'And?' I asked.

'Oh, no proclamation was posted there. The villain behind this was too astute. Instead the proclamation appeared on the door of St Mary Le Bow, another on the cross outside Westminster Abbey. Both carried the seal of Edward V. Both proclaimed Henry to be a usurper, deriding his lack of a son and the sickness raging in London as a sign of God's displeasure. The proclamations were torn down but the whispering has begun.' Agrippa hawked and spat into the river. 'And now another letter has arrived. This time the demand is for two thousand in gold as a punishment. The money is to be delivered in six days' time, on the feast of St Augustine, the twenty-eighth of August: two leather bags in a steel coffer are to be placed near St Paul's Cross as the cathedral bells toll for the midday Angelus.'

'And the letter was dispatched from the Tower?'

'Yes,' Benjamin replied. 'It's almost as if, for the last forty years, this forgotten prince has been sheltering in some secret room in the Tower—'

'But you say arrived?' I interrupted. 'Arrived where?'

'The first one was delivered to the constable of the Tower, Sir Edward Kemble. The second was left in the Abbot's stall in Westminster Abbey.'

'Which explains why we are going to the Tower now?' I asked.

'Ah.' Agrippa pulled his black cloak around him as if the river breeze was cold.

(That's one thing I noticed about Agrippa. He never liked the sunlight. Like some dark spider, he preferred the shadows. I never saw him eat or drink. Oh, he'd raise a cup to his lips, as he did in the garden at Charterhouse, but nothing ever seemed to pass his lips. He always seemed cold, too.) Agrippa pointed to a sandbank in the river on which stood a massive, three-branched gibbet bearing the rotting corpses of river pirates.

'The Tower is full of curiosities,' he murmured. 'A month ago the chief executioner's deputy, Andrew Undershaft, was, somehow, put in a cage at Smithfield and roasted alive over a roaring fire.'

'I was there,' I exclaimed. 'Well, I saw his blackened corpse and helped remove it from the cage . . . What's that got to do with these letters?'

'Perhaps nothing,' Benjamin replied. 'Undershaft died in Smithfield, God knows how. He was seen, the previous day, drinking in a tavern near Cock Lane, and then he disappeared. How anyone could take a burly man such as him, put him in a cage and roast him to death is a mystery. Now the city authorities thought it was revenge carried out by the friends or relatives of a man Undershaft may have executed. However, ten days ago, another member of the Guild of Executioners, Hellbane, was fished from the Thames. According to the surgeon who examined the corpse, Hellbane had been alive when he had been put in the sack. No mark or wound was found upon his corpse, but weights had been attached to his feet. You see, Roger, that's the mystery; two members of the Guild of Executioners suffered judicial murder. They were not knifed or clubbed to death. They were both killed in a way prescribed by law for certain felons. Undershaft died the death of a poisoner; Hellbane suffered the fate of a patricide, someone who has killed his father.'

'And they were innocent?'

Benjamin shrugged. 'As far as we know.'

I gazed at the lonely gibbet. 'Hellbane,' I said. 'What sort of name is that?'

'The city executioners are a rare breed.' Benjamin explained. 'Surprisingly, Roger, despite all the barbarism, very few people want their job. They are marked men, hated and reviled by London's underworld. However, they do a job that has to be done, and business is always brisk.'

(Oh, God bless my master for his truthful heart. During the Great Beast's reign the scaffold and gibbets were never empty. I know of one executioner, an axeman, who became so sickened by the dreadful sentences he had to carry out that he became quite mad and tried to cut his own head off. Poor fellow, he died in chains in Bedlam.)

'Anyway,' Benjamin continued, 'the city hangmen are patronised by the King himself.'

'Like is always attracted to like,' I remarked.

'They meet in a tavern called the Gallows, in the shadow of the Tower. They have their own guild. They wear a chain round their wrists and hold meetings in the nave of St Peter ad Vincula.'

(Now, there's a dreadful place. Under St Peter ad Vincula, the Tower chapel, lies the headless corpses of all Henry's victims; all those who died on the execution block or perished in some desolate dungeon.)

'So,' I insisted. 'Two hangmen have been murdered.

59

They are not the most popular of men.'

'Somehow,' Benjamin replied, 'My Lord Cardinal believes the murders of these two hangmen and the blackmail letters to the King are connected.' He paused as the boat swung in towards the quayside. 'You see, Roger, no one really knows what happened to the Princes in the Tower. They might have been poisoned, strangled or starved.'

'The Cardinal,' Agrippa explained, 'has studied the fate of these princes closely. He has also spoken to Sir Thomas More who is writing a study of King Richard the Third's life. Now More believes that the Guild of Hangmen must have known what happened to the two Princes.'

'You mean a secret passed on from one generation to another?' I asked.

'Precisely,' Benjamin replied. 'John Mallow, the chief hangman, has sworn a great oath that no such secret exists, but, "dearest Uncle" is not convinced. He believes that if the Princes were killed and their bodies removed, someone from the Guild of Hangmen must have been involved.'

'But this is just dearest Uncle's feeling?' I asked.

Benjamin sighed and put his hands together. 'Well, if this villain writing the blackmailing letters is a charlatan, the only way the King could silence him, or so dearest Uncle reasons, is by finding out what really happened to the Princes and proclaiming this to the city and the kingdom. Henry would give his eye-teeth just to find their corpses.'

'And so this same charlatan,' I added, 'is murdering the hangmen just in case one of them has inherited the secret and could reveal the truth?'

'Exactly,' Benjamin replied, peering over his shoulder at the approaching quayside.

'And how many are in the Guild of Hangmen?' I asked.

'There should be seven,' Benjamin replied. 'John

Mallow, he's old and about to retire. Andrew Undershaft, lately deceased. Hellbane, who's also been called to his maker, and four other assistants: Snakeroot, Horehound, Toadflax and Wormwood. And, before you ask your question, Roger, the chief hangman's apprentices are never called by their real names.' He smiled thinly. 'This is to protect them; sometimes they change their minds and decide to take up another profession.'

I looked up at the jutting towers and turrets of the Tower.

'If I had my way, Master,' I grumbled, 'I'd do the same.'

Chapter 4

How can I describe the Tower? A narrow, cruel place. Yet, in 1523, it had yet to acquire its reputation as the Great Beast's slaughter ground. Oh, Edmund Stafford, Duke of Buckingham, had lost his head on the hill outside, but to me it was still a double shield of walls beyond a wide moat; a fortress, strengthened by at least a dozen towers which ringed the great Norman keep that dominated all. It stored the King's arms and artillery, his jewel house, his mint as well as his menagerie, with its lions, apes, pelicans, elephants, bears and other unfortunate animals, sent as gifts by foreign princes. When we approached it after leaving Charterhouse, my overriding concern was about the stench from the moat slimed with green, and the occasional corpse of some animal bobbing on the surface. We entered by the Lion Gate, passing guards who snapped to attention as Agrippa showed his warrant carrying the King's personal seal.

The Tower is like a maze. It draws you in: you become lost, as well as over-awed, by the winding paths along high brick walls, the tower doors, closely guarded, the shutters on the windows firmly bolted. Then, as in a maze, you reach the centre, a great, open, green expanse surrounding the Norman keep: the playground of children of the Tower garrison, who hopped and jumped amongst the mangonels, catapults and other impedimenta of war. Soldiers' wives had put up lines to dry their clothes, whilst the men lazed in the shadows, drinking, dicing, sleeping or gossiping. A homely scene – and that's part of the trap. Around the green are entrances to the different towers. Each of them contains its own mysteries: twisting, mildewed steps which stretch up to cells, or worse, go down to the cavernous pits where the torturers with their instruments wait to search out the truth.

In one far corner, just near the church of St Peter ad Vincula, is a stretch of ground where the grass struggles to grow. Some say it's cursed because that's where the scaffold's erected. I believe this. In my long and troubled life I came to know the Tower well. Sometimes as a visitor, other times as a guest of the King, his prisoner. I have been stretched out on Exeter's Daughter, the great rack which pulls your limbs from their sockets. If you survive and confess, the executioners fix steel plates so your body is in one piece when they cart it out for execution. However, I babble on. On that fine August day, with the sun beaming down, I had no knowledge of the Tower's future. Believe me, if I had, I would have turned and run like a whippet for the nearest gate.

Now, across the green, facing the Norman tower, are the royal apartments, housed in a long, ramshackle building, three storeys high, with a red slated roof, cornices, buttresses and jutting bay windows. A manor house, with black timber and white plaster walls on a red brick foundation. These were the royal quarters where the King's officers lodged.

We went through a bustling entrance and up a broad, sweeping staircase. A guard at the top took our names. He told us to wait on a bench in a small recess, marched down the gallery and knocked at the door. I heard a bell ring, and the guard beckoned at us to approach. We entered a chamber where three men were hurriedly seating themselves around a long, polished table which ran down the centre of the room. They rose as we entered. The man at the top introduced himself as Sir Edward Kemble: fussy, grey-haired, grey-eyed, grey-faced. He was dressed richly in a dark-blue gown lined with dyed black lambswool: however, the jerkin beneath was rather soiled, and the shirt collar which peeped out above looked as if it had missed wash-day. Kemble was one of those worried officials, narrow-eyed from peering over manuscripts. He had an unhealthy pallor and hands which could never stay still. He introduced the gentleman on his right as Master Francis Vetch, his lieutenant or deputy, a bright-faced young man with close-cropped black hair, wide-spaced blue eyes and a pleasant smiling mouth. Vetch was dressed soberly in a dark yellow gown which fell just below the knee. A warbelt was strapped round his middle, but he'd left his sword and dagger lying on a stool just within the door. The man on Kemble's left was Reginald Spurge: a frightened squirrel of a man, with nostrils like a horse, ever sniffing the wind, little darting eyes, and a tongue which reminded me of a cat's, pink and pointed, ever licking dry lips. Like Vetch and Sir Edward, he was clean-shaven. (The King had yet to grow his beard. Of course, what the King did, everyone hurriedly followed suit.)

Spurge was dressed like a dandy, a Court fop, with his tightly waisted jerkin puffed out at the shoulders and clasped round his waist by a narrow jewelled belt. He sported a codpiece a stallion would have been proud of, and tight hose which gave his legs a womanly look. Both Vetch and Spurge murmured their greetings as Kemble chattered on, drowning everyone else.

'I didn't know you were coming. I didn't know you were coming,' he protested. His hands beat the air like a trapped bird. 'Dr Agrippa, Master Benjamin –' Kemble dismissed me with one flick of his eyes – 'if I'd known you were coming, I would have prepared something to eat and drink.'

At last Benjamin was able to placate him, saying we had already eaten and drunk our fill. Only then did Kemble usher us to chairs on either side of the table. He sat down wearily himself, mopping his face with a dirty napkin. He glanced sideways at his companions.

'Master Spurge is our surveyor,' he explained, leaning forward. 'He and Vetch are the principal officers of the garrison.'

Benjamin, sitting next to me, pressed the toe of his boot gently on my foot: I was beginning to snigger at this fussy little man's antics.

'What Sir Edward means,' Francis Vetch spoke up, fighting hard to stifle his own smile at the constable's antics, 'is that Reginald and I, together with himself, are probably the only men in the Tower who could forge a letter claiming to be Edward V and dispatch it to the King.'

'Why on earth do you say that?' Benjamin asked.

Vetch laced his fingers together. 'Master Daunbey,' he replied slowly, 'I have heard of your reputation: you are no fool. I'd be grateful if you would reciprocate the courtesy. Everyone in this room knows a letter was drawn up, sealed, and dispatched from the Tower to the King. Moreover, the first letter was delivered here.' He scratched the tip of his pointed nose. 'Sir Edward Kemble opened the letter in my presence. I had to use smelling salts to bring him out of his faint. I then sent for Reginald and organised the letter's dispatch to Windsor.' He cocked his head to one side. 'You are here, Master Daunbey, about the letter?'

Benjamin smiled.

'Good,' Spurge declared in a high-pitched, squeaky voice. 'There can be no more pretence, can there?'

'Excuse me!' That's me, old Shallot. I was always tactful! The ever-faithful servant. Benjamin allowed me to question others as vigorously as himself, but Kemble didn't know this. He darted a look at me and sniffed as if I was something which had crawled out of his nose. He whispered into Spurge's ear, in that loud, insulting way, asking who I was.

Benjamin tapped the table with the rings on his fingers. 'Master Shallot is my trusted servant in these matters,' he said quietly. 'He is well known to the King and My Lord Cardinal.'

(My master, God bless him, never lied. What he didn't say was what I was known for!)

Kemble's manner changed in a twinkling of an eye. 'Continue with your question, Master Shallot.' He leaned against the back of his chair and stared up at the ceiling as if he secretly wished he or I were elsewhere.

'This letter,' I said. 'It claims to have been drawn up, signed and sealed at the Tower, but how do we know it was?'

Vetch leaned forward. 'Master Shallot, there's no debate about that. My lord constable found it on his desk on the morning of the twenty-ninth of July. You have heard of the sweating sickness in London?'

'I suffered from it and recovered.'

'Then you are truly blessed,' Vetch answered kindly. 'However, from the middle of July until two days ago, the twentieth of August, the Tower was sealed. All gates were closed and padlocked: the drawbridge raised and portcullis lowered. No man nor animal was allowed in. None of the garrison was allowed out: it was our only way of keeping the sickness out. Sir Edward commanded the Tower as if it was a castle under siege.' He shrugged. 'As it was, by Death itself.'

Kemble pointed to a desk in the far corner. 'I had been to Mass at St John's Chapel,' he explained. 'My chamber was always left open. When I returned, the letter was lying on that table.'

'If it was addressed to the King, why did you open it?' I asked.

'If you look at the reverse,' Kemble retorted, 'you'll

notice one phrase: *"de pars du Roi"*, "from the hands of the King". I thought it was a letter from Our Sovereign Lord, so I opened it. At first I thought it was some madcap nonsense, a jest, but when I finished reading it and examined the seals . . .' He shrugged. 'You can imagine my terror. Thank God Vetch and Spurge were here to help!'

'It's the only time we opened a Tower gate,' Vetch explained. 'We sent out our fastest rider to Windsor. On his return, he had to wait in St Catherine's Hospital until the Tower was re-opened.'

'So you see, Master Shallot,' Kemble spoke up, 'no one could have brought the letter into the Tower. Moreover, it stands to reason that only a man of some learning and education could buy the parchment and write in such a courtly hand.'

'And there's no one else who could be the writer?' I asked.

Vetch intervened. 'Well, as I said, there's Sir Edward, myself and Reginald. However, we also have a garrison of professional soldiers. We do not inquire too closely into their backgrounds: former priests, monks, clerks. Anyway – ' he shrugged – 'all were locked in the Tower with us. It's quite possible one of them could have written the letter. Sir Edward's chamber is always open.' He grinned. 'What's the use of guarding galleries and passageways when you are protected by a moat, two curtain walls and a dozen towers, all protected by archers and men-at-arms?'

'Who else is here?' Benjamin asked.

'Well, the mint is empty. The clerks and treasurers follow the King to Windsor,' Kemble explained. 'We had a clerk of the stores, Philip Allardyce. He was our only victim of the sweating sickness. He came back one night after roistering in a tavern in Petty Wales. He fell ill and died: his body was collected by the death-cart for the lime pits.' He shook his head. 'But that was at the beginning of July.'

'Once Allardyce died,' Kemble explained, 'I sent a letter to the King saying that I would seal the garrison in. He agreed, so the Tower was locked.'

'Oh,' Spurge tapped the table excitedly, 'and there's the Guild of Hangmen.'

'Ah yes.' Kemble wiped his mouth on the back of his hand. He smacked his lips and gestured at Vetch to serve some wine. 'Ah yes, the Guild of Hangmen.'

'They stay in the Tower?' Benjamin inquired.

'They are also the torturers,' Kemble explained. 'They are paid from the garrison accounts. There's John Mallow, he's their principal, and his five apprentices: Snakeroot, Horehound, Toadflax, Wormwood and, until recently, Hellbane.' He shrugged. 'They were all bachelors or widowers. They would have to stay.'

'But Andrew Undershaft?' I asked. 'He was found burnt to death in a cage in Smithfield Market.'

'He was different,' Vetch replied. 'Undershaft was a married man. He had his own house in the street of the Crutched Friars on the corner of Poor Jewry. We did not know about his death until the Tower was opened.'

'Hellbane?' Benjamin asked. 'How was he killed?'

'Once the Tower was opened,' Kemble explained, 'everyone was free to come and go as they wished, provided they were not drawn for duty for the day.'

'Let us see.' Agrippa, who had been sitting slouched in his chair, his black-brimmed hat over his eyes, abruptly sat up. He took his hat off, placing it on the stool beside him. 'Let us put things in order, Sir Edward. When did Allardyce the clerk in the store die?'

'Well,' Kemble replied. 'He fell ill on the eighth but died on the tenth when his body was removed. Late in the afternoon, two of the guards took it down to the death-cart waiting near the Lion Gate.'

Agrippa nodded. 'And on the thirteenth of July you sealed the Tower?'

'That is correct.'

'A month passed and nothing untoward happened?'

'No,' Kemble replied. 'We now know that on the sixteenth of July, Undershaft's corpse was found in Smithfield Market.'

'Yes, yes.' Agrippa pressed a third finger. 'And on the twenty-ninth of July the first blackmailing letter was written, sealed and delivered?'

Kemble and his two companions nodded.

Agrippa continued. 'It demanded that a thousand pounds in gold be left within the door of St Paul's on the feast of St Dominic?'

'So it said,' Spurge squeaked.

Agrippa closed his eyes. 'Now, if the gold was to be delivered on that date, the villain expected to collect it. Yes?'

Again the heads nodded.

'Where were you all on the eighth of August, on the feast of St Dominic?' Agrippa asked quietly.

'In the Tower,' Sir Edward Kemble retorted quickly. 'My good doctor, the Tower gates were not opened until the twentieth of August. The same day a herald from the city claimed the contagion was dying and the infection had passed.'

'So you were not in the city?' Benjamin asked. 'Either on the day when the gold was supposed to be left, or on the eleventh, the feast of St Clare, when this spurious Edward V had two proclamations issued: one pinned to the door of Westminster Abbey, the other to that of St Mary Le Bow in Cheapside.'

'And nor was anyone else,' Vetch explained. 'Nobody in the Tower garrison was allowed out until two days ago. God bless the King, but he cannot point the finger of accusation at us.'

I turned and glanced at Benjamin; I gathered from the troubled look in his eyes that we had entered a veritable maze of puzzles.

'The blackmailing letter to the King might have been written and delivered by someone in the Tower,' he

70

declared. 'Indeed, all the evidence points to that being the truth. Yet the gold was to be delivered and those two proclamations were posted when everyone was virtually incarcerated in the Tower.' Benjamin shook his head then turned back to Kemble. 'But it is possible, Sir Edward, that this villainy is the work of two, rather than one person. One in the Tower and one outside.'

'But how would they correspond?' Vetch inquired.

Here I intervened. 'Surely there are secret passageways, postern-gates that are unmanned?'

'All were locked and sealed,' Spurge replied. 'As surveyor of the King's work, I did that personally. Every gate and door was barred, bolted and sealed by the constable. None of those seals were broken. Moreover,' Spurge added, 'you seem to imply that Undershaft's death is connected to this bizarre mystery. But why? And who could kill such a powerful man as Andrew? He certainly would not have gone like a lamb to the slaughter.'

Benjamin toyed with the fur lining of his robe. 'Perhaps the villain is not even in the Tower,' he remarked, then tapped the table. 'You do know a second letter has been delivered? Left in the Abbot's stall at Westminster Abbey?'

'Dispatched from the Tower?' Spurge squeaked.

'Yes!'

'There is another problem,' Kemble pointed out, running one hand through his thinning hair. His face took on a smug look. 'Master Daunbey, like you my career depends on royal patronage, be it here or as keeper of the King's palace at Woodstock. Indeed, at Michaelmas I am to be relieved of this command to join an embassy to the Emperor in Bruges.' The fat little fool preened himself like a peacock.

'What's your point?' Benjamin asked tartly.

'The seals!' Sir Edward declared. 'The quality of vellum is excellent, the wax is the purest you can buy,

71

those seals were no makeshift forgeries. They are the seals of King Edward V: both the signet and the Chancellor's. Now, as you know, they should have been destroyed some forty years ago. Even if they did survive, you know how delicate such seals are? They would be battered and chipped.'

'I can't answer that, Sir Edward,' Benjamin replied. 'But, if it so concerns you, do you have any theories to explain it?'

Kemble shook his head. 'I don't know,' he murmured. 'God forgive me, Master Daunbey, but I don't. Forty years ago a young boy was imprisoned here. For a few weeks, Edward V was the rightful king, but then he and his younger brother disappeared. Now Edward has returned, almost as if he has been on some jaunt along the river and come back to find out what should have been his –' Kemble paused to choose his words carefully – 'has now been taken away.'

'Sir Edward?' I asked. 'How long have you been constable of the Tower?'

'It's two years since I left Woodstock in Oxfordshire.'

'And nothing untoward has ever happened? I mean, involving the long dead Princes?'

'No.'

'And in the Tower, what rumours exist about their fate?' I smiled deprecatingly. 'Every building, be it palace, fortress or church has its own history and legends. Fathers talk to sons . . .'

'There is nothing.' Vetch spoke up. 'Master Shallot, you tread on very thin ice: the two Princes were put here late in 1483. They were last seen with their bows shooting at the butts on the green below. This must have been in the spring of 1484. After that, all is silence. In the Tower there's no whisper or trace; it's as if these boys had never been born.'

'But if they disappeared?' I insisted. 'There must be legends about their possible fate?'

72

'Master Shallot, there are as many theories as there are hairs on your head.' Vetch began to tick the points off on his fingers. 'Some say their Uncle Richard murdered them. Others claim he sent his minions to smother them in their beds. A third theory alleges they died of some sickness, very similar to what has been raging lately in the city. Another claims one of the Princes died and one escaped. You may recall, Master Shallot, how during the present King's father's reign, two impostors came forward, each claiming to be one of the lost Princes. And . . .' He paused.

'And what?' Agrippa asked coolly.

Vetch got to his feet, the legs of the chair scraping behind him. He walked over to the door and pushed it shut. He turned the key in the lock and walked back to his seat.

'Dr Agrippa,' he said in a loud whisper, 'don't play games with us. The common tongue says the Princes were dead before Richard was killed at Bosworth. However, a few point out that it's possible that after Henry Tudor returned from his victory at Bosworth Field, these two Princes were still alive.' He spread his hands.

'Let me finish for you, Master Vetch,' Agrippa intervened. 'There are those caitiffs and knaves who claim the Princes were alive and Henry Tudor did away with them.' Agrippa slipped the ring on and off his finger, turning it round so the precious stone caught the light and sparkled. (One of Agrippa's retainers told me that the magus had a demon trapped there, ready to do his bidding.) 'They say more,' Agrippa continued. 'How King Henry VII, of blessed memory, married the Princes' sister Elizabeth, mother of the present King, so why did he not search for his brothers-in-law?'

Vetch just pulled a face. 'I cannot answer that. Perhaps His Majesty the King, or His Excellency Cardinal Wolsey, may have knowledge of such a search.'

'Let's return to these proclamations,' I said. 'Master Spurge, do you have maps describing the Tower?'

'Yes, I do.'

'And do they reveal anything?'

'Such as what?'

'Secret passageways, galleries?'

'There are sewers,' Spurge replied, 'caverns built by the Romans which run under the royal menagerie.'

'I will need those maps,' Benjamin demanded, rising to his feet. 'But now we must go.'

We murmured our thanks, walked out of the chamber, along the gallery, down the stairs and out into the sun-filled green.

'You perceive the mystery?' Agrippa's voice was half teasing.

'Why doesn't the King just seize these three precious officials, put them on the rack and get the truth?' I asked him.

Agrippa laughed softly, rocking backwards and forwards on his heels. 'Oh, very good, Roger.' He seized my arm and pulled me closer. 'You know our sweet Prince, Roger: he would condemn half of London to the scaffold. However, he needs the evidence, he needs a charge backed up by proof, however spurious that proof may be.' He indicated with his thumb. 'Those men have families and relatives. The more Henry crashes around, the greater the noise. He could kill all three. Extinguish the life of everyone in the Tower garrison as he would the wick of a candle. But the letters could well continue, and Henry's despotic actions would make people wonder. After all, when the proclamations were opened, those officials were innocently here, quietly locked away in the Tower. There's no more secure place in the kingdom than that!'

Benjamin, who had walked away to study the great ravens, now came back.

'Where to now, my good Doctor?' he asked.

Agrippa peered up at the sun. 'We are expected in Windsor by evening. Our barge will take us there. So, let's slake our thirsts, gentlemen, and join the Guild of Hangmen at the Gallows tavern.'

The prospect of a blackjack of ale, even amongst such macabre company, was a bright promise after such sinister tales. Nevertheless, as we walked back across the green and through narrow, winding lanes down to the Lion Gate, the Tower didn't seem so bright and sunny. Just before we turned a corner, I stopped and looked back at the summit of the great Norman keep. Some people claimed it had been built by the Conqueror, others by great Caesar who used human blood to mix in the mortar. Whatever, that keep was a witness to a great mystery. Forty years ago it had looked down upon two young boys playing archery on the green: one was the King of England, the other his younger brother; yet both had disappeared. Or had they? My mind became fanciful. Was it possible that some part of this Tower still housed a great Prince in hiding?

'Roger!' Benjamin called.

I was about to walk on when suddenly there was the most chilling howl. It made me start, curling the hair on the nape of my neck.

'In God's name, what was that?' I exclaimed.

'Henry's wolves,' Agrippa explained. 'A present from the Prince of Muscovy.'

Now at that time I didn't know much about Muscovy or its icy, wild wastes. Nevertheless, ever since my days in Paris during the great famine, I have had a terror of wolves. The city had been cut off by snow and the wolves came down from the forests. One night they hunted me – I was sobbing and crying for mercy as usual – along the foul alleyways of Montmartre. Now their howling awoke old terrors in Old Shallot's soul. I needed no further urging but skipped along, sighing with relief as we crossed the moat and back into Petty Wales.

Apparently Benjamin and Agrippa had changed their minds. Instead of following the Tower wall around to the tavern, we took an alleyway leading into the city.

'We'll first visit Andrew Undershaft's widow,' Benjamin explained. 'Perhaps she knew something the good constable did not!'

I recalled that blackened corpse I'd dragged from the cage in Smithfield and seized Benjamin's arm. He paused and looked kindly at me.

'Roger, what is it?'

'Master, did you believe all that?' I indicated back towards the Tower.

'They are the King's loyal officers.'

'No, no, I am sure they are. Yet how could the Prince have survived forty years? Or, if he didn't, where did those seals come from?'

Benjamin shrugged. His thumb went to his lips. 'Whoever it is knows the King's mind and the nightmares which lurk there. The King has refused to hand over the first amount. I doubt if he will the second.'

He walked on, Agrippa and I trotting behind, struggling to keep up with his long-legged gait. Now and again he stopped to make inquiries. At last a beggar boy took us along a narrow, evil-smelling runnel which led into a surprisingly pleasant open green space. Across this stood the house of Andrew Undershaft.

'He must have hanged many men,' I remarked, pointing to the freshly painted plaster and glass-filled windows.

Benjamin stopped and stared at the tilers busy on the roof, removing damaged slate and replacing it with good. He looked over his shoulder at Agrippa.

'Was Undershaft well paid?'

'Oh, yes, a goodly sum every week. At Michaelmas, midsummer, Christmas and Easter, he'd also be able to draw fresh provisions, fuel and new robes from the royal household.'

'He must have died a wealthy man,' I remarked as we

went through the gate and up the pavement; on either side lay gardens filled with flowers of every kind and hue. Benjamin knocked on the door which was briskly opened by a maid in a white mobcap and grey smock. Benjamin explained who we were. The girl curtseyed as if we were the Great Cham of Tartary. She ushered us into a sweet-smelling passageway, the walls freshly painted, and into a cosy parlour overlooking the front garden. Benjamin and I sat in the window-seat, Agrippa lounged in a chair alongside as the maid hurried off to fetch her mistress.

I heard a child crying, probably from the garden beyond, and two boys playing at the top of the stairs, followed by footsteps and the hoarse whispering of the maid outside. The door was pushed open and Mistress Undershaft came into the room. I immediately rose, sweeping off my hat: she was the prettiest wench you ever did see. Her face was narrow and pointed, the skin ivory pale. Hair the colour of straw peeped out from just beneath her widow's veil. Her dress of black taffeta, mourning weeds, only enhanced her angel-like beauty. She moved delicately with small steps, those lustrous eyes blinking against the sunlight pouring through the window. She glanced at Benjamin, myself and, more than once, at Agrippa, who must have looked like some monstrous dressed spider which had crawled into her house.

'Do I know you, sirs?'

Benjamin made the introductions. The woman's hand went out but not far enough for Benjamin to grip. She smiled quickly, her fingers flying to her lips, then opened the small reticule which swung from the belt round her narrow waist: she brought out a pair of spectacles which she perched on the bridge of that lovely nose.

'I am so sorry, sirs.' Her voice was sweet and low. 'My sight is poor but vanity makes me wear these as little as possible.'

Benjamin bowed from his waist. 'Madam, we have

come to ask you certain questions about your late husband.'

The woman closed her eyes; she clasped her hands together as if in prayer.

'That is difficult, sir,' she whispered. 'I find it so hard.'

She opened her eyes, beautiful, clear pools of light, and Old Shallot saw it. Ever so fleeting! Ever so quick! A look, a cast of the eyes, perhaps a pucker of the mouth. Those little movements you glimpse out of the corner of your eye which tell you that all is not what it appears to be. Agrippa pushed across the chair he had been sitting on and helped her into it, softly murmuring his condolences. The woman looked up, peering over her spectacles at Benjamin, then her gaze slid quickly towards me. I caught it again: a spark of mischief, of hidden laughter. Always remember Shallot's old maxim: 'A charlatan may fool a wise man but he can never fool another charlatan.'

'Sirs, do you wish something to eat or drink?'

Faced with such beauty, I would have stayed to supper, but Benjamin murmured his thanks. 'It is your husband, madam, we have come to talk about. We wish to cause as little pain as possible.'

Mistress Undershaft bowed her head, sobbing quietly. For a while we just sat in silence.

'I am sorry, madam,' Benjamin insisted, 'but we come from the King: your husband's death may not have been a simple act of revenge but connected with something much more sinister.'

The woman's head snapped up, a little too quickly. 'What do you mean, sir?' she stammered.

'Madam, excuse my bluntness, we believe your husband was pushed into a cage at Smithfield and burnt to death not out of revenge, but because of some treasonable activity . . .'

Chapter 5

'Madam.' Benjamin waited for Mistress Undershaft to compose herself. 'Before he died, did your husband act untoward? Did he mention anything? Was he worried about anything?'

'Andrew was a good man,' she replied tearfully. 'He did a dreadful job, though he always maintained that those he hanged or executed fully deserved their punishment. Every Sunday, when he went to Mass at St Peter ad Vincula in the Tower, he always prayed for the souls of those who'd suffered.'

'Precisely so, madam,' Benjamin replied, 'but did he—'

'My husband rarely talked about what he did, Master Daunbey,' she interrupted, a touch of steel in her voice. 'Unlike others of the Guild, he did not boast about how many he had killed, or how he had made such a person suffer by putting a knot in the wrong place. Nor did he refuse those burnt at Smithfield a bag of gunpowder round their necks to hasten their ends.'

(I just sat and shivered to hear this beautiful woman talk so matter-of-factly about her late husband's trade.)

'So you know nothing, madam?'

'Nothing at all.'

'And the night he died?'

'He had been at home a great deal,' Mistress Undershaft replied. 'The Tower was locked and closed. City government had been suspended, the courts had not sat, so he whiled away most of his time digging in

79

the garden or playing with the children.' She pointed to the stool Agrippa was sitting on. 'He had once been apprenticed carpenter. He kept up his old trade whenever he could.'

'And the day he died?' Benjamin insisted.

(Now, my master was a kind man, the essence of courtesy to women, but his grim face and harsh tones showed his suspicions of Madam Undershaft.)

'He stayed in most of the day,' she continued, 'but he became restless. The children were shouting—'

'How many children do you have?' I interrupted.

'Four.' She smiled tearfully at me. 'But they are not mine. Master . . .?'

'Roger Shallot, madam,' I replied.

She leaned a little closer, her bosom heaving quickly. 'Andrew had been married before,' she explained. 'His wife died about five years ago. I became handfast to him three years later. Anyway,' she continued, glancing quickly at Benjamin's impatient face, 'Andrew left the house. He said he was going to drink at the Gallows tavern.' She plucked at the cuff of her dress. 'That was all,' she concluded. 'Later the next day a bailiff came here and told me what had happened.'

'Madam.' I twisted my face into a most sympathetic grimace. 'I had the unhappy coincidence of being at Smithfield when your husband's corpse was removed from the cage. I mean to cause you no distress, but it was dreadful.'

Again that tearful smile of understanding. 'How do you know it was your husband?' I added.

She stared at me, dry-eyed: she opened her mouth to speak but thought different.

'Madam,' Benjamin asked, 'was there any distinguishing mark?'

'Oh Lord have mercy!' she snapped. 'Of course not, sir! I recognised the sole of the boots and the iron guild chain he always wore round his wrist. But no, I could not take a solemn oath and say that he was my husband. Yet, if it wasn't, then I ask you, sir, where is Andrew Undershaft?'

'Your husband was a wealthy man?' Benjamin asked.

'He was prudent, sir. His will left me this house, all his possessions, as well as some silver he had with Thurgood the goldsmith in Cheapside.' Her voice faltered.

'Madam,' I intervened. 'The tilers are busy on the roof, the house is freshly painted. Is this all your husband's legacy?'

Mistress Undershaft made to object.

'We are here on the King's business,' Agrippa declared flatly.

'Andrew was prudent,' she hastily replied. 'He had certain money salted away. However, Thurgood the goldsmith came to visit me two weeks after my husband's death. He said he had received gold and silver from a mysterious donor who wanted to ensure that I lacked for nothing.'

'And who is this kind person?' I asked tartly.

Mistress Undershaft glared at me. 'I do not really know, sir, nor do I really care. My husband was murdered. Perhaps someone's conscience pricks them and this is their way of soothing it. I am a woman left to her own devices with the care of four young children. If Satan came up from Hell with a bag of silver, I'd take it. So ask Master Thurgood: I know nothing about it.'

Benjamin asked, 'Before the sickness broke out and the Tower was closed and sealed, did your husband ever mention anything untoward happening in the fortress?'

'Such as?'

Benjamin shrugged. 'Anything you can remember, madam.'

'He talked little about his work,' Madam Undershaft replied. 'He did not like the Tower, and Sir Edward Kemble in particular. He found him a harsh disciplinarian who loved the exercise of power. Andrew thought the Tower was a cold, narrow place. Unlike his companions in the Guild, he spent as little time there as possible.'

'Did he know the dead man?' I asked. 'The clerk of stores, Philip Allardyce?'

'Andrew was there the morning he fell ill,' she replied. 'Allardyce came down to the Gallows tavern to break his fast. He complained of a thick head and pains in his body. My husband later visited him. He took him a small flask of wine but the fellow was already delirious. My husband recognised the symptoms. He never went back to the Tower again. Allardyce died and the Tower was sealed off.'

'Did he ever mention anything about the Princes?' I asked.

The woman's confused look and shake of her head showed she was no student of history.

'Did you know the other hangman who was murdered? Hellbane?' Benjamin quickly asked.

'I heard rumours,' she replied. 'John Mallow, the chief hangman, sometimes visits me. He brings sweetmeats for the children – yet what can I say, sirs? I can speak for John Mallow: like my husband, he is an honourable man. But the others, with their dreadful names and secret pasts!'

'Secret pasts?' I queried.

'Andrew believed the one who calls himself Toadflax was once a priest in Coventry who turned to black magic. Another, Wormwood, went to the Halls of Cambridge, from where he fled after committing some dreadful crime.'

'And they just told him this?' I asked.

'My husband liked his ale, Master Shallot, and so did they. In every guild they've had their parties and banquets. The last one was on the occasion of the King's birthday, the sixth of June. Apparently Sir Edward

Kemble, according to ancient custom, allowed them to use chambers in the royal apartments. The hangmen brought their ladies, or should I say women of the town?'

'You were not there?' I asked innocently.

'Of course not!' she snapped. 'My husband told me about all the goings-on . . . when he returned,' she added primly.

'Your husband was a carpenter?' I asked. 'He was a literate man? He could write and keep accounts?'

'Oh, of course, sir.' She rose and went across to a chest standing beneath the crucifix. She opened it and brought back a ledger. 'He sometimes sold what he made in the markets. He kept scrupulous accounts.'

I opened the ledger and showed it to Benjamin. He stared at the beautiful copperplate handwriting and smiled.

'Madam,' my master rose and handed the ledger back. 'I thank you for your time in answering our questions honestly. You have nothing further to say?'

'No.'

She darted a smile at me: I quietly wondered whether it would be appropriate for me to visit her by myself.

My master continued. 'Naturally we must make further inquiries of Master Thurgood the goldsmith about this mysterious donor. Perhaps a letter from you?'

Mistress Undershaft nodded and left the room. I wanted to draw Benjamin into hushed conversation, but he shook his head. We waited silently until Mistress Undershaft returned and gave him a square of vellum neatly· tied with a piece of silk ribbon. We made our farewells and left. We walked across the green and back up the alleyway leading to the Tower.

Half-way along, Benjamin stopped and undid the letter. The writing was not as elegant as her late husband's, yet Mistress Undershaft had a good hand for someone who, perhaps, had not been properly tutored. The letters were boldly formed: she simply informed the goldsmith that he should answer any questions the bearer might ask about her mysterious legacy.

'What did you think of her?' Benjamin asked.

'Shrewd,' Agrippa retorted.

'A good actress,' I added. I narrowed my eyes and stared further down the alleyway. 'I don't wish to be cruel, but on the one hand she mourns her husband, yet on the other there is something else. Is it possible that Master Undershaft is not dead? That he killed someone else to take his place and is continuing to send silver to his wife whilst he hides in the city and blackmails the King?'

Benjamin nodded. 'It is true we have no proof that her husband was definitely killed. Undershaft was an educated man, skilled with his hands. He might find the art of forgery an easy accomplishment. His wife could well be party to it.' Benjamin tapped the parchment. 'But that still leaves as many questions as it answers. How was the letter delivered by Undershaft if the Tower was sealed?'

'An accomplice?' I asked.

'Possible,' Benjamin replied, 'but how would they communicate?'

'We have still to study Spurge's maps,' I replied. 'Undershaft could still be alive and the villain of the piece. He might have written that letter before he left the Tower and given it to his accomplice to deliver when the fortress was closed and shuttered. He could then have arranged for the proclamations to be posted after falsifying his own death.'

'I agree,' Agrippa declared. 'Whilst the other hangman, Hellbane, could have been murdered because he knew something? Mistress Undershaft is not what she appears to be, I can see that: her grief is not as deep as it should be. No one identified that corpse as her husband's. We also learnt that Master Undershaft had little liking for Sir Edward Kemble. Moreover, if

Undershaft is supposed to be dead, then that's the best disguise, if you are sending letters of blackmail against the King and leaving them at Westminster or elsewhere. But who the accomplice is and how they communicate is a mystery. And those seals, Roger, are no forgeries. In truth they once belonged to Edward the Fifth. If your theory is correct, how did Undershaft or his accomplice get their hands on them?' He looked up at the sky. 'We must go,' he murmured. 'The King has gone hunting today, as he will tomorrow.' He smiled grimly. 'But he expects to see you at supper tonight, Roger. Moreover, we still have business to do with Snakeroot, Wormwood and the rest.'

We walked back into Petty Wales. Agrippa led us directly to the Gallows tavern which, despite its grisly sign, was a clean, spacious ale-house. The taproom inside was high-vaulted. Bunches of herbs hung in baskets from the rafters, shedding the fragrance of a summer day through the ale fumes and rather greasy odours from the kitchen. The landlord apparently took the sign of his tavern very seriously: the place was decorated with blocks of wood from this gibbet or that. On one wall hung a rope which was supposedly used to kill the great imposter Perkin Warbeck. Above the fireplace a wooden box held – so the notice scrawled below proclaimed – part of the skin flayed from Richard Puddlicott who had tried to raid the King's treasury at Westminster Abbey. A cheerful though gruesome place: skulls had been painted on the floorboards, whilst the wooden pillar in the centre of the room was decorated with knives and daubed with red paint so it looked like a whipping post.

Do you know, over the years I have grown fascinated by human nature. Why do people find the most gruesome things in society so interesting? If I stood up in Cheapside and said I owned the skull of a dog, people would just pass by. However, if I said I was the proud owner of the skull of some bloody-handed murderer, who was also a chaplain in this or that church, everyone would gather round to stare: that's one thing I learnt from my relic-selling days. I sold more skulls, reputedly those of Barabbas or Pontius Pilate, than I did anything else!

Ah well, that's human nature and, little did I know it, my arrival at the Gallows tavern was an introduction to the deep, murderous passions which lurk in the human heart. The Guild of Hangmen were there, seated in a corner beneath a crudely drawn painting of a scaffold. I took one look and thought, oh aye nonny no, here goes Old Shallot again! They were all dressed in black, white shirts peeping beneath the leather jerkins and doublets. (I am always wary of people who dress in the most sombre colours, as if they are in love with death.) John Mallow, the chief hangman, was a grisly-looking soul: small and fat with wizened features, a scrawny beard, smiling mouth, with yellow-gapped teeth and eyes like two piss-holes in the snow. He was the most handsome of them all! Mallow, in turn, introduced his four so-called apprentices: Snakeroot, tall and thin with shift eyes and a slack mouth, a man who'd lurk behind the arras or in the shadows and listen to what you said. Horehound was a tippler; he had a fat, greasy face, greasy spiked hair, a body like a ball of fat with no neck or waist. His chin seemed to rest on his chest. Like me, he had a cast in one eye: not the sort of face to wish you well as you were turned off the ladder at Tyburn or Smithfield! Toadflax was different. He was tall, clean-shaven, bronze-faced. His dyed yellow hair framed his face like that of a girl; his eyes were strange. When he looked at you his mind was elsewhere, as if he lived in a dark world all of his own. Wormwood – well, if I had to choose one of them to go on a journey with, I would have selected him. He at least looked human, with sharp-etched features and cool grey eyes. A man who

86

took meticulous care with his appearance. I wondered why such a man was working as a hangman. One thing I did notice (and I nudged Benjamin) was that Wormwood was writing what he claimed to be a sonnet. Although I couldn't make out the words, I could tell from the script that Wormwood was an educated man who could have secured a benefice in any great nobleman's Chancery.

They all made us welcome enough. Benjamin ordered fresh stoups of ale. Agrippa sat as if he was a shadow. I shivered a little, for Mallow and his four apprentices all concentrated on me. They studied Old Shallot from head to toe as if assessing how much I weighed, how broad my shroud would be, and how long it would take for me to choke on the end of a rope. (Perhaps that was my guilty conscience. During my long and convoluted life I have been condemned to death either in England or abroad at least eighteen times. Sorry, nineteen, I forgot that madcap bugger, the Prince of Muscovy. I've been, no less than eight times, on the scaffold with a rope round my neck.)

Nevertheless, I remained merry-faced. For a while we discussed the sweating sickness, though the conversation was desultory. Mallow and his apprentices seemed highly nervous of Dr Agrippa, and even more so when Benjamin introduced himself as the Cardinal's nephew. I could understand their fear. Hangmen always have a shadowy past. They hide just beneath the skirts of the law and take cold comfort in the fact that, if they are its servants, they are safe. Mallow abruptly made that point.

'We have done nothing wrong, sirs.' He sipped from his tankard.

'No one has said you have,' Benjamin coolly replied. 'But, as St Augustine says, *"Quis custodiet custodes?"* "Who will guard the guards?"' He beat his tankard gently on the table. 'What we do have are villains threatening His Grace the King.'

'We know nothing of that,' Wormwood whispered, his voice no more than a hiss, 'though we heard tittle-tattle about the letters.'

'And the deaths of Hellbane and Undershaft?'

'Again innocent,' Toadflax sneered. 'Master Daunbey.' The hangman leaned forward, I noticed how ink-stained his fingers were. 'We, too, are officers of the Crown. We execute the villains of London. One in three go to the scaffold screaming their innocence: around the hanging tree, their friends and relatives shake their fists and spit at us!'

'Anyone in particular?' I asked innocently.

Toadflax drew his head back, studying me from under heavy-lidded eyes. If he could, he would have spat at me.

Mallow, sniffing and wiping his mouth with the back of his hand, called for more ale before continuing. 'Undershaft and Hellbane were young, powerful men. They would not have given up their lives easily.'

'Hellbane was fished from the Thames,' I replied. 'It's easy to knock a man on the head, put weights on a sack and tip him into the water.'

'If that's the case,' Mallow snapped, 'the list of suspects is endless.'

'Indeed,' Wormwood whispered, 'it could happen to any of us.'

'So, you know nothing?' Benjamin asked, pushing back his stool as if to rise. 'That is the answer we shall give His Grace the Cardinal.'

'No.' Mallow shrugged.

'No quarrel between you, within the guild?'

'None whatsoever. Master Daunbey,' Mallow pleaded, 'it is true that one of us here could have killed Hellbane, but why? True, we have heard of those proclamations pinned on the doors of churches in Westminster and Cheapside, as well as the death of poor Andrew. But, sir, we were in the Tower when all this happened, kept as close and secure as any prisoner.'

'Tell me,' I asked, 'this clerk of the stores, Allardyce: did you know him well?'

Mallow looked at his companions and pulled a face.

'Describe him to me,' I ordered.

'He was tall, about your height,' the hangman replied. 'Long black curly hair, moustache and beard, thick and luxuriant which he liked to oil. He was a happy-go-lucky fellow with no known family and friends. He told us he came from Dover: his task was to keep careful account of the foodstuffs and fodder stored in the Tower. Allardyce would record what came in, how it was distributed. He would also advise the constable or Master Vetch what further supplies were needed.'

'And he fell sick?' I insisted.

'We'd all heard about the sweating sickness, but Allardyce just laughed at it. One day he came down here to break his fast. He said he felt unwell. He was shivering, the sweat coursing down his face like water. He went back to the Tower. Sir Edward Kemble was of a mind to throw him out—'

'How do you know that?' I interrupted.

Mallow pointed to Snakeroot. 'He's well named.' He grinned. 'He slides along galleries and corridors and listens through half-open doors.'

Snakeroot pulled a face. 'I heard Kemble roaring at Allardyce,' he said, 'telling him he should not have come to his chamber. The Tower has a small infirmary, nothing more than a bare cell. Kemble ordered him to go there.'

'Where is this?' I asked.

'Near Bowyer Tower, overlooking the river. There's an old woman, slightly madcap, who calls herself Ragusa. She has some knowledge of physic and looks after those of the garrison who fall ill.' He grinned. 'Sometimes, for a coin, she'll help those lads out who haven't got a woman.'

'And did you see Allardyce there?' I asked.

89

'Oh, for the love of God!' Horehound snapped petulantly.

'I went to visit him.' Mallow spoke up. 'The infirmary's a small, two-storey building. Allardyce was on the upper floor. I went up and left a small jug of wine. The door was open. Allardyce was lying on the bed. He looked like a soaked rag.'

Benjamin drained his tankard and put it down on the table. 'You have nothing to say?' he said again.

They chorused their denials once more, so we thanked them and walked out of the tavern.

'A fine collection, eh, Roger?' Agrippa teased.

'A motley group of moult worms,' I growled. 'I don't like hangmen and that group in particular. Master, they are far too close, their answers are too smooth, well prepared. And, don't forget,' I added, 'that many of them had the education to write those letters, and enough accomplices in the city to assist their nefarious work. Perhaps everyone of them is guilty, and they all conspired to kill Undershaft and Hellbane because they objected.'

I glimpsed the doubt in Benjamin's eyes. 'Though I confess, Master, where they got the seals from and how they were able to communicate when the Tower was locked and sealed is a mystery.'

'Which brings us back to Spurge's maps,' Benjamin said.

He was about to walk on but paused. 'Roger, why did you ask about the clerk of the stores?'

I pulled a face. 'Master, I just wondered. Is it possible that Allardyce did not really die, but that his sickness and death was a sham? He leaves the Tower to act on behalf of his accomplice within?'

Benjamin smiled. 'We'll go back to the Tower. Roger, seek out this old woman Ragusa: have a look at the sick room. Agrippa and I will seek out Master Spurge and demand to see his maps and charts.'

When we reached the royal apartments in the Tower, Agrippa and Benjamin went down to see Spurge. I wandered across the green, past the great Norman keep. A soldier, lounging in the sunshine mending his harness, pointed out the way: I entered a deserted yard, the cobblestones cracked and overgrown with weeds. At the far end stood a small, red-brick building which had been built beside the wall. I went across, pushed open the door, and peered through the gloom.

'Have you come to be milked?' a voice crackled out of the darkness.

An old woman came forward, peering at me. By my own witness I am no beauty, but neither was she. Her hair, a dirty white, hung straggling down to bowed shoulders, her face was deathly pale. She had little black eyes and a thin slit of a mouth under a hooked nose. If I had been asked to name a witch in London, I'd have chosen Ragusa. She was dressed from head to toe in a dark, dirt-stained smock. I tried not to wrinkle my nose at the sour smell, which came either from her or the shabby little room in which she lived. She laughed at me and went back in. I heard a tinder spark as she lit a squat tallow candle. The room looked better in the dark. The rushes on the floor were soiled and looked as if they hadn't been changed for months. Tawdry rags hung on the walls, and in one corner was a cot-bed with a battered trunk beside it which served as a table. There were a few sticks of furniture, and shelves lined the wall, each bearing pots, jugs and small cups, all neatly labelled. The old woman followed my gaze.

'Is it physic you need, Master?' She whined, looking at me from head to toe. 'Physic of the mind or the body?'

'No, just some answers, Mother,' I replied.

'Questions cost money too.' Her face cracked in a smile. I twirled the silver coin before her eyes. She went to grab it but I pulled it away.

'What is it you want?'

'The clerk, Allardyce,' I said. 'You tended him when he was ill?'

'That's right, but there was little I could do for him. He came here on the Tuesday, he was dead by Thursday. Drenched in sweat, buboes in his armpits and groin.' Her thin, bony fingers clawed the air. 'There's no cure for that. I just gave him valerian drops to make him sleep and ease his pain.'

'And you are sure it was he?'

The old woman cackled. 'Why shouldn't it be? Who'd pretend to have the sweating sickness, take valerian, and then offer to die? Are you witless, man?'

'But it was Allardyce?' I asked.

'Of course!' she snapped.

'And you saw him die?'

'Of course I did! I found him in the chamber upstairs.' She pointed to a flight of rickety stairs in the far corner. 'I heard a crash and went upstairs. He was half on, half off the bed, eyes open, blood drooling out of the corner of his mouth. The stench was terrible. I sent for Sir Edward Kemble.'

'And did he come?' I asked.

'Oh no, not that chicken-heart. He climbed half-way up the stairs, took one look at the chamber, and told me to throw a sheet over the man. I did. The following morning two of the soldiers took his sheeted corpse down to the death-cart at the Lion Gate. He was dead as a nail!'

I was about to turn when she caught my sleeve. 'You promised payment. The Tower has many mysteries, Master, but that poor clerk's death was not one.'

'Such as?' I asked, coming back, closing the door behind me. I dropped the silver coin into her hands and tapped my fingers against the dagger in my belt.

'Don't threaten me, Master.' She stepped back. 'I am Ragusa, at least seventy summers old. I have seen all the great lords come tripping through here: Edward the

92

Fourth of blessed memory, his brother Richard of York, the Duke of Buckingham, the present King's father. All come and gone like shadows in the sun.'

'You saw the young Princes?' I asked curiously.

'Aye, poor boys. Oh, they were well looked after, but they were shut up in Wakefield Tower. I saw them playing on the green when their uncle seized the Crown. The elder one fell ill with an abscess in his jaw. I visited him and gave the lad tincture of cloves.'

'But they were in good health?'

'As rude and robust as you are, Master.' She shrugged. 'Then one day they disappeared: that was the end of the matter.'

'Do you know other mysteries?' I asked. 'Tell me, Mother, if all the gates and doorways in the Tower were locked and sealed, could anyone leave or enter?'

'A witch might,' she taunted. 'She might fly over the walls on her broomstick.'

'Witches are burnt at Smithfield, madam.'

'Aye and so are hangmen.' Her wizened face took on a sly, secretive look. 'Oh, we know what this is all about. Sir Edward Kemble's terror when he opened that letter was known by us all.'

I plucked another silver coin from my purse. 'Mother, can you help?'

She knocked the coin from my hand, her hands were so swollen and rheumatic. She scrabbled on the floor for it then stood up. 'No, I can't help. But if things change, you'll be the first to know.'

I turned, my hand on the latch.

'They say there is a secret passageway,' she added. 'Down near the menagerie, under the pits there.' She lifted her stiff, vein-streaked hands. 'But I have told you enough!' she snapped.

I left the old harridan and walked back, following the line of the wall. I went through a small door into an area which overlooked the moat, squeezed between the outer and inner walls. This contained the royal menagerie. A stinking, fetid place, with cages built along the walls holding a mangy lion and a leopard, mad of eye, ribs showing through its coat, pacing up and down. There was a pelican as well as a big, fat brown bear manacled by chains to the wall: the beast hardly bothered to lift its head as I came in to the enclosure. The area was deserted. The keepers, or whoever was paid to look after them, probably drifted away to clear their heads of the smell and bask in the warm afternoon sunshine. On the far side of the enclosure I glimpsed the brick rim of a pit, surrounded by a carpet of sand. I walked across to this, my feet crunching on pebble-covered ground. I gingerly looked over the pit. It must have been about ten feet deep and stank like a cesspool.

At first I thought it was empty, but then a grey bundle which I thought was a collection of rags stirred, and an old, bleary-eyed wolf, tongue lolling between his jaws, looked up at me. I'd seen more vigour in a corpse. I walked round the pit. Although the wolf was old it had a terrible madness all of its own. Moreover, its thick, heavy-furred shoulders, long lean body, drooping brushed tail, erect head and pointed face brought back nightmares from Paris. I walked away, back to look at the lion which had hardly stirred but lay on its side fast asleep. A clink, as if someone had thrown a coin on to the gravel, made me start.

'Who's there?' I called.

No answer. I was about to leave, putting more trust in Master Spurge's maps than my own curiosity when, again, there was a clink. Now, old Shallot has been in many dangerous places before. Someone was here, either hiding in one of the outhouses, or where the fodder and hay was stored. I glanced around and wondered if someone had come along the parapet. My flesh chilled. If someone was waiting for me here, how would they know I'd come? I was sure no one had followed me from

94

Ragusa's hovel. Had someone been listening at the door? I walked slowly back to where the sound had come from. Lying on the sand was a pure silver coin of far better quality than the one I had given the old hag. Now, you know old Shallot: even now my coat of arms includes a jackdaw, because if something glitters, I always look. I snatched up the coin, thick and freshly minted. I saw another one, and hurried to do the same. There was a third just near the rim of the pit and, like a fool, I fell into the trap. The oldest coney-catching device in London: put something precious on the floor and it will always attract the greedy eye and fingers.

I hurried to the rim of the pit. I bent down to pick it up and, as I did so and was half rising, a blow in the small of my back pitched me forward. Now old Shallot is quick of wit with even faster legs, but that blow sent me staggering. I tried to stop myself. I was heading towards the pit, then I was over and falling, my hands flailing the air. I would have gone to the bottom if my fingers had not grasped and held the thick hempen rope which hung there. I hung on for dear life, gibbering with fright. I glanced down. The old wolf hadn't stirred but just stared up curiously. I am sure that, if it could, it would have jumped up and licked my legs. I grasped the rope even tighter, and noticed there was another rope also hanging a few feet away, probably used to lower foodstuffs into the pit. I tried to grab it, hoping I could swing myself up, when I heard a terrible chilling howl. There was another wolf hidden in the cavern running off the pit.

Chapter 6

I stared down in horror. The newcomer was no mangy animal but a great, grey wolf in all its prime, sharp in ferocity and, from the way it was glaring up at me, mad with hunger. One of those magnificent loping beasts from my blackest nightmare. The great ruff on its shoulders stood up. Its jaws were open, lips curled, tongue slavering at the prospect of a piece of Old Shallot for dinner. I screamed and tried to climb even as the wolf sprang, its teeth narrowly missing the heel of my boot. God knows how I did it. The rope burnt my hands, and it seemed like an age as I pulled myself up towards the rim. Again I glimpsed a flurry, a grey shape jumping up almost beside me, snaking its head, its jaws lashing at me. I screamed and climbed faster, ignoring the burning pain in the palms of my hands. The rope was beginning to fray where it hung over the rim of the pit. I heard a snap as strands began to break. The wolf howled and so did I. It lunged again; this time its teeth scored my boot. I closed my eyes and quietly vowed: no more claret, no more wenches, a life of prayer and fasting! The top of the pit seemed as far off as ever. I was terrified I would slip. I screamed and yelled. Suddenly Benjamin was leaning over and, with Agrippa's help, pulled me out. For a while I just crouched on the ground, sobbing for breath. I vomited out of sheer terror. I crawled back to the rim of the pit and shook my fist at the wolf which stood slavering up at me.

'You bastard!'

I fumbled for the hilt of my dagger but Benjamin pulled me away.

'Roger, Roger, for the love of God, it's a dumb animal!'

'It will be a dead dumb animal!' I snarled.

Agrippa came forward. He kicked a long pole which lay near the door of an outhouse, and I realised by what means I'd been pushed into the pit. He thrust a wineskin at me.

'You'll not die here, Roger,' he whispered. 'Drink the wine. Go on,' he urged. 'It's Falernian, the wine of ancient emperors. Pilate drank it when he condemned Christ.'

I lifted the wineskin and let the fragrant juice lap into my mouth. I gave it back, smiled and promptly fainted.

When I revived, I was not in the Tower but in a small ale-house on a corner of an alleyway near Thames Street. Agrippa was pushing a piece of burnt cork under my nose.

'Faugh!' I cursed, and drove it away. I blinked up at my master who was staring at me anxiously.

'Are you well, Roger?' he asked.

'Oh yes.' I straightened up and glared round the small taproom. 'It's not every day you are thrown to the wolves!' I tried to get up but my legs felt a little unsteady. 'How did I get here?' I asked.

'Agrippa and I helped you down to the Lion Gate. We begged a ride from a carter and brought you here.' Benjamin leaned back against the wall. 'Have something to eat, man.'

A slattern came up, bearing a tray of spiced beef, a pot of vegetables and tankards of ale. Now, one of the things about Old Shallot is that if you show me a pretty face or a good meal, danger is soon forgotten. I took my horn spoon out of my wallet and ate as ravenously as any wolf. Indeed, for a few seconds, I could appreciate that beast's disappointment.

'Who did it?' Agrippa asked as I put my horn spoon down and sat back, rubbing my stomach.

'I don't know.' I replied. 'One minute I was picking up silver coins, then a blow on my back with that pole tipped me over. One of those bastards at the Tower must have been hiding in an outhouse.'

'Impossible,' Benjamin replied. 'We were with Kemble, Vetch and Spurge. They never left us, so it couldn't have been one of them.'

'What about the precious Guild of Hangmen?'

Benjamin shook his head. 'As we left the Tower we met them coming in.'

'And I suppose they laughed fit to burst?' I snapped. 'At me being tossed into some cart?'

Agrippa grinned. 'No, they didn't. They declared that if you were being taken to a hanging, could they do it for us?'

'Bastards!' I muttered.

Benjamin grasped my hand. 'Roger, you say someone tried to kill you. You are sure of that?'

'No, Master, I just decided to go down and meet the wolves.'

Benjamin picked up his tankard.

'But if Spurge, Vetch and Sir Edward were talking to you,' I continued, 'and all five hangmen were outside the Lion Gate, who else could it have been?'

A small, black cat appeared from nowhere and jumped into Agrippa's lap. He stroked it, softly talking to it in a language I could not understand. When he glanced up at me his eyes were like the animal's, amber-coloured. I glanced nervously away, taking comfort in the homely atmosphere of the taproom: the onions hanging in bunches from the rafters, the slatterns and scullions chattering near the kitchen door. Two men, leaning over a badger in a cage; a drunk in the far corner; a madcap chattering to himself, waving his hands at some invisible audience. I closed my eyes and thought of that wolf-pit. Who could possibly have followed me, intent on murder?

'Mistress Undershaft was in the Tower,' Benjamin observed. 'As we left Sir Edward, we met her going across Tower Green with two of her children. Apparently, as Undershaft's widow, she still has the right to draw on provisions.'

'But why should she attack me?' I asked.

'You visited Ragusa?' Agrippa asked. 'Could she have followed you?'

I thought of that old woman's shuffling gait, her rheumatic hands and shook my head. Again Agrippa looked at me, his eyes that strange colour.

'What are you thinking, good Doctor?' I snapped. 'That some ghost or ghoul lurks in the Tower?'

Agrippa blinked his eyes, then became bright and merry: as he shifted to put the cat back on the floor, I smelt that strange exotic perfume from his robes.

'It could have been a ghoul or ghost,' he said softly, picking up his tankard. 'What happens, Roger, if the Princes didn't die?' He laughed. 'I am only teasing you, but I believe –' he lifted one black gloved hand – 'that the fate of those two Princes lies at the root of all this mystery. Did Ragusa tell you anything?' he asked.

'She claimed there were secret caverns and passageways beneath the royal menagerie.'

'Yes,' Benjamin nodded. 'Spurge's maps told us the same; that's why we came to the wolf-pit. Kemble maintains that the caverns those beasts live in were once Roman sewers. However, they are now blocked off.'

'I'll take his word for it,' I replied.

'One day we will have to see if that is true,' Benjamin warned. He patted me on the arm. 'But don't worry, Roger, we'll make sure the wolves are caged.'

'And the clerk, Allardyce?' Agrippa asked.

'According to Ragusa, dead as a doornail.'

'Yes, that's what the hangmen told us. They were at

the Lion Gate the morning his body was carried out. They say the soldiers almost dragged it along the cobbles and threw it in the death-cart. There was also a bailiff present.' Benjamin described the same man I had met in Smithfield. 'He declared a proper scrutiny should be made. He climbed into the cart, lifted back the sheet, and pronounced the man dead.'

I remembered my own days working with the death-carts. Usually corpses were dragged out and piled in, but if a city bailiff was present, one of those honest royal officials, this scrutiny was always made. I flung my hands up in the air.

'So Allardyce is dead and my theory with him!' I exclaimed. 'Here we have blackmailing letters being delivered to the King bearing the seal of a prince who was supposed to have died forty years ago. Now, concedo, Master, anyone in the Tower – the hangmen, Kemble or his two associates – could have written them. However, if they did, they could not have sneaked out of the Tower to collect the thousand pounds at St Paul's. They were certainly not there when those two proclamations were posted in Westminster and Cheapside, or the second blackmailing letter which was left in the Abbey. So,' I sipped from my tankard, 'there is either a secret way of entering and leaving the Tower, which I doubt. Or the villain in the Tower has an accomplice outside. Now, we know Allardyce is dead, so it must be Undershaft, or his wife, or both.'

'And Hellbane's death?' Benjamin asked.

'Murdered to silence his tongue.'

'But why?' Benjamin asked.

'I don't know, Master.' I drained my tankard. 'As I don't know who tipped me over the edge of that pit to be devoured by that bloody wolf!'

Agrippa, who had been staring through a window overlooking the garden, abruptly got to his feet.

'It's best,' he warned, 'when we meet the King, that

101

we say nothing of this. We have eaten and drunk enough. We should be gone.'

We arrived at Windsor just as darkness fell. The journey up-river had been quiet and serene enough. Benjamin and I dozed as Agrippa's stalwarts cracked their backs, pulling lustily at the oars. Their master, sitting in the prow of the boat, chattered to himself or stared out across the river, carefully watching the sunset.

The small town built under the soaring keep of Windsor castle was dark and quiet. Agrippa led us up through the steep, narrow streets and across the moat into the Great Beast's favourite palace. Inside all was light and colour: lantern horns hung gleaming like fireflies in the yard. Rich, savoury smells from the kitchen mixed with those in the stables: servants, scurriers, messengers and chamberlains hurried about on this errand or that. The King was in residence and everybody knew it.

Now Windsor is a great sprawling palace: a mixture of fortress and stately manor house with its outer and inner keep, the long connecting galleries, chambers and halls decorated and developed by successive princes. The most beautiful is the Rose Chamber, a long hall or gallery with huge windows on either side. Agrippa led us along this. Outside it was dark, but burning torches and tall yellow beeswax candles turned night into day. Nobody noticed us as we passed; everyone was busy. Agrippa whispered how the King, after his day's hunting, would want his usual dancing and banqueting until the early hours. That was the Great Beast: during the day he'd pursue the fleet-footed stag, whilst at night he would go after the fast-living women of his Court. He'd then arise the next morning complaining about the labours of State and decide to relax with a day's hunting, and so it went on.

Henry had a deep, abiding fear of illness; the very

thought of it and he'd pull up sticks and race off to a place as far away as possible. During that hot, sweaty summer, with the sickness raging in London, he'd moved lock, stock and barrel to Windsor. The Exchequer, Chancery, and even the Court came with him. He also made sure his stay was as comfortable as possible. The walls of the palace were decorated with hangings to be replaced every week by yeomen and grooms of the wardrobe. Furniture from the London palaces filled every room. The royal kitchen, under the command of its French master-chef, worked morning to night roasting beef, mutton, lamb, chicken, pheasants and quails to feed the King and his vast concourse of courtiers.

Of course, poor Benjamin and I got nothing of that. Agrippa handed us over to a royal chamberlain whilst he slipped away. This snotty-nosed little varlet, waving his white wand as if he was king of the fairies, took us to a shabby little chamber in one of the towers: it contained two truckle-beds and a mouldy, worm-eaten chest into which we put our belongings. Thankfully we had not brought much. We never did on these journeys to Court. Henry was a great thief and loved to taunt me. Once I had a fine buckram jacket which disappeared from my chamber when I visited him at Sheen. He just shrugged and said, what could I expect in such a busy place? A few days later I saw it on the back of one of his great hunting dogs, cut and clipped to make the beast feel warm!

Naturally I protested at our quarters, but Benjamin shrugged, murmuring that this was not Uncle's doing; he doubted anyway that we'd stay in Windsor for long. It I had known what the Great Beast had planned, I would have opened the window and dived straight into the moat. It always surprised me that, busy and frenetic though the Court was, Henry always knew when I had arrived. He told me when he grew old, when no one would go near him except old Will Somers, his jester, and myself, that he always longed to see my face. The great turd of a liar! But that's Fortune's fickle wheel, isn't it? In my youth Henry despised me. He baited me and taunted me. The fat bugger even tried to kill me; but when Henry grew old and became imprisoned in his mobile chair, it was Old Shallot who had to push him about. I'd sit with him in the sun-washed tilt-yard at Whitehall. He'd grab my jerkin, those piggy eyes blazing with madness, and push his slobbering lips next to my ear.

'We are so alike, Roger,' he whispered. 'Rogues, but good men underneath.'

(Oh, the gift of self-deception! He'd then go on and list all those he'd once loved who'd failed him: Wolsey, Cromwell, Boleyn, Norris, Howard. Good Lord, my stomach would clench at the long list of men and women he'd used and discarded. Well, Henry's at Windsor for good now. The fat slob is buried there. I personally helped stuff his bloated corpse into the coffin. And it's true, like Pope Alexander VI's, the corpse later blew up and exploded, though by then I was gone, riding for my life from black-garbed assassins. However, that's for the future because, though many don't know it, Henry VIII did not die in his sleep; he was murdered!)

However, on that summer evening so many years ago, my master and I were locked in our little garret, thinking we would have to wait for days before the King summoned us, when a messenger arrived. A royal huntsman, dressed in green velvet with a cap upon his head, adorned with a pheasant plume. (Oh yes, when Henry went hunting he dressed like Robin Hood, silly bugger!) This huntsman, a surly brown-faced fellow, said the King was in his chapel attending a Mass for his dogs. I thought I had misheard him, but as the fellow took us down the stairs and along the gallery, Benjamin grasped my sleeve and whispered that, whatever happened, I was not to laugh. The huntsman took us into the chapel of St George, a beautiful miniature jewel of a church. Its walls and richly decorated stalls were brightly caparisoned with the banners and pennants of the Knights of the Garter. The sanctuary was bathed in light. A priest stood on the altar, ready to say Mass. I glimpsed the back of the King where he sprawled in his throne-like chair, on his right the great Cardinal himself. However, what caught my attention and took my breath away was that the stalls on either side of the sanctuary – two rows, about twenty-eight seats in all – were full, not with chaplains or the King's royal choir, but with bloody great mastiffs and hunting dogs. I just stopped and gaped! The buggers sat there more devout than many a priest, legs together, heads up, ears cocked. You think I joke? I tell you, I half-expected them to burst into the 'Te Deum'.

The chief huntsman turned and glared at me. Benjamin grasped me by the arm and pushed me forward. We went to kneel on the steps before the sanctuary. The King turned to his right, glimpsed me kneeling behind him, snapped his fingers and the Mass began.

It was the strangest ceremony I have ever attended! A simple Low Mass, the priest from the chapel royal devoutly reciting it. The King sat as if he was God himself, whilst Wolsey... well, only the good Lord knows where his subtle mind was wandering. Nevertheless, it was those dogs which fascinated me. I couldn't take my eyes off them. They sat watching the priest as intently as if he were a rabbit hole. Naturally, during the epistle, a couple of them got down to wander off. The King stretched out his hand, clicked his fingers, and back they went. Now the Great Beast loved his dogs. Mind you, I have noticed that about bloodthirsty tyrants. Catherine de'Medici was no different. She'd kill people in batches, only to sit on the floor and weep because her pet lap-dog's paw had been injured.

At last the Mass ended and the priest, before the final benediction, picked up an asperges rod and bucket and blessed each of the animals. I looked at the leader, a great mastiff, almost as big as the lion I had glimpsed in the royal menagerie. I am sure he almost bowed his head. The priest left the sanctuary. The Great Beast rose to his feet and walked along the stalls, patting each dog on its head.

'Lovely boys!' he whispered. 'Lovely, lovely lads!'

The dogs whimpered with pleasure. The King clapped his hands: they all climbed down and followed the huntsman out of the church as devoutly as a line of novices. The King turned his attention on us, indicating that we should come and kneel on the cushions in the sanctuary before him.

I glanced quickly at the Cardinal. He sat sprawled in the throne-like chair, a small purple silk skull-cap pushed on to the back of his black, oily hair. He looked the powerful prince; his features smooth and swarthy like an Italian: red sensuous lips, a slightly beaked nose and dark, lustrous eyes. He was dressed in scarlet trimmed with gold. He caught my eye, winked, and stared piously up at the crucifix in the apse of the church. He would not dare address us until the King had.

The Great Beast proved to be in fine fettle. He was dressed in a lincoln-green jerkin brocaded with silver, matching hose, soft leather boots with an ermine-lined cloak draped over his shoulders. Because he was in church, his head was bare; the only place Henry did not wear those bejewelled bonnets he was so fond of. Oh, but it was his face! Do you know, I have seen Holbein's painting, fat and square with those piggy, slanted eyes. Henry always reminded me more of a Tartar than an Englishman, yet you have to give the devil his due: he had a presence. If Henry had been married to the right woman; if he'd listened to honest men like Tom More instead of the crawlies which swarmed round his court, he could have been a great prince. If you ignored the eyes, his face had a nobility all of its own. A broad brow, powerful jaw, and those lips always clenched; when they opened to speak, everyone's heart skipped a beat. He glanced down at Benjamin and proffered his hand, his fingers shimmered with light from the precious jewels clustered there. Benjamin edged forward and kissed them, then Henry turned to me. I came forward. He patted me on the head as if I was one of his dogs, and Great Wolsey tittered at the joke.

'We will talk in here.' The King spoke in a hoarse whisper. He glanced sideways at Wolsey. 'This is the one place I know there are no peepholes in the walls.' His eyes slid to Benjamin. 'Master Daunbey, our good Doctor Agrippa has told you everything?'

'We have seen the letter, Your Grace. We also know about the proclamations the traitor has posted against you.'

Henry shuffled his feet, the fury blazed in his eyes. 'Traitor it is!' he rasped. 'And, as God be my witness, I want him seized, taken to Tower Hill, half-hanged, cut down, his body ripped open, his innards plucked out and burnt before his eyes.' Henry leaned back in his chair, breathing noisily.

'What have you discovered, beloved Nephew?' Wolsey tactfully intervened.

'Beloved Uncle,' Benjamin replied, kneeling back on his heels, 'nothing but a riddle. The first letter was delivered when the Tower was sealed. Moreover, that same place was locked, and everyone confined within, when the gold was supposed to have been collected from St Paul's and those two other proclamations appeared.'

'I know that,' Henry snarled.

'We think,' Benjamin continued hurriedly, 'that there are two, not one traitor involved. One inside the Tower, one without.'

'Who?' Henry rasped.

'Your Grace, we do not know.'

'Your Grace, we do not know. Your Grace, we do not know,' Henry mimicked. He stretched out his boot and kicked me on the shoulder. 'And you, Shallot, with your cunning face and twisted eye?'

'I am Your Grace's most humble servant.'

'Oh piss off!' Henry snorted. 'Everyone's my humble servant – ' his voice was shot through with self pity – 'until I need help and assistance.'

'Are the deaths amongst the hangmen connected with this villainy?' Wolsey asked.

'Beloved Uncle, we do not know. We can't even prove that it was Undershaft's corpse taken from the cage.'

'Do you suspect anyone?' the King asked, leaning forward.

Benjamin shook his head. 'But, Your Grace,' he added hurriedly, and glanced quickly at his uncle, 'these letters and proclamations are issued in the name of a long-dead prince, Edward V.'

Henry bared his lips, reminding me of a mastiff. The very mention of the Yorkists could send him into a paroxysm of rage.

'Continue, beloved Nephew,' Wolsey said smoothly.

'Surely the Crown and its spies at the House of Secrets must know something about the fate of these two Princes?'

'We have combed the records.' Wolsey stopped speaking and looked round the darkening church.

'Your Grace, the door is sealed.' Agrippa, standing at the back, shouted from the darkness. 'No one can hear.'

The Cardinal leaned forward. 'Then listen well, Nephew. I shall tell you about those two princes. They were last seen in the summer of 1484, then they disappeared. The King's illustrious father, after his great victory against the usurper Richard the Third at the battle of Bosworth, came into London and lodged at the Tower. He announced his betrothal to the Prince's sister, Elizabeth, our noble King's illustrious mother: at her insistence, he organised a most thorough search of the Tower and its precincts.'

'Who was constable under Richard the Third?' Benjamin asked.

'Sir Robert Brackenbury,' Wolsey replied. 'But he, too, was killed at the battle of Bosworth and could not be questioned. Now the search organised by the King's father found nothing. The most industrious of his spies, both here and abroad, could elicit little more.' Wolsey paused. He glanced at the King but Henry had his eyes closed. 'Now, our King's illustrious father and his good wife spent twenty-four years of his reign wondering what had happened to those two Princes. Matters were not helped by a succession of pretenders, the most serious being the Flemish boy Perkin Warbeck. He claimed to be the younger prince Richard. As you know, for a while Warbeck flourished. He was supported by both France and Scotland, who accepted his explanation that he had escaped from the Tower whilst his brother had been murdered. Now Warbeck was captured and executed.'

'Not before he confessed to being a Fleming of low birth,' Henry snarled.

'Precisely,' Wolsey continued, 'but the mystery still remains. Some say the Princes were murdered by their uncle, Richard the Usurper. Others that they escaped.'

'Is there any truth in the latter theory?' Benjamin asked.

'We do know,' Wolsey replied, 'that in January 1485, Sir James Tyrrell, one of Richard's henchmen, took three thousand pounds abroad. Some people say that this huge fortune was because Richard allowed his nephew to go abroad to live a life of wealthy but relative anonymity.' Wolsey shrugged his shoulders. 'But, there again, there are other stories that, on the morning of Bosworth, the usurper Richard was seen in his tent conversing with a young, silver-haired boy whom many thought to be one of the Princes.'

'So they could be alive?' Benjamin asked.

'Tom More doesn't believe that,' Henry declared, squirming in his chair. 'He learnt a different story from Cardinal Morton, my father's principal minister. According to him, the three thousand pounds Sir James Tyrrell received in January 1485 was a reward for smothering both Princes in their beds.'

Wolsey took up the story. 'Sir Thomas More believes that the usurper Richard sent his agent John Greene with orders to the constable to kill the Princes. Brackenbury refused, so Richard dispatched Sir James Tyrrell together with two assassins, Dighton and Greene, into the Tower, where they smothered the Princes and buried them in a secret place.' Wolsey smiled bleakly. (He had little love for Sir Thomas More!) 'There's no evidence for such a story,' he continued. 'Sir James Tyrrell was arrested by the King's father in 1502 for conspiring with Yorkists abroad. Some say he confessed to the murder of the Princes, but that is more fanciful thinking than fact.'

'The Tower grounds have been searched,' Henry declared. 'No remains were ever found.'

'What about those servants who waited on the Princes?' Benjamin asked.

'All are long dead.' Wolsey replied. 'And they could tell the King's spies nothing . . .'

'They are dead! The Princes are dead! They are dead!' Henry pounded his fists on the arm of the chair. He glared at the crucifix as if he expected confirmation from God Himself.

'My Lord King.' Wolsey turned and bowed. 'I fully agree with you, but where do those seals come from? If the Princes were killed, those seals would have been destroyed. If the Princes escaped, they might well have taken them with them.'

Henry glared at his first minister, his face mottled with fury.

'Your Grace,' Wolsey whispered, 'I am as desperate as you are for this villainy to be unmasked.'

'Show them the second letter,' the King growled.

The Cardinal put his hand into his silken robes and drew out a roll of parchment which he handed to Benjamin, who studied it and, ignoring the King's hiss of anger, passed it to me. The letter was couched in the same kind of language as before: the writing beautifully elegant, the bottom of the letter bore two seals. It purported to be from Edward V, King of England: it called Henry a usurper, fulminating against his perfidy. Imperious in its demand that two thousand pounds be left in front of St Paul's Cross on 28 August, the feast of St Augustine. It closed with the arrogant phrase, 'Given at our palace at the Tower during August in the fortieth year of our reign.'

'Will you pay?' I asked. The words came out in a rush.

Henry leaned down. 'Pay, little Shallot! You, my little pickle onion! My little dropping! You, a stain on my court! You will take the two thousand pounds at noon on that day, but you shall arrest the villain responsible.'

The threat seemed to sweeten Henry's mood. He smiled brilliantly at Wolsey, kicked me once again and rose to his feet. He patted his stomach.

'Did you like my Mass, Shallot? Asking God's blessing on my hunting dogs?' He patted my head. 'Tomorrow you shall hunt with us, but tonight we will feast.'

He swept out of the chapel. Wolsey stopped to sketch a blessing in the air above his nephew's head. He followed in a billow of scarlet silk gowns. Agrippa opened the door for them, grinned at us, then slammed it behind him.

'I'll kill him!' I whispered, getting to my feet. 'Benjamin, he treats me like a dog.'

'Roger! Roger!' Benjamin slipped his arm through

mine as we walked down the church.

'Mind you,' I scoffed, 'he's frightened, isn't he? Terrified of the Yorkist ghosts? Do you think it could be a plot?' I added. 'Remember, Master, years ago, the Brotherhood of the White Rose? Yorkists plotting against the Tudors?'

Benjamin pulled a face. 'Time has passed, Roger. The House of York is a withered root. No flower, no fruit grows there. The fate of the two Princes,' he added quietly, stopping to admire a tapestry hanging on the wall just above the door, 'that is of interest, but only because of those seals. Where a king is, so are the insignia of office. However, what we are hunting here, Roger, is a blackmailer and a murderer, and a very clever one at that. But come, the trumpets will bray and Uncle wishes to see us at supper.'

We scurried back to our chambers. Like good little boys, we changed and went down to the hall or, should I say, one of the halls in the inner keep. A magnificent occasion. The room was lit by so many candles you'd think it was daytime: their flames dazzled the gold and silver plate stacked high on shelves and chests around the room. Pure woollen carpets with silk fringes covered the floor. The best Flemish tapestries hung on the walls. Silver and gilt vases full of blooming red roses filled the air with their perfume. (Another sign of Henry's madness. He was so determined to stamp out the White Rose of York, every bloody building had red roses carved in the ceilings or walls. Henry had six craftsmen skilled in carving them. Mind you, one of the funny things about the Great Beast's palaces were his changing wives. He would be carried away in such a flood of affection, he'd insist that the initials of himself and his current queen be placed everywhere. He had six queens! So many he became tired of changing initials. I thought it was particularly amusing that his last queen, sharp-faced Catherine Parr, had the same name as his first. If he had chosen a line of queens with the same name, he would have saved himself a lot of money.)

The supper party that night was not one of Henry's great banquets but a small, intimate affair. The King, of course, had his table on a dais, with a large, throne-like chair in the centre, under a white silk canopy adorned with red roses. Wolsey and some of his cronies sat alongside him. Benjamin and I sat at one of the two tables just below this. Nonetheless, Henry liked his feasting and this occasion was as glorious as any. The plate was of heavy gold or silver, the tablecloths white satin. The meats – venison, boar, swan – were all professionally cooked in tasty, rich sauces, and followed by delicious confectionery, cakes, custards and trifles, whilst the wine flowed like water.

I confess I was in a foul mood. I don't like being treated like a dog. I was also still trembling after my escape from that wolf, so I drank deeply. After Henry's interminable banquets, there was always singing, dancing and card-playing. Sometimes the King liked to regale us all with stories. On that particular night he had the past in his mind. He talked tearfully of his mother and even spoke eloquently of his own father. He patted the hand of his dumpy wife Catherine and recalled his elder brother Arthur who had died so young. The fat Beast lolled in his chair, playing with the gold tassels on the arm.

'So long ago,' he crowed self-pityingly. 'So many shadows, so many regrets.'

A chilling silence greeted his words. A few guests looked sly-eyed at poor Catherine of Aragon, who'd failed to produce a living son.

'Fourteen years,' the beast went on. 'Since my glorious father's death and my accession.'

'Yet many more to come,' a brown-nosed flatterer cried out. 'Sire, you are only in your thirty-first year!'

The King's fat face creased into a smile. He nodded imperceptibly, acknowledging the plaudits of his flattering courtiers.

'The sixth day of the sixth month of the sixth year of

113

your father's reign.' Norris, one of the King's oldest cronies, was shouting, dramatically extolling the date of the Great Beast's birth.

Now the good Lord knows what got into me: wherever the Great Beast was concerned, I always put a foot wrong. Perhaps his treatment of me in the chapel had violated Shallot's one and only virtue: I don't like being bullied.

'Aye,' I cried, my belly full of wine, 'the sixth day of the sixth month of the sixth year. Six, six, six; the sign of the Great Beast in the Book of the Apocalypse!'

The banqueting chamber fell so quiet, you could have heard a fly fart. Henry glowered down the hall. My master put his face in his hands; even Wolsey raised his napkin to his mouth and gazed fearfully at me.

The King lifted a hand. 'Music, let the dancing begin: tomorrow we hunt!' He glared murderously at me: the Great Beast was about to strike.

Chapter 7

I went to bed as drunk as a bishop. All I could recall was Benjamin taking me upstairs, laying me down on the bed and looking nervously at me.

'Roger!' he hissed. 'What on earth made you say that?'

'Devil's bollocks!' I muttered back. 'It's the truth.' And, crossing my arms. I slipped into a wine-drenched sleep.

My awakening was not so graceful. The sun had not yet risen when royal huntsmen, cowled and hooded and carrying torches, burst into our chamber. Benjamin sprang from his bed, but one of them pressed a dagger against his cheek.

'Stay where you are, Master Daunbey,' he warned. 'Your beloved Uncle sends a message. If it were not for you – ' he pointed to where I hung, half-dazed, between the arms of two burly verderers – 'Master Shallot would swing from the highest gallows in the castle for his crime of lese-majesty.'

Do you know the bastard was right? I had committed misprision of treason by casting a public slur on the King's date of birth. However, in doing so (and the good Lord moves in mysterious ways his wonders to behold), my jest was to unlock the dreadful bloody puzzle which confronted Benjamin and myself.

However, at five o'clock in the morning, when I was cold, terrified, and my head still thick with wine fumes, I really didn't give a damn. I still believed I was going to hang. I thought of pleading. I opened my mout' they thrust me out of the chamber, locking the door behind me, but one of the huntsmen smacked me in the teeth. I could see he was not open to reason, so I hung listless as they carted me downstairs, along empty galleries and into one of the castle's great stableyards. Nearby were the royal kennels, and the blood-curdling howls of the hunting dogs awoke strange fears in my soul. It was that eerie time between night and day. The sky was clear, but only a light-reddish hue indicated where the sun was about to rise. The huntsmen gathered round me like a group of leather-garbed devils. A few of them were grinning. One or two looked sadly at me, the rest worked like professional mercenaries: they had a task to do and they would do it. I was stripped of every article of clothing: that's the last I saw of my Italian silk shirt, fine Flemish hose and expensive linen under-garments. (Take Shallot's advice. Never sleep in your clothes. So, when the bastards come to collect you in the early hours, they can't steal your under-garments.)

I tried to object. A huntsman smacked me across the mouth with his leather gauntlet, so I shut up. I was doused under a pump; the cold water sent my heart fluttering and my wits racing. After that they brought a tub of grease, rancid and foul-smelling. I was daubed with this from head to toe. A pair of roughly fashioned sandals were thrust on my feet and I was covered from head to toe with deer-skin. I tried to make a run for it but they caught and held me fast, tying my ankles and wrists together. At last they were finished and stood back, admiring their handiwork.

'One of the strangest beasts I have ever seen,' a huntsman remarked.

'I wonder,' one of them commented, 'how long it will be able to run for? Mind you –' he came closer and dabbed some more grease on my face – 'we can always mount his head beside a boar's!'

The joking stopped as a massive figure swept through

a doorway and strode across the cobbles. It was the Great Beast himself, dressed in his Robin Hood garb, lincoln green, with a silly bonnet which had a white swan's feather clasped to it on his head. He came closer and peered at me.

'Master Shallot, you should hang for what you said!'

'Some of us hang, some of us don't,' I replied cheerfully. The King spread his lips in a grimace but the fury boiled in his eyes.

'Today we hunt: not the deer or the boar, but those who should know their place and keep a still tongue in their head. Open your mouth, Master Shallot.'

I did so and the King poked his gloved fingers in and seized my tongue. He dragged it out and pulled me closer.

'When a deer is brought down,' he hissed, 'it's the prince's privilege to cut the tongue. Remember that, Shallot.'

I did what I always do when the fat Beast threatened me. I farted, loud and clear, like a bell tolling across the square, a long, fruitful blast of protest. The huntsmen sniggered. Henry snapped his fingers.

'Bring out the dogs!'

Two verderers went behind the high palings and brought out two of the great beasts I had seen in the chapel the night before. I thought they might recognise me, so I forced a smile, but the evil-looking bastards just growled, their forelips coming back to display white, snarling teeth.

'Let me introduce Death and Pestilence,' Henry taunted. 'They are also figures in the Apocalypse, Master Shallot. They are German hunting dogs, the best in the field.' He crouched down and stroked both of them. 'Once they sniff you and have your scent, they'll pursue you to the rim of the world. When the hunt begins you will start running. You can run for your life and these dogs will pursue you! Climb a tree and they'll sit at the bottom! Take off those deer-skins and they'll still follow the grease on your body. Jump into a river and try washing it off: impossible. By the time you do, they will have caught you and pulled you down!'

'What chance do I have?'

'Very little,' the Beast replied. 'But if you can come back here to this stable, dressed within those skins, you will win your life and a purse of gold.' The cruel bastard wagged a finger in front of my face. 'You are not to take those skins off, nor seize a horse, nor attempt to ride in any cart.'

My heart sank. Of course, as the Great Beast had been talking, I had been pondering all the possibilities. The easiest would have been to lurk by some trackway and steal a mount. Henry's words dashed these hopes, as did his warning that I could not remove the skins. After all, it would have been pleasant to put them on some wandering friar and scuttle back to Windsor whilst some fat priest raced for his life. Instead I had to stand and shiver as the sun began to rise. Henry and his select band of courtiers, the usual gang of sycophants, saddled and horsed, drinking their cups of hot posset. They looked me up and down as if I was some prize buck or barnyard fox.

At last the bastards were ready. Two mounted huntsmen put a cloth sack over my head and, holding me between then, left the castle, skirted the small town and took me into a wide, sweeping meadow still wet with the morning dew. At the far end of this stood the edged of the great forest where Henry loved to hunt.

'Run for your life, Master Shallot.' One of the verderers pulled the sacking from my head and pointed towards it. 'The King has agreed to give you an hour's start. You'll hear the horn and the baying of the dogs.'

I looked at the man's companion: he was one of those evil, narrow-eyed caitiffs. I glanced up at the huntsman and saw kindness in the rugged, sunburnt face.

'What can I do?' I whispered. 'This is against the law and all usages.'

The fellow shook his head. 'You are not the first, nor will you be the last to take part in a death hunt.'

'What can I do?' I begged.

The man leaned down from his saddle. 'This is the royal forest,' he whispered, 'only the King's law rules here. The last poor creature hanged himself. Whatever you do, don't let the hounds catch you. They'll tear you to pieces.' He squeezed my shoulder. 'Run!' he added. 'Run like the wind! Don't try and hide. Those hounds have your scent and they'll never forget!'

He turned his horse and, followed by his companion, galloped away. There was I, poor old Shallot, dressed in deer-skin, frightened as a fawn, trembling from head to foot. I stared up, the sky was a deep blue and the sun was beginning to strengthen. A beautiful summer's morning. I could hear the wood pigeons cooing and the chatter of grasshoppers. It was the sort of day you'd take a lovely lass out for a walk in the meadow, with a jug of white wine, two cups, and sit on the bank of some stream and tickle the lazy trout. But not for Shallot! Oh no, I was about to die! I did what I always do in such straitened circumstances. I collapsed to my knees and blubbered. I prayed earnestly to God's own mother, reminding her that, though I was a sinner, I was more sinned against than sinning. (Another phrase I have given to Will Shakespeare.)

And then I was off, running like a hare through the grass, aiming true as an arrow towards that dark fringe of trees. The wine fumes cleared from my brain and my sharp wits began to assert themselves. (Oh, just a minute, I can see my little clerk begin to snigger. There's nothing the little bumsqueak likes to hear about better than his old master having to run for his life. I'll just give the little mouse-dropping a rap across his knuckles with my cane. Good, that will teach him to respect his betters.)

I reached the trees, stopped, and looked along the trackway which snaked through the forest. I was tempted to plunge into the undergrowth, but that would have been foolish. The brambles and weeds would ensnare my ankles, lash my legs, impede my progress and the dogs would be on me. I ran on, cursing and muttering, deeper and deeper into the dark forest. I splashed across streams, through dark quiet glades, desperately seeking some place to hide, anything to escape the death which would soon be pursuing me. Yet this was a royal forest, Henry's hunting preserve: there would be no villages, no lonely farms, or occasional woodcutter's hovel, or charcoal-burner's hut. I was alone. On and on I ran, my heart beating fast, my legs beginning to grow weak. I reached one glade and was half-way across when the horseman emerged from the trees. I looked at him and fell to my knees. I thought I'd died and gone to Hell. The rider was dressed completely in black. His warhorse was of the same dark hue, eyeballs rolling, sharpened hooves scraping at the moss-covered ground. The rider was a vision from Hell. A black mask covered his face. On his head, the long horns of a great stag rose up on either side like branches curling towards the sky.

'Go no further!' he shouted.

'I didn't intend to,' I whimpered back, staring up at this macabre vision.

'I am Herne the Hunter,' the figure went on, his voice low and hollow. 'What are you doing running in my forest?'

'I am going to bloody die!' I screamed back. 'That Great Beast of a King is hunting me!'

I measured the distance between him and myself. I fleetingly wondered if I could try and unhorse him: spectre or no spectre, that horse was real enough. I could be at the nearest port before Henry found out. The huntsman seemed to read my mind; a crossbow appeared beneath the cloak and an arrow whistled over my head.

'No further!'

I sat back on my heels. 'Help me!' I whimpered.

The rider threw a sack down on the ground and, turning his horse's head, galloped back along the forest track. I let him go then, half crying, half laughing, crawling towards the sack. I undid the cord. As I did so, something scratched my arm. I plunged my hand in and drew out a long bow, the wood of polished yew with a strong handgrip and a quiver carrying six goose-feathered arrows. I also drew out a mask and, fastened to the boiled leather on either side, antler horns. There was also some biscuits coated with sugar and a small flask of wine. Now you know old Shallot: never look a gift horse in the mouth! My prayers had been answered, even if my benefactor was Herne the Hunter.

For a while I just stared at what the sack contained. I then wolfed down the biscuits, emptied the wine flask and wondered what I should do. Help had arrived, but why like this? Why Herne the Hunter? I recalled the legends about this mythical figure, supposedly the ghost of a huntsman unjustly hanged from a great oak in Windsor Forest hundreds of years before. He was supposed to still haunt there, with demon hounds and devil riders.

I drew in my breath, great sucking gasps, calming my heart, clearing my mind. Of course, the Great Beast was as superstitious as any old gypsy woman, and I knew what my anonymous benefactor intended. I had been given wine and food to build my strength, a mask bearing antler horns, a long bow and a quiver of arrows. I was no longer to be Roger Shallot but Herne the Hunter.

I made sure there was no wine left in the flask. I

pushed that back into the sack, together with the woollen cloth which had contained the biscuits, and hurled the whole lot among the bushes. I heard the long wailing blast of a hunting horn and, on the breeze, the strident, whining howl of the dogs. The hunt was about to begin, but who was to be the hunter?

I ran on, confident I'd escape. I splashed across a small brook and climbed a bank; my legs and hands were caked with mud. The King had instructed me not to remove the deer-skin, but he had not told me what I could put on it. I jumped back in the stream and, scooping up handfuls of mud, began to coat myself from head to toe. By the time I had finished, I did look like some woodland demon sprinting through the trees. Behind me the deep bellows of the dogs grew nearer. As they did, Shallot the coward was replaced by Shallot the cunning.

There was a break in the forest. I scampered up a steep hill and squatted in the bushes at the top. At last the two great hell-hounds came like arrows through the trees. They stopped at the foot of the hill, casting around for my scent. I was pleased to see the mud had at least confused them. Now, despite my poor eye, I was a consummate archer. I came to the brow of the hill, notched an arrow, and drew it back. I tested the wind against my cheek. The breeze was light, hardly noticeable. Now I love animals, and dogs and horses are my favourites, but those two great mastiffs Death and Pestilence were set to tear me limb from limb. I drew in a deep breath and let the arrow fly. Down it sped, catching one of the hounds deep in the throat. The dog jumped up and fell on its side. The other gave a howl of rage and charged up towards me. Another arrow was notched. I no longer felt afraid. My only regret was that it wasn't Henry but some poor dog coming towards me. Again I loosed, but the dog was moving too fast and the arrow skimmed above his head. Other members of the pack were now breaking through the trees. I seized another arrow, took aim, and hit the animal full in its slavering jaw. It swerved, crashed, the slid back down the hill. The other hounds, sensing that something had gone wrong, milled about at the bottom. Their keeper gazed fearfully up at the apparition at the top of the hill.

'I am Herne the Hunter!' I bellowed, my voice sounding muffled behind the mask.

The hunter dropped his whip and stared up at me. I notched another arrow to my bow and took the bastard full in the shoulder. After that, I sprang up, did a strange dance, and disappeared behind the bushes. Well, what more could I say? Of course, the hunt was finished. The leading hounds were dead. One huntsman was wounded. I now began to double back, thoroughly enjoying myself. Near the forest edge I glimpsed the soaring battlements of Windsor Castle.

I doffed the mask, hid the bow and quiver-arrows in the undergrowth, washed off the mud in a nearby stream and walked, cool as any courtier, back through the village. I ignored the astonished looks of traders and hawkers as I strolled back to the castle. Oh, how my blood sang and the fire burned in my belly! Chamberlains and servitors looked at me as if they had seen a ghost. I found my way back to the stableyard and imperiously demanded a cup of sack and a dish of stewed meat. I sat down with my back to an outhouse wall and ate and drank my full in the warm sunlight.

The hours passed. I grew a little cold. There was no sign of the hunt returning, so I seized a cloak and began to wander the palace. Rumours of my escape had already swept the royal household and, although the day before, people would have seized me and escorted me to the nearest horse-trough, now they left me alone. I returned to the tower, but the staircase to Benjamin's room was still heavily guarded. I decided not to exert my new-found authority, but at least I knew that my mysterious benefactor in the forest could not have been Benjamin. I went on to the kitchens, bullied some more meat and drink from a terrified cook, and roamed the palace once more.

That particular day was important to me, not just because I had escaped Henry's wrath: it was also closely entwined with the bloody murders which puzzled Benjamin and myself. I must have been in the main keep, going along a wooden gallery, when I glimpsed a large framed picture at the end, mounted against the wooden panelling. It depicted the Great Beast's mother, Elizabeth of York. I went along and stared up at her beautiful, thin, ivory-white face, her famous golden hair tightly bound under a jewelled cap. Behind her, in the background, were pictures of her family: these were fairly indistinct, as the painting had gone dark with age and was covered with dust. (It just goes to show you the manners of the old Beast! He never cared for his father or his mother. When his commissioners under Cromwell began to destroy the abbeys and churches, Henry actually dug up his great-grandmother, leaving her coffin to be abused and rifled by any passing villain. Years later I intervened, and begged Elizabeth to have the remains properly coffined and reinterred.)

I pulled up a stool and climbed up to clear away the dust for, in the background, playing in a field, were two young boys: Elizabeth's two brothers, the Princes in the Tower. I thought the picture might give me some clue, then the stool slipped and I fell against the wooden panelling. My flailing hand must have caught some secret lever, the panelling moved inwards, acting as a secret door. I looked around. No one was present so I went in. I jammed the stool between the door and the lintel lest it close and seal me in for ever.

Inside was a small, musty chamber. Straining my eyes, I could make out a table, a chair and, in the far corner, a small truckle-bed. I stretched my hand out across the table. I grasped a thick, squat candle and, beside it, a tinder with flint. After a great deal of difficulty, I lit the candle and the chamber flared into light. God knows what I expected, but all I found was an earthernware pot, a few rags on the bed, a stained pewter jug and the remains of a cup which had apparently fallen from the table. Nevertheless, the chamber looked as if it had been occupied, though not recently. I blew the candle out, left the chamber, and quietly resealed the panelling.

I was about to continue my wandering when I heard the faint sound of a hunting horn. I scurried back to the stableyard, taking up position at the very spot where the King had last threatened me. I breathed in deeply to calm my thudding heart as the King and his cronies, spattered with mud and rather subdued, swept into the yard. Henry slid down from his horse and ordered the wounded verderer to the castle infirmary, and the corpses of his two great mastiffs to be laid out in the castle chapel. The Great Beast swaggered towards me; his cronies, faces tense, eyes watchful, crowded behind him.

'So, Shallot, you escape yet again?'

'Yes, your Grace.'

'And how?' The Beast thrust his face towards me.

I acted all coy and frightened, opening my mouth to reply, then closing it with a sigh.

'You know what happened to my hounds?' the King barked.

I shook my head fearfully.

'Or my verderer?'

I began to sob.

(Kit Marlowe once told me I would have made a fine actor. I could change my moods at the drop of a coin. Believe me, on that day at Windsor I was acting for my life!)

I knelt on the cobbled yard before the Great Beast. A nice touch! Henry liked to see people abase themselves before his majesty.

'What is it?' Henry barked.

'You'll not believe me.' I grasped his boots and glanced up fearfully. 'What I saw, Your Grace, was most fearful! A vision from Hell.'

Oh, my arrow struck its mark. Big, fat Henry! As superstitious as any gypsy.

'On your loyalty,' the Beast barked.

'I was in the woods, Your Grace. I was running for my life, aware of how my clacking tongue and stupid wits had brought this sad fate about.'

'And?' Henry asked.

'A rider came out of the trees. Oh, Your Grace, he was fearful. The horse was black as coal, its eyes like burning embers. The harness was ribbons of fire and the saddle was fashioned out of human skin.' I paused for effect. 'Your Grace, I fell into a swoon.'

Henry crouched down beside me. 'And what happened then?'

'When I awoke the rider had dismounted. He was towering over me, tall, dark, black. Only Your Grace,' I added falteringly, 'has ever appeared more fearful to me.'

Henry smiled knowingly. I knew I had hit my mark.

'And what did this figure say?' Henry asked.

'I am Herne the Huntsman.' My voice rose. 'His voice was like yours, thunderous and majestic, roaring like the sound of cannon-fire at the height of battle.'

'And how was he dressed?' the King urged.

'Black as night with a great pair of sweeping antler horns on his head. He carried a bow, so huge only someone like yourself could have stretched it.'

'And what did he say?' someone shouted.

Henry turned round and glared. 'Tell me, Shallot.' He scratched my head as if I was a dog.

' "I am Herne the Hunter," the figure repeated. "You,

Shallot, are a base-born rogue. You have deserved to die for offending the King's greatness. However, I am here to show you great pardon and mercy. You shall not die today." ' I paused, swallowing hard.

'Go on!' Henry hissed.

I glanced up. ' "You are to be my most faithful emissary," Herne proclaimed. "The servant of my beloved, England's greatest King." ' I lowered my voice. ' "You will free him from his present troubles." '

Henry was now beaming from ear to ear.

'Continue,' he urged.

'I am to serve you all your days,' I continued.

'And did he promise anything?' the Great Beast urged, like a child begging for a sweetmeat.

'Greatness of days for yourself, Sire,' I replied. 'A lusty son and a long line. I asked him for a sign,' I whined.

'And?' the Great Beast asked.

' "Have I not given you a sign already?" Herne replied. "Did I not rescue you from the sweating sickness in London?" '

(Oh, a beautiful touch! Will Shakespeare would have loved it, for it brought 'oohs', 'aahs' and knowing nods from Henry's companions.)

The King squeezed his lower lip between his fat fingers.

'True, true,' he muttered. 'I had heard of that. Go on.'

' "I shall deliver you from this hunt," Herne promised. "I cannot touch my beloved Henry, but I shall punish those who put this idea into his head. Tell the King that when my punishment is done, the matter is forgotten." '

I stared up, my eyes full of tears. 'Your Grace, I just ran on. I seemed to fall into a deep slumber, as if I was in a trance. I could hear the dogs behind me, then I found myself on the outskirts of Windsor and walked back here. I am sorry – ' a delicious quaver entered my voice – 'about the death of your hounds.'

I stared into the Great Beast's eyes. He continued to

squat there, scratching his chin. I could see suspicion but, there again, what could he do?

'I have also won my wager,' I whispered.

Henry got to his feet and pulled me up by the shoulder. 'We saw Herne the Hunter,' he declared. 'As you describe, on the brow of a hill.' He snapped his fingers; one of the huntsmen brought forward three arrows. Henry held them up. 'I have never seen the likes of these before,' he remarked. 'Beautiful, steel-tipped.' He threw them back. 'Norris!' He shouted without turning round. 'You remember that purse of gold you won from me at gambling last night? Well, now it's Shallot's, give it to him.'

Red-bearded Norris came forward and sullenly handed the prize over. I guessed he must have been the architect of today's villainy: he put the idea in the King's mind that it would be better to hunt poor old Shallot rather than some old boar who would probably have loved a sprint through the woods. The Beast clapped me on the shoulder.

'Faithful, faithful, faithful Roger.'

Again I caught the suspicion in his voice, but he then dismissed me and I returned to my chamber. My master took one look at me, hugged me, then pushed me away, studying me from head to toe.

'Roger, did they hurt you? I heard what happened.' He held his hand up. 'No, don't reply. I'll wait.'

Benjamin went to the door, shouting for servants to bring buckets of hot water. My master waited until I was soaking under deep, thick suds, a bowl of sack in my hand, before continuing his questioning.

I told him everything that had happened. Every so often, he'd go and check the door to ensure there was no eavesdropper. Benjamin heard me out and whistled under his breath.

'Who was it?' he asked.

'Herne the Hunter as far as I am concerned,' I replied.

'That's my story, Master, and I am not changing it.'

Afterwards, feeling heavy-eyed and sleepy, I dressed in the new clothes sent to me by the King and went down to the Great Hall where I was toasted and cheered. People came up to me, slapping me on the back, saying what a good fellow I was. The whole palace had now heard the news, and everyone thronged about to ask about Herne the Hunter. I told my story, embellishing it where I could; now and again I caught the Great Beast's sardonic glance. I could see he was puzzled, but he couldn't come up with a solution. Afterwards, my belly full and my purse swollen with gold and silver, I stumblingly followed Benjamin back to my room. Agrippa was sitting on the bed waiting for us, a large leather sack tied at the neck on the floor between his feet.

'Beloved Uncle sends his compliments, dearest Nephew,' he intoned. 'Tomorrow you are to take this gold into London. You are to leave it on the steps of St Paul's Cross as the cathedral bell tolls the midday Angelus.'

'And the King will do nothing?'

'Oh, the King will do everything. The place will be swarming with sheriff's men, all in disguise. Royal archers will guard and seal every gateway at the Tower from ten o'clock in the morning onwards.' Agrippa's face broke into a lopsided smile. 'The King has great confidence in you, Roger. Herne the Hunter has favoured you and vowed you will bring the King safely through this crisis.'

I groaned and slumped down on a stool. The great bag of wind had closed the trap. If Herne the Hunter had appeared to me, then tomorrow I would be successful. If not, I'd be running for my life again!

Chapter 8

We left by barge the following morning, just as dawn was breaking. Agrippa walked us down to the quayside, humming some little song under his breath. He helped me to the barge, grasped my hand and pulled me towards him.

'Next time you meet Herne the Hunter,' he whispered, his eyes bright with merriment, 'do give him my regards.'

I sat down, gaping in surprise as the barge pulled away: Agrippa simply lifted his hand, turned and disappeared into the early morning mist. I'll be honest. I have always wondered whether he was Herne the Hunter. Years later, when old Tom Wolsey had fallen into disgrace because he couldn't get the King a divorce and journeyed south to York to stand trial for treason, I accompanied him. I was there in Leicester Abbey when he fell suddenly sick. (Oh, yes, he was poisoned and, no, it wasn't me.) I knelt by Wolsey's bedside as the death rattle began in his throat, and he confessed all his sins. I squeezed his fat, podgy hand.

'Tell me, Tom,' I asked. (By then I was on first-name terms with everyone; even the Great Beast let me call him Hal!) 'Tell me, Tom,' I said. 'As you hope to meet your Saviour, did Agrippa dress as Herne the Hunter?'

Fat Tom shook his head. 'Impossible,' he whispered. 'He was with me all that day, closeted on the King's business.'

Ah well, maybe Agrippa got one of his bully-boys to dress the part. I never have found out.

We reached St Paul's Wharf just as the city church bells tolled for mid-morning Mass. Benjamin had remained quiet during the journey, but now he stirred himself: gripping the bags of gold, he ran up the quayside steps and stared anxiously around.

'What's wrong, Master?' I asked, following him quickly.

Benjamin hid the gold beneath his cloak and stared round anxiously.

'Roger, I feel uneasy!'

I pointed to the halberdiers and archers still on the barge.

'They'll be with us,' I declared. 'And the King undoubtedly has others hidden around St Paul's Cross.'

But Benjamin would not be comforted. The royal bodyguard quickly formed a screen around us and we went up towards the towering mass of St Paul's. The city had returned to some form of normality. Traders, hucksters and merchants were busy behind their stalls. Dung-collectors were cleaning the public latrines: they dressed like lazars, covered from head to toe in rags against the foulness and the fetid smells which cloyed the air and caught the throat. There were no signs of any death-carts or red crosses daubed on doors. I glimpsed two cunning men, pickpockets, and idly wondered where Quicksilver was. I still harboured a deep desire to shake him warmly – by the throat! However, as the psalmist says: 'Sufficient unto the day is the evil thereof', and Benjamin and I were busy.

We turned on to Paternoster Row and went up St Paul's Alley which led straight into the cathedral. As we passed, I studied the famous wall paintings of the Dance of Death: grotesque, macabre skeletons leaping and cavorting as they led hundreds into the great dark pit of Hell. I simply mention it because it has gone now. The Duke of Somerset pulled it down. We went into the cathedral along the nave, Paul's Walk, where men of the city strode, showed themselves, gossiped and did a little business. The choirboys were out in force, looking for anyone silly enough to wear spurs, for they had the right to demand 'spur' money as a fee. At the west end of the nave, about two dozen scribes sat at small tables scribbling letters and legal documents. Benjamin made his escort stop and stared at these industrious scribblers.

'I wonder,' he whispered, 'if our blackmailer uses them?'

'No, Master.' I pointed round. 'Just look at the rogues and rapscallions gathered here. Servants for hire, ragged-arsed lawyers looking for clients. If the scribe didn't betray their hirer, these would.'

Benjamin agreed. We went up to the sanctuary dominated by the gorgeously carved and decorated tomb of St Erconwald. A busy-looking cleric, hopping from foot to foot, was waiting for us there. He beckoned us quickly into the sacristy where a liveried thug introduced himself as John Ramasden. A captain of the guard of the King's palace at Whitehall, Ramasden was dressed in chainmail, a heavy warbelt slung round his waist. A hard-faced, lean, mean-eyed, fighting man. He ignored our introductions and came swiftly to the point.

'My orders are simple,' he barked. 'When the cathedral bell tolls the Angelus, you are to go into St Paul's churchyard, carrying the gold. You are to place the gold on the steps of St Paul's Cross.'

'And then what?' I asked.

Ramasden pushed his face close; his blood-filled eyes reminded me of the King's.

'I don't give a rat's turd what happens!' he replied: then he grinned. (He had one good tooth in his mouth and his breath was foul.) 'Some villain will try to pick up the sacks. I and my men will seize him and any accomplices, then it's heigh ho down to the Tower. Until

133

then,' he pulled a face, 'we wait!'

And wait we did: the minutes seemed to last for hours. Benjamin, lost in his own thoughts, crouched on a stool, cradling the gold. Every so often he would look at me, shake his head and mutter.

'But how could it be done? How on earth, Roger, could it be done?'

To be truthful, even my sharp wits were dulled. I jumped as the bells began to toll. Ramasden hustled us out by a side door into the vast expanse of St Paul's churchyard. Now, those of you who have been there, know the area is a small town in itself. It stopped being used as a cemetery years ago, and became a shabby market where all the thieves congregated to share their ill-gotten gains. They're protected by some stupid city ordinance which stipulates no lawman or sheriff's officer can enter there in pursuit.

On that particular day, business was brisk. The air stank with a variety of smells: sweaty bodies, stale food being cooked over open fires, perfumes from the whores, whilst our ears were dinned by the clack of tongues and shouts of traders. A few people looked askance at Ramasden. However, he was wearing the royal livery, so no one dared accost him as we threaded our way past the battered stalls to where St Paul's Cross soared high above the graveyard. Now the cross was where heralds came to report news of great victories; the birth of a prince; to announce the sentencing of some great noble, or to give a lurid description of his death by disembowelling on Tower Hill. Around the cross were the bookstalls and pamphleteers whose clerks would sit and listen to such information and, within hours, be writing some broadsheet to sell in the streets outside. Above us the bell kept tolling as I anxiously searched the crowd, seeking a face I could recognise. At last, the chimes began. Benjamin and I counted aloud.

'Ten, eleven!'

And then, like the knell of death, the final one. Benjamin quickly moved forward and placed the gold on the steps of the cross. I was wondering how long it would stay: with every rogue in London milling about, any sack left unattended would disappear in a twinkling of an eye. I watched one sharp-eyed caitiff come from behind a stall and edge towards the sack. I started as a woman screamed.

'The sweating sickness! The sweating sickness!'

Her screams were drowned by a deafening explosion, as if someone had fired a cannon. Everyone scattered. Benjamin and I dropped our guard and, when we looked back, the bags were gone. I ran to the cross, up the steps and gazed over the crowd. Of course, everybody was running: either terrified that an infected person was near, eager to get away from the explosion, or determined either to guard their possessions or plunder someone else's. The scene was total chaos. Men and women fighting each other, stalls knocked over, knives being drawn, bottles hurled, children crying, women screaming, men cursing and shoving at each other. I glimpsed Ramasden, his sword drawn, beating people away from the cross.

'The sacks have gone, Roger!' Benjamin shouted. 'And God knows who took them!'

'But how?' I screamed back.

Benjamin sat on the bottom step, head in hands. It seemed to be the only thing to do, so I joined him.

'I never thought of that.' Benjamin raised his head, staring at the chaos around him. 'What are all Londoners frightened of, Roger? The sweating sickness and fire.' He got to his feet. 'We are wasting our time here!'

He went across and spoke to Ramasden, then beckoned to me to follow him back into the cathedral which was also deserted.

'I am not a prophet,' my master remarked, squatting

at the base of the pillar. 'But I wager a tun of wine, Roger, that Ramasden comes and tells us there is no one ill of the sweating sickness, whilst the explosion came from a trail of gunpowder carefully laid in some enclosed space.'

Benjamin was correct. Ramasden followed us into the cathedral, swearing and cursing fit to burst.

'The bastards!' he screamed, walking up and down in front of us. 'The misbegotten turds!'

'Are you talking about your men?' I asked. 'Who allowed the villain to escape?'

Ramasden ceased his pacing. He came over and kicked me on the sole of my boot.

'No, sir, I am not. I'm talking of the stupid drunk, sweating like a pig, who fell into a swoon just inside the churchyard. A silly woman believed a beggar who examined the man and said he was infected.'

'And the explosion?' Benjamin asked.

'A trail of powder,' Ramasden replied. 'Laid in a gulley which ran into one of the derelict tombs.' He shook his head. 'Nothing but a magnificent fart.' He hawked and spat on the church floor. 'Didn't you see him?' Ramasden stared accusingly at us. He squatted down and poked me in the chest. 'How do I know you didn't take it yourself?'

'If you poke me again . . .!' I shouted.

'If you poke me again,' Benjamin repeated, 'I'll see you in the Tower, sir!' My master got to his feet, dragging me with him, and stared coolly at Ramasden. 'The gold has been taken by a subtle device and the rogue will be long gone. I shall report as much to my uncle the Cardinal.'

Ramasden stepped back, muttering apologies. Benjamin ignored him. He plucked at my sleeve and almost hurried me out of the cathedral, down past Paternoster Row to a small tavern built alongside Blackfriars Wall.

'Now's not the time for eating and drinking!' I moaned.

'There is little more we can do,' Benjamin replied.

'We could search for that beggar who raised the alarm, or make inquiries about who laid the gunpowder.'

Benjamin smiled. 'Roger, do you think anyone in St Paul's churchyard saw what happened and, if they did, would any of those wolvesheads tell us the truth? We could spend hours making fools of ourselves.'

'But it must be someone from the Tower,' I said. 'Gunpowder is stored there.'

'Aye,' Benjamin sighed. 'But it can also be bought, stolen, or even made. What we have to do, Roger, is discover whether Kemble, Vetch, Spurge, Mallow, or any one of those hangmen, were absent from the Tower this morning.'

'And if they are not?'

'Then, dear Roger, we are truly in a pig's mess. Uncle will be furious. The King's rage . . .'

He paused as a servant brought us a tankard of ale and a platter of stew and vegetables.

'The King's rage can only be imagined!'

I dropped my horn spoon and gripped my belly. Once the news reached Windsor, the Great Beast would be bellowing. Herne the Hunter had publicly promised that I would bring the King safely through his present troubles. Now he was two thousand pounds poorer and the rumours of this blackmail were spreading further. I picked up my horn spoon again. 'Then it's back to the Tower, Master.'

'Oh no. We first have to check on Mistress Undershaft's new-found wealth.'

I ate morosely. After we had finished, I followed Benjamin along the busy, crowded streets, up through the dirt and mess of Newgate and down into Cheapside. An apprentice boy pointed out Thurgood the goldsmith's shop. We found him in his counting-house; a thick-necked, fleshy-faced man, with eyes which could assess

137

your wealth in a few seconds. He took one look at us and returned to his ledger, so Benjamin whispered in his ear and Thurgood sprang up like a jack-in-a-box, all servile and eager to please.

'Oh, yes, yes.' The words came out in a hiss of pleasure. 'Mistress Undershaft.' He moved the manuscripts from his table, pulled out a calf-bound ledger and opened it. 'Just after her husband's sad demise.' The goldsmith's eyelids fluttered in what he thought was a look of condolence. 'A beneficiary deposited a hundred pounds in gold in her name.'

Benjamin whistled under his breath. 'But that's a fortune!'

The goldsmith spread his hands. 'Such bequests are not unknown.'

'When was it made?' I asked.

Thurgood leafed through the ledger and pointed to an entry; the date was about a week after her husband's death. It showed the amount deposited under Thurgood's seal.

'And before you ask, good masters, the person wished to hide his identity. He was cloaked, cowled and masked. The transaction was very swift: the gold was in good coin.'

'Didn't it concern you who he was?' Benjamin asked. 'And wasn't a receipt sought?'

'Master Daunbey, Master Daunbey.' The fellow smiled like a schoolmaster facing a thick-headed pupil. 'I am a goldsmith; such transactions are common.'

'How would the beneficiary know you passed the gold on?' I asked crossly.

'Because I issued a tally receipt,' Thurgood snarled. 'All it gave was the date, the amount received, and who was to receive it. I then informed Mistress Undershaft.' He drew his head back as if I stank. 'If I'd failed to carry out the request,' he snapped, 'I'd be no more than a felon – and that, sir, I am not!' He threw the ledger back on the table. 'I can tell you no more.'

Benjamin and I left his shop and walked into Cheapside. A young girl ran up, dressed shabbily, her face blackened with dirt. A little boy, probably her brother, grasped one hand; her other hand held a small inflated bladder. She stopped in front of Benjamin, put the bladder down, and pushed a scrap of parchment into my master's palm. Then, before he could stop her, she grabbed her young companion and the inflated bladder and disappeared into the crowd. The parchment was screwed up tightly. My master unfolded it and we both stared at the message inscribed in elegant pen strokes:

'On behalf of my noble master, Edward King of England, Scotland, France, etc. I accept, as his due, the two thousand pounds returned to its rightful owner: signed Francis Lovell, Viscount Titchmarsh. Given at the Tower this twenty-eighth day of August'.

'Who, in heaven's name, is Lovell?' I asked.

Benjamin stared down at the message.

'Haven't you heard the doggerel rhyme, Roger? "The cat, the rat and Lovell the dog rule all England under the hog". The hog or boar was Richard the Third's emblem. He had three henchmen: Ratcliffe, Catesby and Sir Francis Lovell. The first two died at Bosworth in 1485, but Lovell escaped the battle and supported later Yorkist plots against Henry the Seventh. He invaded England in 1487 and fought at the battle of East Stoke in Nottinghamshire: afterwards he disappeared.' Benjamin shook his head. 'It can't be him, surely? If he was still alive, Lovell would be ancient.'

'They are mocking us,' I exclaimed. 'Master, they are mocking us.'

Benjamin just shook his head and walked off into the crowds. Muttering and cursing under my breath, I followed. Now and again I turned round to see if anyone was watching us. If I had caught the bastard who had sent that message, I would have dirked him on the spot, but there was no one. We hurried down to Queenshithe and hired a wherry to take us up-river to the Tower. We found the fortress heavily guarded, drawbridge up, portcullis down. It took a great deal of screaming and shouting at a guard who peered out at us from the Lion Gatehouse before Kemble appeared and gave us permission to enter.

The drawbridge fell in a rumble of chains, the portcullis creaked up like the jagged teeth of some dragon. Benjamin became even more disconcerted.

'It cannot be anyone in the Tower, Roger,' he muttered. 'Beloved Uncle gave orders that, on this particular day, no officer or member of the Tower garrison should enter the city.'

'So, the villain who collected that money and sent that impudent message . . .?'

Benjamin shrugged. 'We have to accept it, Roger: whoever he or she is, they do not live in the Tower.'

Kemble was waiting for us beyond the gateway. He took one look at Benjamin's face and shook his head mournfully.

'The gold was taken!'

'Yes, it was stolen!' Benjamin snapped.

Sighing heavily, Kemble took us up into his chamber in the royal quarters where Vetch and Spurge were also waiting. They had apparently been spending their time feasting; the ragged remains of a pheasant lay on a platter. Kemble was sobersided, but Vetch and Spurge looked flushed and bright-eyed.

'So they can't arrest us,' Vetch muttered, once we'd announced what had happened. He got up and shakily filled two goblets, brought them back to the table and pushed them towards us.

'Someone will hang for all this,' Spurge squeaked. He looked slyly at me. 'And it won't be us.'

'What happened?' Kemble asked.

Benjamin told him in quick, clipped tones. The

constable leaned back in his chair, whispering under his breath and shaking his head. 'And you have no suspicions?' he asked.

'Two villains are at work here,' Benjamin explained. 'One in the Tower and another outside. However, I have not any evidence to point the finger of accusation.'

'Did anyone leave the Tower?' I asked.

Kemble shook his head. 'You saw for yourself, Master Shallot, all doorways were barred and bolted. Men patrol the ramparts and towers, two soldiers guard each postern-gate.'

'And the hangmen?' I asked.

'They are in their quarters. Every hour, on the hour, at least until noon, Vetch went round and checked.'

My master sipped at the wine cup.

'What do you think, Master Daunbey?' Vetch asked.

'I am wondering where the rogue is who took the two thousand pounds' worth of gold,' Benjamin replied. 'And will he be satisfied with that or strike again?' He put his cup down on the table. 'Sir Edward, how long have you been constable of the Tower?'

'About two years this Michaelmas,' Kemble replied.

'And you have heard no legends or stories about the Princes?'

The constable shook his head. 'I have told you, as I have told others, their fate is a complete mystery.'

'But you know the story of Tyrrell?' Benjamin insisted.

'Aye, he was alleged to have been involved in smothering the Princes, but the King's father made a careful search. No remains were ever found.'

Suddenly there was a drumming of feet on the stairs outside and Mallow burst into the room, his face white as a sheet. For a while he just stood there trembling, then he came forward like a dream-walker.

'Sir Edward,' he muttered, 'you'd best come. All of you!'

Benjamin sprang to his feet and grasped Mallow's hand. 'It's as cold as ice!' he exclaimed. He forced the

141

man to sit down on the chair and thrust the wine cup to his lips. 'Drink, man!'

Mallow blinked.

'Come on, drink!' Benjamin fairly poured the wine into the fellow's mouth.

Mallow coughed and shook himself. 'It's Horehound,' he whispered. He stood up, swaying slightly. 'You must come!'

'We'll never make sense out of him!' Vetch snapped. He grasped Mallow by the jerkin. 'Where is Horehound?'

'The cellar,' Mallow muttered. 'The death cellar in Beauchamp Tower.'

'It's where the execution block and axe are kept,' Vetch explained.

And, leaving Mallow, we all left the room. Outside, on the green, the news of something dreadful had already spread. Soldiers, servants, even masons who were preparing a stretch of the inner wall, were hurrying towards the huge, forbidding Beauchamp Tower. When we reached it, the rest of the executioners were gathered round the door; a royal serjeant was trying to hold the people back. The fellow was pallid-faced, slack-jawed, his mouth still stained with vomit. He glimpsed Sir Edward and pointed with his thumb towards the half-open door.

'Sir Edward,' he exclaimed, 'there's a demon in the Tower!'

Kemble led us into the stairwell and down to the basement. Someone had lit the sconce-torches on the wall. The shadows flickered and danced as if ghosts had come to plague us. At the bottom was a small cellar or cavern. In one corner stood a huge block, cut from some massive oak, with an axe in it. I also glimpsed in the poor light a massive, metal-studded door, almost covering the floor.

'What's all the fuss about?' I asked.

Benjamin pointed. I grabbed a torch from the wall and

stared; on either side of the door a hand stuck out and, at the far end of the door, the top of Horehound's head. I took a step nearer. My boots squelched in the blood and I became aware of a fetid smell. Benjamin remained, but Kemble and his two officers had already gone out to vomit in the small privy chamber.

'Lord have mercy!' Benjamin breathed. 'The poor bastard's been pressed!'

Now I shall spare your sensibilities, but pressing is the most terrible of deaths. It is carried out in three places in London: the yards of Fleet and Newgate prisons, or in the Tower. It's not a torture but a special punishment reserved for those who refuse to plead either guilty or not guilty. In my long and troubled life I have been in many a scrape but, when taken before the justices, I would never refuse to plead. Once you do that, you have very little chance. Sometimes the press can be heavy boards which are weighted with bricks on top, but the pressing door in the Tower was of a special kind. Small wheels were fixed on the bottom, and a rope fixed to the top. This ran through a pulley system, so it could be lowered gently on to the victim who would lie spread-eagled on the ground. No such delicacy had been shown to Horehound.

Benjamin pointed to the pulley hanging from the ceiling, and explained. 'Horehound must have been laid out on the ground. The door was tipped and the rope cut till finally it slammed down, reducing his body to a bloody pulp.'

Kemble and his two officers returned, accompanied by Mallow, who looked as if he had drunk the wine jug dry. Toadflax, Snakeroot and Wormwood, under Kemble's direction, slowly lifted the door, pushing it back on its wheels and leaning it against the far wall. On the inside of the door were small arrow points of sharpened steel; these had turned Horehound's body to a tangled, gory mess. Once the corpse was exposed, all stood away: even the hangmen, experienced as they were in death, could not bear the sight. My stomach heaved, though, I'll be honest, at that moment in time, I was more terrified of the Great Beast than the pulpy remains of one of London's hangmen. Benjamin showed no fear but crouched down, ignoring the mess: he carefully examined Horehound's wrists and ankles.

'He wasn't fastened down, was he?' Wormwood came forward.

'No, he wasn't,' Benjamin replied. 'There are no marks round his wrists or ankles.' He pointed to the iron chain hanging on a wall which would be used to secure a prisoner about to be pressed.

'Then how was it done?' Kemble's voice was muffled behind a pomander he held to his nose.

'I don't know.' Benjamin replied. 'But Horehound was a man capable of taking care of himself, yes?'

Wormwood nodded. Snakeroot and Toadflax also agreed.

'So how could the killer lie him out on the ground?' Benjamin sounded puzzled. 'Horehound must have made no objection or tried to get away.'

'Perhaps he was already unconscious,' Vetch remarked from where he stood in the doorway. 'A knock on the head or a dagger in the back. His corpse is so torn we cannot tell.'

Benjamin got to his feet and, taking a sconce-torch from the wall, carefully walked round the chamber. He shook his head.

'There's nothing here.'

'We'll seal the chamber,' Kemble announced. He took a coin from his purse and tossed it at Wormwood. 'He was your friend. Bury him!'

'He was no friend of mine,' Wormwood snapped. He looked coolly at Sir Edward. 'Don't you know, Master Constable, hangmen don't have friends?'

'Well, he was in your guild!' Kemble snapped.

'Don't worry, don't worry.' Mallow came forward, hands flailing. 'I'll take care of poor Horehound.'

We left the Tower. I was grateful to be out, breathing God's fresh air. The guards had driven off the curious onlookers. Benjamin pointed across to the church of St Peter ad Vincula.

'I have further questions to ask,' he declared. He stared round. 'Of all of you!'

No one objected, and we walked into the church as dutifully as a congregation on a Sunday morning. Benjamin led us into the sanctuary, indicating the stalls on either side. We sat down. If I wasn't so frightened, I would have burst out laughing. There we were, Constable and officers of the Tower, the hangmen of London and Old Shallot, the greatest rogue in Ipswich, sitting in benches facing each other like a hanging jury ready to deliver its verdict.

On any other occasion there would have been vociferous objections, but Horehound's ghastly death had knocked any querulousness on its head.

Benjamin sat in the sanctuary chair. 'Gentlemen.' He began softly, yet his words echoed round that cavernous church. 'Gentlemen, there is villainy here, the likes of which I have not seen before. This morning Master Shallot and I took two thousand pounds in gold to St Paul's Cross. We were guarded and protected by royal soldiers, as well as other agents of the Crown. However, a cry about the sweating sickness and an explosion caused by a small trail of gunpowder, led to that gold being taken.'

Toadflax was about to spring to his feet and declare his innocence; Benjamin shook his head.

'I know. I know,' he continued. 'All the hangmen were in the garrison refectory.' He turned and pointed at Vetch. 'You, Master Vetch, can vouch for that.'

The constable's lieutenant nodded slowly. 'Yes, I can. As I can also vouch for Sir Edward, myself and Master

145

Spurge. We were in the constable's quarters.'

'I accept that,' Benjamin agreed quietly. 'Later on, the villains who stole the gold had the impudence to send me a letter whilst I was in Cheapside.' He paused to collect his thoughts. 'Now, until our arrival here, the Tower's gates and postern doors were all sealed and barred, so no one could have left to commit such villainy.' He smiled bleakly. 'And there's the rub. I believe there's one rogue in the Tower and another, his accomplice, in the city. Sir Edward.' Benjamin turned to Kemble. 'We are the only ones to enter the Tower today?'

The constable nodded. 'Once you were in, Master Daunbey, the portcullis was lowered, and the guards have not been relieved of their duties. Even the masons working outside on the scaffolding were forced to sleep in the cellars, or in any nook or cranny they could find. They will not be allowed out until this evening.'

'Yet Horehound was killed,' Benjamin went on. 'By whom?' He stared at Mallow and his apprentices.

'As you know, Master Daunbey,' the chief hangman replied, 'we all supped and dined together at midday.' He scratched his head. 'But then we went about our different duties.'

'Such as?' Benjamin asked.

'Cleaning our quarters, sleeping off what we had eaten and drunk.'

Wormwood sniggered behind his hand at that.

'And when was Horehound last seen?'

'About an hour before Mallow found him,' Snakeroot declared. 'He'd been drinking, as usual. I saw him staggering across the green.'

'Did anyone else see him?'

The hangmen all shook their heads and started shouting out where they were and what they were doing.

Benjamin clapped his hands for silence. 'I don't think you understand the point I'm making.' He got to his feet.

'Which is what?' Mallow shouted.

146

'Today the King's gold was stolen,' Benjamin explained, walking over towards him. 'And, Master Mallow, one of your hangmen died. Don't you see? They are both linked. So, if more demands are made, more of you will die.' His words created a pool of silence in the chapel. Benjamin wiped his mouth on the back of his hand. 'I can do little to protect you,' he said, 'so I strongly advise you not to go anywhere alone, either here or in the city.'

'Is there anything else we can do?' Snakeroot snivelled. He looked so frightened that I thought he'd fall into a swoon.

'Yes,' Benjamin replied. 'Tell me something about the three hangmen who died.'

'We know very little,' Mallow whined. 'Undershaft was my assistant. He was a family man. He kept to himself.'

'And Horehound?'

'He was a tippler, a sot,' Toadflax replied, tossing back the curls on his head. 'He stank, never washed; even the whores used to stay clear of him.'

'That's why he was by himself,' Wormwood continued, 'wandering the Tower this afternoon. His breeches stank like a midden: when he was drunk, he lost all control of himself.'

'Hellbane was different,' Toadflax offered. 'He had a woman, a whore; he brought her here into the Tower when we celebrated the King's birthday on the sixth of June.' He closed his eyes, drumming his fists on the stall. 'What was her name? Ah, that's it, Marisa! She's a slattern down at the Monkshood tavern. Looks like a gypsy she does: green eyes and raven-black hair.'

'But you can tell us nothing else?' Benjamin looked to where Kemble and his two officers sat quietly. 'Anything at all?' Benjamin pleaded.

Again there was silence, abruptly broken by the harsh cry of a raven outside.

Chapter 9

Benjamin and I accompanied Kemble and his two officers back to the royal apartments. Spurge, at Benjamin's request, produced his plan of the Tower from a coffer. This was copied on a great roll of vellum which he spread out on the table, using candlesticks to keep it down at each corner. The drawing was very precise, everything clearly marked.

'I did it myself,' Spurge declared proudly. 'The ones Sir Edward gave me when I took up office here were highly inaccurate.'

'Not very good at all,' the Constable agreed. He pointed to the small postern-doors indicated on the map. 'These, for example, were not on it.'

'Nor this.' Vetch pointed to a dotted line drawn through where I knew the royal menagerie stood. 'This runs under the royal menagerie; part of it is now used as a wolf-pit.'

I glanced quickly at Benjamin but held my peace.

'It's part of the old Roman sewer system,' Spurge explained.

'And, before you ask,' Vetch added, 'early this morning I had the wolves confined. Spurge and I went down there. There are two tunnels: both are bricked off. Not even a mouse could get through.'

'So, you are sure that there are no secret entrances in or out of the Tower?' Benjamin asked.

'None whatsoever,' Spurge declared. 'I'd put my life on that.'

I pointed to the small postern-gates, some overlooking the moat, others the river. 'And this morning all these were guarded?'

'They still are,' Kemble replied proudly. 'I, for one, wish to be above suspicion, Master Daunbey. Don't forget, even if someone could leave or enter the Tower secretly, such comings and goings would eventually be noticed.'

Benjamin tapped the map with his hand. 'May we borrow this?'

'I'd prefer it if you didn't,' Spurge replied. 'In a way, it's as costly as any portrait or tapestry.'

'I won't leave the Tower,' Benjamin promised.

Spurge reluctantly agreed.

'Do you wish me to accompany you around the Tower?' Kemble offered.

'No, Sir Edward, I don't. However, I would be grateful for quarters, a chamber for myself and Shallot.'

Kemble smiled. 'The most spacious two are in the Wakefield Tower. I'll have them prepared. Master Daunbey,' he continued, 'can I ask your advice?'

'Of course.'

'If I keep the Tower locked and barred much longer,' Kemble declared, 'people will begin to chatter and the gossip might spread.'

'Then you had best open it,' Benjamin answered.

And, taking our leave, we left the royal quarters. Once we were out on the green, well away from any window or door, Benjamin stopped and beat the rolled-up map against his leg.

'There must be two villains,' he said. 'One stole the gold in the city and the other killed Horehound. But why kill a drunken hangman?' He continued hoarsely.

I stared at a raven hopping towards me, its cruel yellow beak held out like a lance. I stamped my boot and shooed the bird away. (God forgive me, I can't stand ravens: they are birds of ill-omen. Ah, my little chaplain

150

asks me why? It's the way the bastards look at me with their beady little eyes: as if they are truly disappointed that my head is still on its shoulders and not hanging on some pole where they can peck it to their hearts' delight).

'What have we established?' Benjamin asked impatiently.

'Well, we know there are two people, partners in villainy,' I replied. 'One is here in the Tower. He sent the first letter and tried to kill me by throwing me into the wolf-pit. However, on the latter occasion, Kemble and his officers were not involved. When I was screaming for my life in the wolf-pit, you were with them. The same is true when Horehound's murder happened. All three were with us. So, Master, it must be Mallow or one of his hangmen.'

I stopped as the people I was talking about came out of the Beauchamp Tower bearing Horehound's corpse, neatly wrapped and hidden by a canvas sheet which was lashed by cords at top and bottom. They took it over to a cart. Mallow climbed into the seat, cracked his whip and, with his three apprentices walking beside, made his way down to the Lion Gate.

Wormwood stopped, shading his eyes against the sun, and called out to us, 'We are going to bury him in the cemetery of the Crutched Friars. Say a prayer for the poor bugger,' he added.

Benjamin and I nodded and watched the miserable procession continue.

'I am sure of it,' I whispered. 'One of them is the killer, but God knows who their accomplice is!'

'Mistress Undershaft!' Benjamin replied. 'We must speak to her again about her mysterious legacy. First, let's study Spurge's map.'

We walked round the Tower. As we did so, I became more heavy-hearted. Kemble was true to his word. Men-at-arms and archers guarded every entrance, water-gate and postern-door marked on the map.

'You couldn't smuggle a rat in here,' I grumbled. 'Do you believe the underground tunnel is sealed off?'

'Of course,' Benjamin replied. 'If Spurge and Vetch were lying, they'd lose their heads.'

We did the full length of the Tower, coming back to where we started, then walked down to where the builders and masons were working on scaffolding up against a wall. They seemed a cheerful bunch of rogues, covered in dust, swearing and cursing as they scrambled about like monkeys. Benjamin called the master mason down.

'What do you want?' the fellow asked, shaking water from a pannikin over his face and wiping the dust from his wrists and arms.

'How long have you been working here?' Benjamin asked.

'Oh, must be a week now, sir.' He looked up. 'Martin!' he shouted.

A crop-haired, cheery-faced fellow came to the edge of the scaffolding and smiled down at us.

'We've been here a week haven't we?' The master mason shouted.

'Aye, it's about that.' The fellow's rustic accent seemed out of place, warm and friendly.

'Why?' the builder continued. 'Don't say we've got to stay another bloody night here?'

Benjamin shook his head. 'And you've seen nothing untoward?' he asked the master mason.

'Sir, we have come in to do the walls, and the walls we will do. Master Spurge has given us directions. We work from dawn till dusk, then – ' he raised his voice – 'we are supposed to go back to our homes. Last night we found the gates sealed and Sir Edward said none of us could leave and so here we stayed.'

Benjamin thanked him and moved off as the mason, cursing under his breath, climbed the ladder back on to the scaffolding. We returned to the royal quarters, gave Spurge his map back and left the Tower. Kemble had already ordered the main gates to be opened. We went along winding streets to Petty Wales and into the Monkshood tavern.

If Marisa had been Hellbane's doxy, she had soon forgotten him. We found her in a corner, sitting in the lap of a chapman who was plying her with drink. At first the ruffian was going to object, but when my hand fell to the hilt of my sword, he scampered off muttering that we were welcome to her. Marisa was one of those young women with an old face; hair as black as night falling down to her shoulders, a thin white face, a narrow slit for a mouth and the green eyes of a nasty-tempered cat. She wore a stained blue dress with the bodice cut low; it was rather dirty, but revealed all her charms. When Benjamin put a coin on the table, she leaned a little closer and became much friendlier.

'I very rarely take two at a time.'

'Shut up!' I snarled. 'It's not your body we are after!'

'Then what?' she snapped and, before I could intervene, her fingers had grasped the silver coin. 'I am a good girl.' Her voice rose to a screech in an attempt to gain the attention of the landlord who had been standing watching us. I turned and glared at him: he moved to wipe the top of a beer-barrel as if his very life depended on it.

'Sit down, Marisa,' Benjamin ordered quietly. Another silver coin appeared between his fingers; this time it was held well away from her. 'You knew one of the hangmen at the Tower? A gentleman called Hellbane?'

Marisa's face softened. 'His real name was Crispin,' she whispered. 'He was a printer. Did you know that? He came from Southampton where he had killed two men. He fled abroad but he said it was better to starve to death in England than do so in some foreign city, so he came back.'

153

'Did he enjoy his work?' I asked.

'Sometimes.' Marisa crossed her arms and sat back, blinking furiously at the tears welling in her eyes. 'He did love me,' she whispered hoarsely. 'He even said he'd marry me. He talked of earning enough, then we'd leave London and the Tower, travel north, go somewhere where no one would know us. Start up his old trade again.'

'Did he have friends?' Benjamin asked. He leaned across and gently caught her hand. 'Tell us, Marisa, please. We want to catch his killer.'

She forced a smile. 'I thought a gentleman always brought a lady a drink?'

Benjamin called the landlord across and, at Marisa's request, ordered three cups of white wine.

'And your best!' Marisa screeched. 'None of that bucket-swill! We are going to toast Hellbane's soul!' She turned to Benjamin. 'You asked if Hellbane liked his job, and the truth is no. He hated it. He said when he turned people off the ladder, he always closed his eyes. However, he thought being a hangman was the best protection against the sheriff's warrant. As for friends . . .? People like Hellbane don't have friends. Sometimes he'd go with that ridiculous guild, but he spent most of his time with me.'

'And the day he was killed?' I asked.

'We were to meet here one evening. He never came. The next morning they fished his body from the Thames. Someone had knocked him on the head but had not bothered to steal a penny from his purse or the rings from his fingers. He'd been put into a sack with weights and tossed into the Thames.' She paused as the landlord brought across the wine which she grasped and drank greedily. 'All I could think was that someone had wanted revenge. What does the Bible say, sir? Eye for eye, tooth for tooth?'

'I don't think so,' Benjamin retorted. 'I think Hellbane

was killed because of what he knew.'

My master grasped her hand. 'Marisa, did he ever remark on anything strange happening in the Tower?'

'He hated the place,' she whispered, turning her cup. 'He claimed that, at night, ghosts walked. He heard strange sounds and cries ... But no, he didn't mention anything in particular.'

'And he drank with the rest of the hangmen?' Benjamin asked.

'Oh yes, and sometimes they drank deeply. I joined them. The last occasion was the sixth of June, the King's birthday. It's the ancient custom for the constable to host a banquet for the Guild of Hangmen in the royal apartments.' She smiled thinly. 'A macabre affair, Masters. Mallow, Hellbane and the rest, all dressed in their hangmen's costumes, black leather jerkins, belts, swords; they even wore their masks and hoods. I and the other girls were quite frightened.

'And what happened?' I asked, curious at the thought of hangmen sitting at a table, masked and cowled, feasting and drinking.

'Well, Sir Edward's a good man and the wine flowed. Afterwards, well, we played Hangmen's Bluff. The men hid and their girl friends, we had to search for them.' She sipped from the cup. 'You can imagine, sirs, the squealing, the kissing, the slapping and tickling! The galleries and corridors were dark, and each of the men masked!'

'Was Undershaft there? Mallow's lieutenant?' I asked.

'Oh yes, but he was by himself. The others called him a spoilsport so he took part for a while and then went home.' She smiled to herself. 'We did drink deeply that night.'

'Did Hellbane say anything?' I asked, an idea forming in my mind. 'Did anything untoward happen during those festivities?'

Marisa tossed her head and rubbed her face. 'I can't

remember much. Sir Edward Kemble and his officers were there. The wine flowed like water. Undershaft left early, I remember that. Others were lying in corridors or galleries, drunk as sots. That's all I know.'

Benjamin handed the silver over and we made to leave.

'Sirs!' she called.

We went back to the table. She stared up at us and said, 'Hellbane thought Undershaft's death was curious: the man didn't have an enemy in the world. He kept to his woman and children.' She paused. 'You might be right, for all I know; both he and poor Hellbane could have been party to some dreadful secret but what it was, I don't know.'

I leaned across the table, kissed her cheek, and pressed a coin of my own into her hands. 'I am sorry I was rude,' I whispered.

'You must come back to the Monkshood some time,' she smiled. And, for a while, her eyes softened as her soul reappeared.

We left the tavern and walked back through the streets towards the Tower.

'What do you think this secret is?' Benjamin asked.

'I disagree with Marisa,' I replied. 'But what happens, Master, if, during those festivities on the King's birthday, the hangmen did see or learn something mysterious? Perhaps they don't even realise it?'

'And?' Benjamin asked.

'Well, they were all masked and hooded,' I replied. 'Perhaps one of them stumbled on something. In their disguise and the poor light, the holder of this mystery decided it was best if they all die, just to ensure he kills the right one.'

'But, if that's the case, my dear Roger, the hangmen who did stumble on that secret would realise they were being pursued and act accordingly.'

I couldn't answer that.

'Let's visit Mistress Undershaft,' Benjamin declared.

We found the good widow woman sitting in a parlour embroidering a piece of linen. In the rooms above, we could hear the maid shooing the children into bed. Mistress Undershaft was welcoming enough, offering us ale and bread, but Benjamin refused. We sat opposite, watching as she continued to thread the needle for the cloth.

'You have great skill, Mistress,' Benjamin remarked.

'My mother taught me,' she replied smilingly. 'But you are not here to praise my needlework, sirs.'

'No, Mistress, we are still puzzled by the strange bequest to you.'

'As I am,' she replied. She lay the piece of cloth in her lap and stretched one hand out towards the fire, half listening to the sounds above. 'I have told you, sirs, the bequest was made to goldsmith Thurgood. Who am I to object? There's no crime in that.'

I caught the lilt in her voice and asked if she was born in London. She shook her head.

'No, my family are from Lincoln, they're clothmakers. I met Andrew there some years ago, before we came to London.'

'Was he always a hangman?' I asked.

She blushed and her hands shook. 'He was a priest,' she replied quietly. 'Yes, sir, a defrocked priest. He killed a man in his own church and fled. I came with him to London. For a while he did some labouring before taking up his post as an apprentice hangman and joining the guild.' She shrugged. 'The rest you know.'

'But the children?' I remarked.

'Andrew was one of those priests who did not follow canon law,' she answered. 'He had his woman, she gave birth to children. Go round the churches of England, Master Shallot. It's none too strange. That's how he killed a man,' she continued. 'Andrew was a good priest. He worked hard for his parishioners. He was a carpenter

157

by trade and sold what he made so his children were not a burden on the parish. His wife died. Two years later he met me. One day, a parishioner accosted him in the nave of the church and called Andrew filthy names. Knives were drawn. For a while Andrew took sanctuary. I gathered up his possessions and children and fled south.'

'And you know of no reason why someone should kill your husband so barbarously?' Benjamin asked.

'I have told you, sir. Andrew was a private man. He kept to himself. He did not talk much about his trade. Sometimes he drank with the guild.'

'And the festivities on the night of the King's birthday?' I asked. 'Your husband attended?'

'Yes, but he left early.'

'Did he remark on anything untoward?'

She shook her head. 'Nothing, except to say that his comrades were as drunk as pigs and were lewd with their women.' She picked up the embroidery and jabbed at it with her needle. 'I tell you, sirs, I have nothing to say. I cannot help you. If I . . .' She stopped speaking as a little girl burst into the room chased by a boy, his fingers covered in ash.

'Simon! Judith!' Mistress Undershaft stared down at the children. 'What on earth are you doing?' She grabbed the little girl, and her nightdress came loose exposing one thin white shoulder.

'It's Simon,' the girl squeaked, pointing at her brother. 'He's trying to draw on my shoulder.' She pointed to the dirty charcoal mark in the shape of a 'W'. The boy stood, hands by his side, looking fearfully at his mother.

'Simon, you should not have done that!' Mistress Undershaft, highly agitated, began pushing him towards the door.

'But Simon says you've got one,' the little girl replied. 'You have a letter on your shoulder.'

Mistress Undershaft fairly pushed them out of the

158

room into the arms of the waiting maid. She slammed the door behind them, leaning against it, her face white as chalk, eyes closed, that lovely bosom heaving as if she had run a mile. I got up and walked towards her.

'You heard?' she whispered without opening her eyes.

'Aye, Mistress, I did. Is it true? Does your shoulder bear the brand of a whore?'

She nodded, walked back, and slumped into the chair. Her shoulders began to shake as she wept.

'I have told you the truth,' she said between sobs. 'Both Andrew and I came from Lincoln. He was a priest, his woman died, and then he met me. He was kind and generous-hearted. He told me he could not live a life of celibacy. Yes, I was a whore,' she continued softly. 'I was born and raised as a seamstress, but times became hard.' She swallowed, wiping her eyes with her fingers.

'That's what the quarrel was about, wasn't it?' Benjamin asked. 'When your husband killed that man in his church?'

'Yes, it was about me,' she replied. 'Then Andrew took sanctuary.' She raised her face. 'You know the law, Master Daunbey: either you surrender yourself to the royal justices, in which case Andrew would have certainly hanged, or you are given forty days to leave the kingdom. The friends and relatives of the man he killed would make sure he never left the city alive. So I organised everything. I didn't love Andrew but, there again, no man had ever stood up for me as he did. I smuggled him and his family out of Lincoln.'

'And the money left at Thurgood's?' I asked. 'That's yours, isn't it?'

She nodded. 'I was a very good seamstress, Master Shallot, but I was an even better whore. The great and rich of Lincoln sought my favours. I kept my monies hidden. Andrew was proud and refused to touch my money. When he died, I simply drew it out of my secret place and took it down to Thurgood's. I dressed and acted as a man. I didn't think anyone would show much interest.' She sighed, put the embroidery down on the chair and walked over to make sure the door was closed. She came back and stood over us. 'I could tell the day you first came that you were suspicious that I was not the grieving widow.' She crouched down before me, the skin of her beautiful face tight and glistening with sweat, those beautiful eyes begging and pleading with me. 'God be my witness, I did not love Andrew Undershaft. He was a good man, but he knew what I was. Now he is dead. I don't know why, God rest his soul. However, for the first time in my life, Master Shallot, I am free of the past. I am a woman of good standing in my community. I have a house, I have children, I have my trade as a seamstress and monies with the goldsmith. I can start again . . .' She paused. '. . . If I am allowed to.'

I stroked her hair, took her hand and made her stand. I kissed her on each cheek.

'Your secret's safe, Mistress Undershaft.' I tapped her shoulder lightly. 'There are good physicians in the city. They could hide that for you.'

Benjamin also took her hand, vowing what she had told us would remain a secret. He made her promise that, if she remembered anything untoward, she would tell us.

When we left the house, darkness had fallen. Benjamin linked his arm through mine and we walked back towards the Tower.

'What do you think, Roger?'

'I believe her, Master. But, there again, if she can lie once, she can lie a second time.'

'But you don't think that?'

'No, Master, I don't. I still wonder about her husband. Was that really his corpse discovered at Smithfield? Or is he the villain? An ex-priest, a violent man by all accounts.'

Benjamin stopped and leaned against a garden wall, listening to a nightingale which was singing so beautifully in the trees above his head.

'All things are possible, Roger. However, let's remember the three men who have been killed. They are all fairly young, tough, probably violent. They wouldn't give up their lives lightly. Ergo, were they murdered by someone close to them?'

'Not necessarily, Master,' I replied. 'Undershaft, if it was he, could have been drugged or knocked on the head before he was burnt. Remember, his body was bundled into a cage at the height of the plague. No one would care a whit: Horehound and Hellbane could have gone the same way. I still believe we should ask the sheriff to search for Undershaft. Remember, he was a priest, skilled in matters of the Chancery. The drawing up and sealing of letters would be easy for such a man. But God knows where those blessed seals came from . . .'

'Aye, that's the stumbling block,' Benjamin agreed. 'Those damn seals.' He came closer. 'I asked Agrippa about that. He confirmed the King had made a search of all Chanceries. Nothing remains from the reign of a young boy who ruled only for a few months some forty years ago.'

'Henry will now be dancing up and down in fury, or gnawing on the rushes at Windsor, threatening to have my head on a pole,' I added bitterly.

Benjamin grinned and slapped me on the shoulder. 'Don't worry, Roger, the game's not over yet.'

Well, it nearly was. My master was far too trusting. We went down another alleyway, intending to enter the Tower by the Lion Gate. It was a quiet night, well away from the taverns and cheap markets of Petty Wales where you can buy or sell anything until the early hours. I was trailing slightly behind Benjamin, kicking at anything in my path, and wondering if I should suggest that we take a journey abroad. After all, we could be in

Dover within a day, and in France by the end of the week. I was about to suggest this when a crossbow bolt flew by my face and cracked the plaster in the house alongside. I stopped.

My master pulled me down just as another bolt came whirring through the night air. We crouched like two little schoolboys, staring into the darkness, straining our ears for any sound.

'It came from the riverside,' Benjamin whispered.

I could hear the lap of the water and the faint cries of a boatman, but nothing else.

'The assassin could be anywhere,' I whispered.

Through the darkness came a whistle, full and merry on the night air, as if some lad was sitting on the quayside, a fishing rod in his hands. I recognised the tune, a lilting song, sung in the London taverns, about a young girl and her love for a great lord. Well, I did what I could. I whistled back. Once again an arrow smacked into the plaster above our heads.

'Who's there?' Benjamin called.

The whistling began again, but this time it was chilling. I could imagine the assassin walking up and down, soft-footed, notching another bolt into the groove. The plaster of the house was white, and that was what he was watching. If we moved, he would see our silhouettes from where he stood with his back to the river, cloaked by the night.

'Whistle again,' Benjamin ordered.

I tried to but my mouth was dry, and all I could do was croak. All the old signs of Shallot's terror were beginning to manifest themselves: a tightening of the stomach, a loosening of the bowels, and this overwhelming urge to run.

'For the love of life, whistle that bloody tune!' Benjamin whispered.

This time, panic lent its aid. I wet my lips, recalled the tune, and whistled it back. I also made the mistake of moving, and a crossbow bolt streaked across my hair. If it had been a barber's knife, I would have lost some of my lustrous locks.

'Now!' Benjamin screamed. 'Charge!'

I had no choice but to follow him and, even as I did, I recognised my master's wisdom. We were now away from the wall and the assassin would have to retreat. We streaked like greyhounds towards the river, shouting and yelling so loudly that even a sentry on the walls of the Tower called out to ask what was the matter. We reached the quayside: to my right I heard the faint patter of retreating footsteps. There was nothing, only a few boats tied to their poles, bobbing in the full evening current. Benjamin stopped and crouched down to ease the cramp in his legs and snatch gulpfuls of air.

'Well, well, Roger.'

He didn't have to commiserate with me. I was on my knees retching and coughing. I looked around, a postern-door in the Tower opened, and soldiers ran out towards us, carrying torches, swords drawn.

'Master Daunbey! Master Shallot!'

I glanced up.

Vetch came forward. 'What's the matter? You were attacked?'

'No!' I snarled, getting to my feet and helping my master up. 'We always do this just before we retire to bed!'

Pushing our way through the soldiers, we made our way into the Tower. I was convinced it was time for old Roger to leave. As I settled on to my pallet-bed, I firmly resolved that, the first thing I would do the next morning, would be to persuade my master to join me.

Chapter 10

'No, Roger, I will not.' Benjamin sat on his bed in our chamber in the Wakefield Tower and shook his head angrily.

We had spent most of the morning sharing a wineskin I had filched from the Tower kitchens, and discussing who the assassin could be. Now tired, our wits dulled, our heads thick, Benjamin and I just sat in our comfortable quarters and wondered what to do next. Benjamin had been so morose, I'd tentatively put it to him that perhaps we should spend a few months beyond the seas.

'Roger,' he exclaimed, 'that would be betrayal of beloved Uncle's trust!'

'Damn him!' I cried. 'Master, in the last few months I have been hounded from Ipswich by the Poppletons, almost poisoned by Quicksilver, nearly died of the sweating sickness, pushed into a wolf-pen, and now someone is shooting arrows at me. Not to mention,' I continued bitterly, 'my desperate run through Windsor Forest which, if the King gets his hands on me, I am doomed to repeat!'

'How far would we get?' Benjamin retorted. 'Don't you think the same thought has occurred to dearest Uncle? The ports would be watched. We would be arrested and back in the Tower, not as guests, but as prisoners. Moreover, if we journey abroad, how will we live? When could we come back? Moreover,' he added bitterly, 'you

165

know the King's mind. He might start wondering who really is behind these blackmailing letters and demands for gold.'

'He wouldn't blame us!' I cried.

Benjamin glanced at me: I knew he was right. In his present mood, the Great Beast would be only too willing to point the finger.

'Ah well,' I sighed. 'What do we do next?'

Benjamin stared round the chamber. 'We are well looked after,' he remarked. 'Let's wait here and think. Our enemies are bound to make a mistake.'

I reluctantly agreed: after all, Kemble was a perfect host.

Now, you young men who know the Tower might think it was all gloomy, wet, mildewed walls, draughty cells, narrow cold passageways and creaking doors. Oh, there's plenty of that, but our rooms in the Wakefield were spacious, well-lit by windows, all filled with glass and protected by shutters. Tapestries hung on the wall, we had soft beds, tables, chairs, a large aumbry for our clothes, as well as chests and coffers. In many ways it was a home from home, except for the problems which faced us. Cooks and servitors brought us wine and food, and Kemble issued an open invitation to dine with him or in the garrison refectory. However, for the next few days we kept to ourselves. Benjamin paced up and down. He slept, muttered to himself, or studied Thomas More's *History of Richard the Third.*

In any other circumstances I would have gone wandering into the city looking for mischief, but I was frightened. Benjamin kept to his studies: he borrowed parchment, quills and inkhorn from the Tower stores, and began to scribble furiously. On the morning of our third day he finished. I came back from my usual walk on the Tower Green, where everyone could see me, to find him sitting on the bed, studying what he had written.

'What if,' he began, 'the young Edward the Fifth did survive? Or his younger brother, or both? They kept their seals and now work in the Tower garrison as humble soldiers or servitors?' He took one look at my face and grinned. 'It was just an idea,' he declared. He swung his legs off the bed. 'This is the problem, Roger. Forty years ago, the two sons of Edward the Fourth, his eldest boy, also named Edward, and Richard Duke of York, were locked up in the Tower by their Uncle Richard. They disappeared. They could have been murdered, or they could have escaped. We know that, for most of Henry the Seventh's reign, the King's peace of mind was plagued by pretenders who claimed to be the lost Princes. Even our present King has had to face conspiracies from the secret Brotherhood of the White Rose.'

Benjamin walked to the window and looked down at the soldiers practising their archery on the Tower Green. 'Now, I think both Princes are probably dead. However, their seals, which should have been broken and defaced, are being used to blackmail Henry. The sequence of events is as follows, correct me if I am wrong. On the sixth of June last, the Guild of Hangmen celebrated the King's birthday in a banquet which turned into an orgy. The hangmen were dressed in their official garb. It's possible that one of them saw something in the Tower which put the whole company at risk. Time passes: the sweating sickness breaks out in London, but the garrison only suffers one casualty, Philip Allardyce, clerk of the stores. He falls ill and is looked after by the crone Ragusa. We know he was ill from the testimony of witnesses. The old woman claimed he died: his sheeted corpse was taken to the death-cart at the Lion Gate, where a bailiff also pronounced him dead.'

'Aye, that road is closed,' I agreed. 'We know Allardyce was ill and died. He can't possibly be the villain in the city.'

'The sweating sickness begins to rage,' Benjamin continued. 'Kemble sealed the Tower as if it was under siege. He and his two principal officers stay here, as do Mallow and his guild. No one is allowed to enter or leave. Then the first blackmailing letter arrives. It was left in Kemble's chamber, so the writer must be someone in the Tower. However, he must also have an accomplice in the city who can issue those proclamations and demand the money be left near St Paul's. We also think the same villain is behind the death of the hangman Andrew Undershaft, whose blackened corpse was found in a cage at Smithfield. Agreed?'

'Yes, Master.'

'And what else, Roger?'

'The sweating sickness passes and the Tower is opened. Another hangman is murdered, knocked on the head and drowned in a sack in the Thames, whilst a further blackmail letter is left on the Abbot's seat at Westminster. We, unhappy two,' I continued bitterly, 'have the miserable task of taking the gold to where the blackmailer wants it at St Paul's. By subtle trickery, the villain seizes this and also taunts us. Once again we know it could not have been anyone from the Tower as, for most of that particular day, the Tower was locked and sealed. Nevertheless, we come back here, Horehound is horribly murdered. We are none the wiser, except that we know someone in the Tower, and another outside, are working in partnership.' I paused.

Benjamin walked back to his bed and sat down, head in hands. 'I was with Kemble when you were thrown into the wolf-pit,' he said, 'and we were both with the officers when Horehound was killed.'

'So?' I asked. 'Are you saying the malefactor must be amongst the hangmen?'

'I think so,' he replied, and smiled at me. 'I am also beginning to wonder if you are correct, Roger. Is Andrew Undershaft really dead?'

'One thing does bother me,' I replied. 'Granted, the hangmen have been slaughtered because one of them saw something untoward, but why kill them in such barbarous and grisly ways? It's as if the killer is imitating every type of execution: burning in a cage, drowning in a sack, or being pressed to death under a heavy door. There's a malicious relish here,' I declared. 'As if the assassin is determined to kill the hangmen in the most barbaric way possible.'

'For revenge?' Benjamin asked.

'Possibly,' I replied. 'We should have another word with Master Mallow.'

'As the King wants a word with you!'

I spun round. Agrippa stood in the doorway, his black, broad-brimmed hat clutched in his hands.

'You've come from Windsor?' Benjamin asked.

'Aye.' Agrippa walked across and sat down on a stool, staring at us with those strange eyes.

'Tell us the worst,' I moaned.

'The King is furious. He's talking of treason, dereliction of duty by faithful servants. Do you remember the captain of the guard in St Paul's churchyard? What was his name?'

'Ramasden,' I replied.

'Well, Ramasden's no more. He was hanged on the common gallows outside Windsor. The King is threatening to do the same to you, Master Roger. What's worse –' Agrippa pulled a small scroll from beneath his cloak and handed it to me – 'yesterday morning this was handed to one of the royal justices as he left Westminster Hall.'

I gazed down at the elegant writing. 'To the King' and the red silk ribbon like a circle of blood around the scroll.

'Not another letter!' Benjamin exclaimed.

I undid the ribbon. The letter was shorter than the first but couched in the same arrogant, impudent tones.

'From Edward V, King of England, etc., etc., To one

Henry Tudor, calling himself King. . .'

The date given was two days earlier at the Tower. The threat was the same: the writer accused Henry of trying to trap him, and therefore imposed a fine of one thousand gold coins. This time the money was to be left at the foot of the gallows at Tyburn.

'On your allegiance to Us,' the letter concluded, 'do not attempt to obstruct or impede our rightful collection of these taxes.'

'The monies are to be left there at Michaelmas,' Agrippa explained.

I looked up. 'Two weeks hence.' I threw the letter at Benjamin. 'Master, what can we do?' I went and sat next to him on the bed and gazed bleakly at Agrippa. 'What's the King so frightened of?' I shouted. 'Why doesn't he just refuse to pay the gold and tell the villain to go hang?'

Agrippa shook his head like a benevolent schoolmaster facing a dim-witted pupil.

'You don't understand, do you? In his father's reign a kitchen boy pretended to be a Yorkist prince. A mere kitchen boy, Roger! Yet he won the support of powerful princes abroad. He invaded from Ireland. Henry's father met him at East Stoke in Nottinghamshire, and nearly lost the battle to a kitchen boy who could produce very little proof of his scurrilous claims! A few years later, Perkin Warbeck, the son of a Flemish weaver, came forward and claimed to be one of the younger Princes, Richard of York. And, for almost ten years, harassed the King's father to the point of distraction. Even now Henry is busy watching anyone with Yorkist blood in him.'

Agrippa beat his hat against his knee. 'Can you imagine, Roger? Must I keep repeating it? What would happen if such letters, signed and sealed by a Yorkist prince, began appearing all over London? Letters bearing the royal seal, proclaiming Henry as a usurper and alleging that the burdens the country is facing are

170

because of his father's usurpation? Henry would spend tens of thousands raising troops and crushing revolts. No, this villainy must be stopped, the perpetrators captured and hanged immediately.'

'And is that all you can say?' I yelled back.

He spread his hands. 'I can only say what I know.'

'Listen.' Benjamin, who had been studying the manuscript carefully, rolled it up and handed it back to me. 'My good doctor, whatever this villain says, I believe the two Princes in the Tower are dead. The constable, Sir Robert Brackenbury, who looked after them, was killed at Bosworth. Sir James Tyrrell, who may have had a hand in their murder, is also gone. However, Sir Thomas More, in his *History of Richard the Third*, alleges two common malefactors were involved in the Princes' murders, Dighton and Greene. Does anyone know of their whereabouts?'

'My Lord Cardinal has already thought of that,' Agrippa answered. 'Careful search has been made amongst the public records. Dighton was a northerner, he may have been executed in Durham but we have no real proof. Greene was a Londoner, a young man, a rogue. After Bosworth, a hunt was mounted for him. All we have is a description: lean, narrow-faced, with a terrible scar on his right wrist.' Agrippa sighed and got to his feet. 'But that's all I know. Now I have to report back to Windsor. You have the letter and the King's instructions. I wish you well.'

I made an obscene gesture as the door closed behind him. 'Shall we go to France?' I asked.

Benjamin sniffed the air. 'Isn't Dr Agrippa's perfume strange?' he muttered. 'Some say it is pleasant but others claim it's foul.'

'The same goes for a hanging!' I snapped. 'It's pleasant if you're watching, or so they say, but dreadful to experience.'

Benjamin got to his feet, picking up his doublet. 'All

paths are closed,' he declared, 'except one which you, Roger, have opened.' He smiled down at me. 'Let's ask Master Mallow a few questions.' He picked up the scroll Agrippa had brought and pushed it into one of the saddlebags hanging from a peg on the wall. 'We've some time yet.'

We left Wakefield Tower. It was strange to be surrounded by the daily retinue of the garrison: soldiers cleaned their equipment whilst children chattered and played in the sun: a cartload of provisions trundled towards the kitchens; masons banged and sang on the scaffolding. Benjamin made inquiries and discovered the hangmen had been busy carrying out executions and would be at the Gallows tavern. We went there but found it empty. Benjamin ordered ale, the landlord assuring us that, before the hour was out, Mallow and his apprentices would arrive. We sat sipping morosely at our ale until they did, coming through the doorway like a collection of demons. This was the first time I had seen them dressed in their official garb: black, high-heeled boots, long leather jackets of the same colour, hoods with a half-mask over their faces. They looked sinister and, as they walked across towards us, I realised how difficult it would be to tell one from the other in some darkened gallery or half-lit room. They greeted us cheerfully enough, pulling back their cowls, taking off the face masks, wiping the sweat from their faces as they shouted for ale.

'A good day's work?' I asked.

They acted like labourers coming in from the fields rather than executioners who had just been dispatching men on the gallows.

'Good?' Mallow queried. 'Of course, it's good, Shallot. London is a safer place. This morning we hanged nine river pirates near Wapping: that's why we were all there.'

'A bad time for river pirates,' I observed.

172

Mallow smirked and sipped at his tankard. 'Less of the sarcasm, Shallot. Now the sweating sickness is over, the justices of gaol delivery have been busy at the Fleet, Newgate and Marshalsea, so now we are going to be very busy over the next few weeks. Well –' he put the tankard down – 'what can we do for you? As you can see, we are all alive and kicking.'

'Unlike the river pirates,' Wormwood quipped. 'They are just kicking!'

'It's about the murders of Hellbane, Horehound and Undershaft,' I began.

'We've told you all we know,' Snakeroot sneered.

'Tell me,' Benjamin asked, 'how does the Guild of Hangmen function? I mean, who decides which executions will be carried out?'

'That's my decision,' Mallow replied. 'I work with the under-sheriffs. Naturally, sometimes we are busier than others. After the quarter sessions or commissions of gaol delivery, execution days are fixed either at Tyburn, in St Paul's churchyard, Smithfield, or at any of the crossroads leading into the city. There is a roster of duties.'

'Yet today you have all been busy?' I inquired.

'As I have said, the plague is now over. Commissioners of gaol delivery sit at Westminster and the Guildhall, whilst the King's ships have been busy in the Thames estuary. River pirates have been caught and have now been hanged, either at Wapping or along the riverbanks.'

'So,' Benjamin asked, 'are you ever threatened by friends, relatives, or members of the gangs?'

Mallow grinned and sipped from his tankard. 'Now that's strange,' he declared. 'Oh, yes, sometimes. However, Master Daunbey, we are masked and hooded, whilst most felons and cut-throats see capture, imprisonment and execution as an occupational hazard. Amongst the outlaws and wolvesheads there is only one law: don't be caught.' He shrugged. 'And if you are, you pay the price. Why, where are these questions leading to?'

'We believe that the murders of members of your guild are definitely linked to the blackmailing letters being sent to the King. Now,' Benjamin paused to collect his thoughts, 'God knows the reason, though I suspect it might be connected to the events which occurred in the Tower on the night of the King's birthday.'

'What do you mean?' Wormwood snapped.

'If I knew, I'd tell you,' Benjamin declared. 'Nevertheless,' he continued, 'Undershaft, Horehound and Hellbane were all slain with a malicious relish. Each of them suffered execution as laid down by the law. Undershaft was burnt in a cage. Hellbane drowned in a sack, and Horehound pressed to death. We believe the assassin has a grudge against all of your company.'

'But, as we have said –' Snakeroot's shifty eyes gazed blearily at us, his mouth slack and dribbling '– the villains of London leave us alone.'

'Think!' Benjamin urged them. 'Think! Have there been any executions, carried out by all of you, where vengeance was promised?'

Benjamin's words hung like a hangman's noose over this sinister group of men. They had walked into the tavern the roaring, bully boys, used to exercising the power of life and death. Now they were being confronted with the prospect of their own executions, and macabre ones at that.

(Oh, I see my little clerk is tapping his quill. A sign he wishes to ask a question. 'Have you ever been an executioner?' he squeaks. I am tempted to rap him over the knuckles with my ash cane for his impertinence: the answer is no! In all my adventures, despite all the extremities I have been pushed to, I have never taken a life unless I have had to. There, he can shut his mouth and I'll continue.)

'Think!' Benjamin repeated.

174

'The Sakker Gang!' Toadflax spoke up, running his hands through his yellow hair.

'Of course!' Mallow breathed. 'The Sakkers!'

'Who are they?' Benjamin asked.

'A Kentish gang,' Mallow replied slowly. 'A father and five sons. They owned a tavern on the London to Canterbury road. They used to prey on pilgrims. The sheriff of Kent and the local law officers could do nothing against them. They robbed, plundered, raped and ravished. At first no one suspected them. They owned a tavern near St Thomas's watering-hole. Pilgrims would stop there. The Sakkers wined and dined them, carefully scrutinising their intended victims. The following morning, after the pilgrims had left, the Sakkers would take a short cut through the forest and ambush them: heavily armed pilgrims they left alone. They preyed on those little groups: families, merchants alone with their wives. Sometimes they would just rob. However, if they thought there was danger of being identified, they would kill with a cold ruthlessness.'

'And no one suspected them?' Benjamin asked.

'Well, no. As I have said, it was a father and five sons. The eldest, Robert, would stay in the tavern and pretend that his father and brothers were with him. They'd amassed quite a fortune. One day a merchant stayed at the tavern, months earlier one of his comrades had been attacked and killed. Now this merchant had given his friend a bracelet, a midsummer present which he saw on the wrist of one of the Sakkers. The merchant immediately returned to London and laid this information before the sheriffs. The gang was caught by Theophilus Pelleter.'

'Who?' I interrupted, intrigued by such a strange name.

'Theophilus Pelleter. One of the under-sheriffs,' Mallow replied. 'He lives with his daughter in Catte Street.' His eyes softened. 'A good man, straight and true. I understand that when the plague visited the city, Pelleter stayed at his post and did what he could.'

I stared across the tavern where a cat, a rat caught between his jaws, padded out from the kitchen and disappeared into the stableyard.

'Anyway,' Mallow continued, 'Pelleter laid a trap. The entire gang was rounded up and appeared before King's Bench where, because of their crimes, the judges ruled that their tavern be levelled to the ground. They were to be hanged on special gibbets constructed on the site.'

'And did they all die?' Benjamin asked.

'That's when the threats were made!' Wormwood snapped. 'The father and only four of his sons were captured. The eldest, Robert, escaped. Apparently, the night Pelleter and his men ringed the tavern, Robert was away. He returned to find his father and brothers captured.'

'So, why didn't he swear vengeance against the under-sheriff?'

Mallow looked shamefacedly away. The rest of his guild shuffled their feet and stared into their cups.

'Well?' I asked.

Mallow looked up. 'To answer your question, the under-sheriff and the other law officers were responsible for taking the gang back to the tavern and making sure lawful execution was carried out.'

'Yes, yes, I can understand that,' Benjamin replied.

'Before the tavern was razed,' Mallow continued, 'we er . . .'

'Helped yourselves?' Benjamin asked.

'Well, we claimed the prerequisites of our office. Most of the tavern had been looted. What was left we took. Pelleter refused to have anything to do with it.'

'But hangmen always claim their dues,' I insisted.

'Oh, tell him!' Wormwood snapped. 'Tell him what really happened!'

'I will,' Snakeroot declared. 'When you hang a man,

Master Daunbey, you can do it fast or do it slow. The Sakkers were an evil, malicious coven. By slipping the knot around the back of their heads, we ensured they strangled slowly. All five of them took a long time dying.'

'And the under-sheriff allowed this?' I asked.

Mallow answered. 'Like any law officer, once the ladder was turned and the men were hanged, he and his assistants rode back to London. If you look at the rules, Master Daunbey, the hangmen must attend the bodies until they are dead.'

'And the threats?' I asked.

Mallow breathed out a sigh. 'The executions took place at noon. Three or four hours later, as we prepared to return to London, a mysterious archer began to loose arrows at us from the trees. We concealed ourselves behind the death-cart, then we heard a man shout. He was Robert Sakker and he vowed he would seek vengeance for what we had done. We waited a while, then we left for London.'

'And you've heard nothing of it since?' I asked.

'A few days later,' Toadflax replied, 'the sheriff of Kent came to inspect the corpses we had gibbeted; he found all five had been removed for secret burial. A note, signed by Robert Sakker, declared vengeance against those responsible for the slow and malingering death of his father and brothers. The note vowed that the perpetrators would suffer just as bitterly.'

'And was Undershaft part of this?'

'Oh yes,' Mallow answered. 'Like me, he knew about the Sakker crimes. The women who had been raped, their throats cut. Master Undershaft believed in the notion of "eye for eye and tooth for tooth". He was party to what we did. But nothing happened, even though we received many threats.' He stared round at his companions. 'We forgot it.'

'Do you think?' Wormwood interrupted. 'Sakker is behind the deaths of our colleagues?'

177

'It's possible,' Benjamin replied. 'He may have come into London to pursue a path of retribution.'

'But you said that these deaths are linked to the blackmailing letters being sent to the King,' Mallow said.

Benjamin looked at me and shook his head. 'I believe so, but I have no proof.' He replied. 'That is a complete mystery.'

'What was Robert Sakker like?' I turned to Mallow.

The chief hangman shook his head. 'I don't know, sir. You'd have to ask Pelleter, the under-sheriff.'

'Do you have anything else to add?' I asked.

'We've spoken enough,' Mallow replied. He leaned over and pushed a stubby finger into my chest. 'We've talked to Sir Edward Kemble,' he continued. 'The constable says you were sent into London to end this villainy, yet you haven't.' He waved round at his companions. 'We are still being threatened and the letters are still being sent.' His words dropped to a whisper. 'You should be careful, Master Shallot; otherwise we may have a meeting of a different sort.'

I stood up, kicking the stool away, my hand going to the dagger in my belt. Benjamin intervened. He rose, genially thanked Mallow and his companions and, tugging me by the sleeve, took me out of the tavern.

'I could tickle his ribs with my dagger!' I swore.

Benjamin stopped. 'And that will get us nowhere. I understand your fear, Roger. The King will not forget our future.' He pulled me into a corner of a narrow, dark alleyway, staring around to make sure we were not being followed. 'If we can make no progress in this,' he whispered, 'then, Roger, I will follow your advice. I have money with a goldsmith in London. If we have to flee beyond the seas, then we shall do it, but it shall be in my way and at a time of my own choosing.'

'And what now?' I asked desperately.

'We go and see Pelleter.'

We found the under-sheriff's house just near the

178

Guildhall. Benjamin, hoping the law officer was at home, pounded on the door of the thin, narrow house which looked as if it had been pushed in between the mansions on either side. It was not well kept: the hall windows were dusty and holed, the beams cracked, whilst the front door hung askew on its hinges. Benjamin knocked again. We heard a soft footfall and the door was opened by a young woman.

Oh, the precious sight! Even now, down the long, dusty corridors of the years, I can picture her. How can you describe a song in flesh? She was about seventeen or eighteen years old, tall and slender. Large, beautiful brown eyes in an angel's face: the hair was a dull gold, her skin glowed. Benjamin and I just stood there like two schoolboys drinking in the sheer beauty of her: high cheekbones, perfectly formed nose and the sweetest of mouths. She stared coolly back, though you could see the laughter in her eyes.

'Good morning, sirs!' Her voice was soft and rich. 'Good day, sirs!' she repeated. I saw a flicker of alarm in her eyes as she went to close the door.

'I am sorry,' Benjamin stammered. 'We need to see Under-sheriff Pelleter.'

The laughter returned to those beautiful eyes. 'I'm his daughter. Miranda.'

'We are from the Tower,' Benjamin explained.

Miranda smiled. She was dressed simply enough in a blue gown, not too tightly fitting; really it hung on her like a sack, whilst the ruff round her neck had seen better days. But that smile! Like the sun coming out from behind the clouds! She laughed softly and beckoned us in; her eyes never left Benjamin and a stab of jealousy made me catch my breath. (No, Benjamin was not the most handsome of men. He was tall and strong and his black hair tended to straggle but his eyes were good and clear. Women were always attracted to him. And me? Oh, poor Shallot! I look what I am, a rogue born and bred! Attracted to the doxies, the molls, the besoms, the saucy tavern wenches, but women like Miranda? Miranda! Miranda! She still lives, you know? Well, not in the flesh: read Shakespeare's play *The Tempest*, you'll find her there with old Prospero.)

Ah well, on that summer's day so many years ago, she took us along a dusty passageway and into a small writing office at the back of the house. The man seated at a desk beneath the window, rose as we came in. He was dressed in the city livery, a chain of office round his neck. His square, honest face and clear eyes were a testament to his strength and integrity. He shook our hands, asked Miranda to pull up stools and bring refreshments for his guests. He turned his chair round to face us and sat down grimacing, favouring his back.

'You are in pain, sir?' Benjamin asked.

'I was attacked.' Pelleter replied. 'About two weeks ago, an assassin outside Whitefriars. A flesh wound, but the pain is still there. Well?' he asked, pausing as Miranda returned with a tray bearing jugs of ale.

She served us delicately, smiling at her father, though her smile widened as she handed Benjamin a tankard. She didn't ignore me, but stared shyly at me from under her eyelids. She then sat on a stool beside her father and returned (oh Lord save me from jealousy!) to studying Benjamin. My master, too, was distracted. Pelleter leaned forward and tapped his tankard against my master's.

'Your good health, Master Daunbey. You know who I am, where I live. You know I have a pain in my back,' he smiled. 'And you have met my lovely daughter, the light of my life. But why are you here?'

'Robert Sakker,' Benjamin declared brusquely.

Pelleter groaned and sat back in his chair, favouring his wound.

'God have mercy!' he breathed. 'Sakker's responsible for this!'

Chapter 11

We must have sat there for at least two hours whilst the under-sheriff described the depredations of the Sakker gang on the Canterbury road. I must admit I did not object. Why should I? Miranda was sitting there like a rose in full bloom, as fascinated by Benjamin as he was with her. I knew why jealousy is such a terrible sin. My stomach curdled, my blood boiled. I heartily wished that Benjamin wasn't there. She seemed impervious to me, apart from the odd kind smile or an offer to fill my tankard. Now and again Benjamin would turn, gaze adoringly at her, then return to questioning her father. When he had finished, Benjamin told Pelleter the reason for our visit: the blackmailing letters sent to the King and the grisly murders of the hangmen. Pelleter leaned back in his chair, whispering under his breath and shaking his head.

'I always thought Undershaft was a good man,' he said quietly. 'So his death was murder.'

'But do you know he's dead?' I asked. I was tempted to tell him how I had seen Undershaft's corpse, but I was fearful this might lower my status in Miranda's eyes.

Pelleter looked at me, bushy eyebrows raised. 'What makes you think he isn't?'

I explained about the blackmailing letters: how both Benjamin and I believed there was one villain in the Tower and another outside.

'In which case I'll make inquiries,' Pelleter offered. 'I'll ask the bailiffs and wardsmen to keep their eyes and ears open. But – ' he pointed a finger at Benjamin – 'if I follow the gist of what you are saying, you believe Robert Sakker's involved in this villainy?'

'Do you think it's possible?' Benjamin retorted.

'Robert Sakker was the most intelligent member of the gang. He went to Stapleton Hall in Oxford. He was quite skilled as a clerk and served for a while in one of the royal palaces.'

'So, he could draft a letter?' I asked.

'Possibly, but where would he get the seals of Edward V?'

'What did he look like?' Benjamin asked.

'Like all his family: tall, dark with reddish hair, clean-shaven, deep-chested; a merry-looking rogue despite the scar on his cheek. The sort who'd smile as he slipped a dagger between your ribs. A man who could act many parts: the boisterous soldier or the crafty clerk.'

Benjamin and I glanced at each other: the description fitted no one we had met in our inquiries.

'And so he escaped?' Benjamin continued. 'And has now threatened you?'

Pelleter put his cup down and spread his hands. 'Master Daunbey, I have no real evidence, but there was an attack on me recently. On two other occasions I've had scraps of parchment pushed into my hands. One was of a gibbet with me dangling from it.' He paused and glanced sideways at his daughter. 'The second, well, it was my daughter. That's what made me think it was Sakker.'

That beautiful smile faded from Miranda's lovely face, but I could see the steel in her eyes and the determined set to her jaw. She leaned over and kissed her father on the cheek.

(Oh, most fortunate of men!)

'Have you made inquiries?' I asked.

Pelleter snorted with laughter. 'Of course. I offered rewards, even the prospect of pardon from the Mayor and Aldermen to any felon who could give me the smallest scrap of information.' He shrugged. 'But I couldn't discover anything.'

'What happens if Sakker isn't living in London?' I asked. 'What if he has returned to his old haunts.'

'The Sakkers' tavern near St Thomas's watering-hole has been torn down,' Pelleter replied. 'Though they did have a lair: an old hunting lodge deep in the forest.'

'Could we go there?' Benjamin asked.

Pelleter blew his cheeks out. 'Not today: it's too late and I have other business. But tomorrow at dawn? I'll meet you at the tavern in Southwark.' He grinned. 'The Tabard, the place Chaucer's pilgrims left from. Now, sirs, I do have other business.'

Benjamin and I made our apologies. My master grasped Miranda's hand and kissed it. My heart skipped a beat! She held his fingers much longer than courtesy demanded. She was kind to me, proffering her hand. I lifted my head to murmur how pleasant it had been to meet her, but her gaze had already returned to Benjamin.

We left Pelleter's house. Benjamin was pleased, rubbing his hands in satisfaction.

'We have flushed a coney from the hay, Roger!' he exclaimed, slapping me on the back. 'Oh, the evidence is meagre, the proof paltry, but I believe Robert Sakker is involved in this villainy.'

He paused on a corner of an alleyway and watched as two officials of the city seized a wandering pig, thrust it squealing to the ground and cut its throat. I turned away as the hot blood rushed out.

'And Mistress Miranda?' I asked.

Benjamin's face grew serious; he grasped me by the shoulder.

'An angel, Roger. Have you ever seen such eyes? The

183

sheer harmony of her features!'

'You were taken by her?'

'Ravished,' he replied.

I glanced away, thrusting my hands between my cloak so my master would not see my fists curled in fury.

'And you, Roger?'

I stepped back and his hand fell away.

'She was comely enough,' I muttered. 'Master, should we not return to the Tower?'

Benjamin, the innocent, unaware of the black storm raging in my heart, gazed back in the direction of Pelleter's house.

'Do you realise, Roger,' he whispered, 'if this Sakker is involved, if he's hunting our under-sheriff, perhaps at this very moment, he is not far away.'

I didn't care. I had to hide my envy and resentment and said we should leave. It was a fine day so we decided to walk down Lombard Street and into Eastcheap, the most direct path back to the Tower. Benjamin chattered like a magpie, unaware of my seething passion. (I once told Will Shakespeare about this in a tavern on Bank Side. He'd asked me what was the most powerful emotion a man could feel? Lust? Anger? The desire for riches? I told him jealousy! I sat back against the tavern wall, the tears streaming down my face, and told him about Benjamin and Miranda, that golden couple who lived so long ago. Will heard me out in that quiet attentive way of his, his olive-skinned features betraying nothing. Then he nodded and murmured that he would remember what I had said. Go and see his play *Othello*, about the Moor of Venice, the wicked Iago and the lovely Desdemona. I never asked him who Iago was! Last Yuletide, I hired a troupe of actors and made them recite the lines whilst I sat and quietly cried about the lovely Miranda.)

Anyway, on that day we returned, hot and dusty, to the Tower. We were almost through the Lion Gateway

184

when a woman stepped out of the shadows and caught me by the arm.

'Mistress Undershaft,' I exclaimed, though in truth I felt no pleasure: after seeing the marvellous Miranda it was like comparing candlelight to the sun.

'Master Shallot,' she whispered, 'Master Daunbey. I have something to show you.' She gazed fearfully around. 'I have heard about Horehound's death.' She continued hurriedly. 'I need to speak to you, repay you for your kindness.'

She took us back out, across the drawbridge, and down near the river. I gazed around but, apart from fishermen sitting on the quayside mending their nets, and an old beggar man pushing a barrow laden with half-ripe apples, I could see no one to be wary of.

'Let's stroll,' Benjamin suggested, 'as if we were taking the air and enjoying the afternoon sunlight.'

Mistress Undershaft agreed, though she first pushed a square of parchment into Benjamin's hand. 'I went amongst my husband's belongings, looking for something which might help you.'

Benjamin opened the parchment. He studied it, then passed it to me. It was nothing much, a square about nine inches by nine, yellow and greasy, the ink marks poor and faded. A rough drawing of the Tower: underneath, a shape like the letter 'T', with a cross where the two lines met. Next to this was a large question mark.

'What does it mean?' she asked Benjamin.

'I don't know, Mistress.'

'Neither do I.' I pushed the parchment into my pouch. 'What makes you think it's so important?'

'Oh, at first I didn't,' Mistress Undershaft replied. She kept gazing fearfully around, as if someone might be watching her. 'I was going to throw it into the fire. After all, Andrew often made drawings of one of his carvings or some piece of furniture. However, I remembered the day after the King's party, Andrew was in the garden. He liked to sit there admiring the flowers. On that particular morning, he was poring over that piece of parchment, as if it held some great secret. When I asked him what it meant, he shook his head and mumbled it was best not to know. For the rest of that day he was withdrawn.' She stopped. 'Masters, that's all I can tell you.'

And, before we could stop her, she slipped away along the quayside. Benjamin and I went and sat on a small, grassy bank overlooking the river. I pulled out the scrap of parchment and stared at it.

'There's a rough drawing of the Tower,' I declared, 'but that holds no secret.' I pushed it closer so my master could see it. 'And there's the letter "T", done in square fashion, the lines scored time and time again.'

'And what do these mean?' Benjamin pointed to the stem of the 'T', where small dashes marked the right-hand side.

'I don't know,' I said. 'Yet it disturbed Undershaft and set him wondering. Perhaps he was the executioner who saw something untoward that night?'

Benjamin lay back on the grass and stared up at the fleecy clouds.

'This is luxury, Roger,' he murmured. 'A warm day: listen to the bees humming. The river is quiet, the sky is blue. I have just met the fairest lady in the world.' He sat up and rubbed his face. 'Every Paradise has its serpent.' He leaned over and tapped the parchment still in my hands. 'And this is the very devil. Now, Roger, I agree something happened during those festivities. But remember they were held not in the Tower proper but in the royal apartments: the mystery lies there. But come!' He got to his feet. 'We have a hard day tomorrow.'

We returned to the Tower and managed to beg some dried bacon, bread and wine from the kitchens. We sat outside and ate. Benjamin was still taken by Miranda, though now and again he would return to ponder the problems confronting us. I grew tired of his company. When he returned to our chamber, I mooned about like a love-lorn swain, though I stayed in full view of the guards: I hadn't forgotten the recent attack on me. I joined some soldiers and drank their coarse ale before staggering back to my chamber. Benjamin was already asleep. I threw myself down on the straw mattress, blissfully unaware of the horrors which were to occur that night.

Benjamin must have got up early the following morning. He was already washing and changing when a clamour broke out on the stairs outside. Vetch's pounding on our door sent me scurrying, heavy-eyed, from my bed.

'You'd best come!' Vetch declared hoarsely. He glanced quickly at me. 'And, if your stomach's fickle, you'd best hold your mouth!'

We went downstairs, across the mist-shrouded green and into the base of Bowyer Tower. It was very much like the cellar we had visited at the Beauchamp, but this one was well-lit by torches. Kemble and Spurge stood just within the doorway, as did a pallid-faced Mallow.

At first, because my head wasn't clear, all I could see was a faint figure in the gloom, lying on what I thought was a bed. When I went down the steps and looked more carefully, I realised the full horror of the scene. Now many of you young men have seen hangings and decapitations, men quartered and disembowelled, but a man stretched out on 'Exeter's daughter' is a most hideous sight. (Oh, excuse me if I digress! My little chaplain is quite ignorant as to what 'Exeter's daughter' is. According to legend, during the reign of Henry VI, the Duke of Exeter introduced the rack into England, hence the name.) The rack was shaped like a bed with posts at each end. On that sun-filled morning, in the centre of the rack, sprawled Wormwood's body. Someone had slipped his wrists and ankles into the loops of heavy hempen rope, and then turned the wheel at either end, so the rack stretched, cracking muscle and sinew. Wormwood's face was a mask of indescribable horror; eyes popping, mouth open. His legs had been stretched, one arm had been pulled out of its socket. His entire torso looked as if it had been pummelled and beaten. I rushed back up the steps and cleared my stomach of what was left of that stale ale. Benjamin, though as gentle as a fawn, found such sights easy to stomach: he and the rest later joined me outside where I crouched, my back to the wall, gulping air.

'Who did that?' I stammered.

'I don't know.' Kemble scratched his unshaven cheek. 'Very much like Horehound. A young girl found the door open and went inside. The torches were lit, Wormwood's body lay stretched on the rack. The rest you know.'

'And no one heard anything?' Benjamin exclaimed. 'Such cruelty would have provoked the most hideous of shrieks. It's a wonder he wasn't heard in Petty Wales.'

'I have already investigated that,' Kemble replied. 'The guards on the ramparts heard nothing but an owl shriek.'

Other members of the garrison were now hurrying across.

'This is not the place to discuss it,' Kemble muttered. 'Vetch, Spurge, Master Daunbey, we shall meet in my quarters.' He turned and went down the steps where Mallow stood, leaning against the door. 'I want the members of your guild to join us.' Kemble ordered.

Mallow nodded, wiping his mouth on the back of his hand. I hastened back to our quarters where I hurriedly shaved, washed and changed my soiled jerkin, then joined the rest in Kemble's chamber.

'How could this have happened?' the constable began. Mallow and his hangmen, grouped in a frightened cluster at the foot of the table, mumbled under their breath.

'Well?' Vetch barked. 'Are you going to answer the constable's question?'

'Oh, don't come the high and mighty with us!' Snakeroot snapped. 'We were all in the Tower last night. Wormwood was alive – drunk, but very much alive!'

'Who saw him last?' Vetch asked.

'We were all drinking outside Bowyer Tower,' Toadflax replied. 'Then we went to our quarters. After that, you know as much as we do. Why?' He leaned on the table. 'Are you going to claim Wormwood was killed by one of us? Sir Edward, you were in the Tower last night, as were Vetch and Spurge.' His eyes slid towards us. 'Not to mention our guests.'

Benjamin scraped back his chair, stood up and walked over to the window. 'There's a killer in the Tower,' he said softly, speaking over his shoulder. 'A man whose real name is Robert Sakker.'

I gazed round quickly: Mallow and his executioners looked disconcerted.

'Sakker!' Toadflax exclaimed. 'Here in the Tower!'

'Who is this man?' Kemble demanded.

'He was an outlaw, the only surviving member of a gang who terrorised pilgrims going to Canterbury,' Benjamin replied. 'Mallow and his confederates hanged the rest of his family. Robert Sakker has returned to wage war against these executioners.' Benjamin walked back to the table. 'Somehow, Master Constable, I believe Robert Sakker is involved in the blackmailing letters being sent to the King.'

'But there's no Sakker on the muster roll,' Kemble retorted. 'I, alone, am responsible for that!'

Benjamin shrugged. 'The felon's probably using another name. Under-sheriff Pelleter described him as a tall, red-haired man with a scar across his chin.'

'I have seen no one like that,' Vetch replied, 'either

amongst the garrison or the servants.'

'Or the masons working on the wall,' Spurge spoke up.

Kemble, balancing a quill between his fingers, sat back in his chair, staring narrow-eyed at Benjamin. 'But you, Master Daunbey, believe he is in the Tower?'

'Yes I do,' my master replied. 'And that wouldn't be hard, now the gates are opened.'

'But he would need a pass, or the guards would refuse him entrance,' Kemble pointed out.

'Well, I believe he's here,' Benjamin said once more. 'And last night he went hunting poor Wormwood. Master Mallow, Wormwood had been drinking, yes?'

The chief hangman nodded.

'So.' Benjamin took his seat. 'Let's just imagine Wormwood staggering round the Tower in the dark, in very much the same condition as poor Horehound. Somehow or other, he is lured into some dark corner. He's knocked on the head, his body dragged and strapped to the rack. The man's half-conscious, drunk, gagged! Small wonder we heard no screams. Whoever killed him must have enjoyed every second!' Benjamin drummed his fingers on the table-top. 'It must be Sakker!' He glanced across where the sunlight was pouring through a half-open window. 'Sir Edward, I want you and your officers to scrutinise every man in the Tower. You have Sakker's description. I want guards put on every postern-gate.'

'You can't order—!'

'Yes, I can,' Benjamin replied. 'Or I'll ride to Windsor and bring the King himself back here.'

Kemble hastily agreed. 'You say he's red-haired, scarred?'

'Yes, across his chin,' Benjamin replied.

Now I had been sitting there, as usual, watching everybody. God knows the workings of my own mind, but the mention of Sakker's scar made me think of

Greene. You may remember, Sir Thomas More said he was one of the murderers who killed the little Princes. According to Agrippa, Greene had an ugly red scar across his wrist. I remembered being back in our parish church at Ipswich when I had been baiting the Poppletons. Old Quicksilver, outside in the graveyard, hands stretching out to take the purse, the way he covered his wrists, then his drunken boasting about serving in the Tower when the Princes were confined. I was so excited, I sprang to my feet, clapping my hands in glee.

'The rogue! The villain!' I exclaimed. 'The sparrow-turd! The ancient pig's-dropping!'

'What on earth?' Kemble half rose from his chair. 'Master Daunbey, has your servant lost his wits?'

Benjamin was staring at me curiously. 'What is it?' my master asked.

And then I made my terrible mistake. Oh, I have these bright flashes of intuition, a keenness of wit, a prodigious memory, but I also babble too much, I know that. And that day was no different: I sat down chattering like a child.

'Master, you remember Dr Quicksilver?'

'How could I forget?' Benjamin caustically replied.

'He's a quack, a cunning man,' I explained to the rest of my bemused companions. 'He was always boasting about what he did in his glorious past. Now I rejected it because Quicksilver is a liar, born and bred.'

'What on earth has this got to do with the matter in hand?' Vetch snapped.

I explained. 'Quicksilver is well past his sixtieth year. However, he once told me that he visited the Tower when the Princes were imprisoned here. He talked of secret passageways and chambers. I dismissed this as mere ranting, but I also noticed he kept his hands and wrists always covered. No matter what he did or where he went, his wrists were always hidden.'

Benjamin clapped me on the shoulder. 'Of course, Roger.' He squeezed my shoulder, his face wreathed in smiles. 'According to beloved Uncle, Greene had an ugly scar on his wrist. You are saying Greene and Quicksilver are one and the same?'

'I do,' I replied. 'Sir Edward,' I glanced at the constable, who slumped, half-bored, in his chair, 'of your goodness, please send a message to Under-sheriff Pelleter in Catte Street. Ask him to inform his bailiffs and criers throughout the city that a charlatan known as Dr Quicksilver is to be arrested immediately.'

Kemble's fat face threatened to turn sour, clearly resentful at having to take orders from the likes of me.

'Do it!' Benjamin ordered. 'And it must be done quickly. Master Shallot and I are to meet the under-sheriff very soon; there's no time to lose!'

Kemble nodded at Vetch, who hastened from the chamber.

'And what about us?' Mallow wailed. 'If Sakker is hunting us, how safe can we be?'

'You are in the Tower,' I snarled, 'the king's principal fortress. You should heed my master's advice. Go nowhere by yourself.'

'We'd best go,' Snakeroot whispered. 'Wormwood at least deserves a Christian burial.'

'Your numbers are declining, Master Mallow,' Spurge taunted.

The chief executioner stopped and gazed hatefully at the King's surveyor of works.

'Oh, don't worry about that, Master Spurge. Haven't you heard the old proverb: for every villain there'll always be a hangman?' And, with his two apprentices trailing behind him, Mallow strode out of the chamber.

Benjamin waited until he had gone, then whispered for the piece of parchment Mistress Undershaft had given us. I passed this to him and he tossed it to the constable.

'Sir Edward, does that drawing mean anything to you?'

Kemble opened the parchment, smoothing it out on the table-top.

'A rough drawing of the Tower,' he muttered. 'And the letter "T". Master Daunbey, what is this nonsense?'

'Master Spurge?' Benjamin asked.

The surveyor grabbed the piece of parchment, studied it, shook his head and passed it back.

'What does it mean?' Kemble asked.

'I don't know, Sir Edward, but when I find out . . .' And Benjamin rose, indicating for me to follow him from the chamber.

'I think I know who the assassin is,' Benjamin whispered as we went down the stairs and out into the sunlight. 'Roger.' He gently tapped my chin. 'Close your mouth or you'll catch flies!'

'You know who the assassin is?' I gasped.

'So do you,' Benjamin replied. 'It's Master Spurge!'

'Spurge!' I exclaimed.

'He's the surveyor, Roger. He knows all the secret entrances.'

'But we've seen his map, Benjamin,' I replied. 'There was nothing hidden there. Remember when the villain collected the gold in the city, when I was pushed into the wolf-pit, when Horehound was crushed to death; Spurge was always elsewhere.'

'Of course he was.' Benjamin linked his arm through mine and walked me back across the green to our chamber. 'What I am saying is that there must be a secret gate or postern-door which Spurge deliberately omitted from that map: probably overlooking the moat or the river. Somehow or other, Spurge struck up an unholy alliance with this Sakker, whom he can bring in and out of the Tower whenever he so wishes. Sakker was watching you that day near the wolf-pit. He also killed Undershaft, Horehound and Hellbane, as well as poor Wormwood. He collected the gold at St Paul's. He also delivered those blackmailing letters and proclamations to frighten the King.'

'Two cheeks on the same arse,' I replied. 'Spurge and Sakker working together.' I squinted at the clear blue sky. 'But how would they meet?' I replied. 'Why should they trust each other? Sakker may enter the Tower secretly, but this is a close community, people would recognise a stranger. And, above all, where on earth did they get those seals from?'

Benjamin paused, finger to his lips. 'Roger, do you remember when you were at Windsor and you discovered that secret chamber? What happens if there was a similar room here in the Tower? And, let us say, someone found a pouch or casket in that chamber bearing the seals of this long-dead Prince? What better person than the surveyor of the King's works, whose job it is to know every nook and cranny of this sinister fortress?'

Benjamin stopped speaking as Ragusa came screaming across the green, rags flying out like banners behind her. Her stiff, vein-streaked hands were beating the air like the wings of a pinioned bird; behind her hurried Mallow. The old woman's mad gaze caught mine and she stopped.

'You are the handsome youth who visited me,' she screamed. 'You came to ask old Ragusa questions. Remember?' She drew closer: in the daylight she looked even more hideous, and made the air about her foulsome. 'Help me!' She turned as Mallow caught up with her. 'Go away!' she screeched. 'Go away, leave old Ragusa alone!'

Mallow stopped, hands on his hips, chest heaving. 'For the love of God, woman!' he grated, 'we will pay you well.' He glanced at us. 'Someone has to dress poor Wormwood's body for burial.'

'All flesh and gore! All flesh and gore!' Ragusa

shrieked. She held up her hands. 'Stiff and cold they be, stiff and cold! They can't feel flesh, be it alive and quick or cold and dead.'

I grasped her hands: they were cold and hard, like stones on a freezing winter night. 'You'll be paid well,' I said.

Her mad eyes caught mine. 'It'd best be me,' she muttered. She turned on Mallow. 'For two silver coins,' she demanded.

Mallow, swearing she would get all she wanted, thanked me and led her away. I watched them go. Something pricked my memory, but I was in too much of a hurry to leave to recall what it was. We were to meet Pelleter: I hoped against hope that young Miranda would be there waiting for us.

We packed our belongings and made our way down to the Wool Quay. At Custom House we hired a skiff to take us across to Southwark. The river was busy with barges and ships, so the morning was half-way through before Benjamin and I reached the Tabard to find Pelleter and the beautiful Miranda waiting for us.

'I got your message,' the under-sheriff growled. 'My bailiffs are out looking for this Dr Quicksilver.'

Benjamin thanked him.

'And I have hired horses,' the under-sheriff continued.

Again, Benjamin absentmindedly murmured his appreciation, though, like me, he only had eyes for Miranda, who sat on a gentle brown cob looking more beautiful than ever. There was the usual hurly-burly as our horses were saddled, panniers thrown across and directions taken before we left. The old jealousy sparked in my heart. I found myself riding next to the under-sheriff whilst, in front of us, Benjamin escorted Miranda. I won't bore you with the details of the journey. A beautiful, sun-filled golden day. The trees and flowers were in full bloom, but there was a touch of autumn, a glimpse of gold amongst the green as we trotted down the old pilgrim way towards Canterbury. Our pace was brisk. We were not travellers set for the Becket shrine. We did not stop and tell each other tales. Nor were we hindered by pack animals. Pelleter was eager to help, and Miranda, God bless her, was fascinated by Benjamin's discourse. And old Shallot? Well, just to be with her was pleasure enough. If I'd had my way, we would have ridden all the way to Canterbury and worshipped before Becket's tomb and seen that brilliant diamond, the Regal of France, dazzling in the darkness. (It's all gone now. The Great Beast put paid to that. He destroyed the tomb, seized the gold and the Regal of France. Well, to be honest, I have that, but I won't tell you how, that's another story!)

By late afternoon we'd reached St Thomas's Watering Hole on the Canterbury road. Pelleter took us to where the Sakkers' tavern once stood: now it was nothing more than a blackened piece of land littered with scraps of timber and burnt plaster. A cold, eerie place, full of ghosts, a blight on that golden day. Pelleter pointed to where the scaffold posts had stood. The under-sheriff then took us off the road and into the forest. We were hardly in the trees when we met a party of royal verderers, all dressed in lincoln green.

'Where are you going?' the leader asked, planting himself in front of us.

Pelleter leaned down and explained.

'Sakker!' the verderer exclaimed. 'Robert Sakker! Are you witless, man?'

'What do you mean?' Pelleter snapped.

'Why, sir,' the fellow replied, 'Robert Sakker was killed eight months ago outside Maidstone.'

Chapter 12

Despite Pelleter's insistent questioning, the verderer was adamant.

'It's well known,' he explained. 'Sakker became a poacher. We often hunted him; fleet of foot, he was. Then one day a chapman, making his way from Dover, stopped at one of the hostelries on the road and told us the news: Sakker was slain in a tavern brawl.' He shrugged. 'That's all I know.'

Pelleter thanked him. We rode on, following the track deeper into the forest, its dark greenery filled with birdsong and the occasional bright spots of sunlight. We rode silently, listening to the chattering birds: all the time I kept my eyes on the fair Miranda's slender neck. So close! So soft! I felt like stretching out my hand and touching her. But, of course, Shallot could not. Instead I was drawn into conversation with the under-sheriff about what the verderer had told us, whilst the light of my life talked to Benjamin. Now and again I caught her gaze, I glimpsed the admiration in her eyes as Benjamin explained to her the mysteries of alchemy, or made her laugh with the stories from the schoolroom at our manor.

At last we entered a clearing larger than the rest. In the centre stood the ruins of an old hunting lodge which, Pelleter explained, dated from the days of Henry VI. The stockade fence had long disappeared, as had the bothies, byres and stables. The lodge itself still stood, but the roof was holed and the windows were mere gaps in the wall. We hobbled our horses and went inside. The stairs were usable but there were gaps in the roof and puddles of mildewed water on the floor.

'This is where Sakker and his gang often hid,' Pelleter explained. 'I now know the woodland path, but it's easy to get lost in the forest. The Sakkers would gather there, plot their ambuscades and retreat from any possible pursuit. Young Robert stayed at the tavern, shielding the rest of his family.' He took us across and pointed to where the floorboards had been ripped up. 'This is where we found most of their plunder.' He smiled thinly. 'God knows what happened to that: the King's commissioners probably took it.'

(Oh aye, I thought and, knowing the Great Beast as I do, I doubt if any of it found its way back to the rightful owners.)

At first I couldn't understand why Benjamin had insisted on coming here. True there were scorch-marks on the floor, bits of rotting food, traces of people having lived there, but these could have been due to the verderers or any of the forest people. Nevertheless, Benjamin began to search the house carefully, scrutinising every nook and cranny. At last he paid heed to my insistent questions.

'Roger, we know this place is now the haunt of owls and bats –' he looked round and shivered – 'but it was also the lair of the Sakkers. People never change. Old habits die hard. Robert Sakker must have come back here. Even if it was just to search for some of the plunder his family had hidden.'

I glanced across where Pelleter and Miranda were sitting on a crumbling doorstep, leisurely eating the provisions they had brought.

'Master, what is the use? You heard the verderer. Sakker is dead and I am hungry!'

Benjamin plucked at my sleeve. 'I don't think Robert Sakker's dead,' he replied, then cautiously climbed the battered wooden staircase.

I groaned and reluctantly followed. The second floor was positively dangerous, with gaps and sagging timbers. Benjamin went into the chambers on either side. I still did not know what he was looking for. As our search continued, the shadows grew longer and that old hunting lodge creaked and groaned. A tingle of fear ran up my spine. After all, this was an ancient house. God knows what terrible things the Sakker gang had done here. Were their ghosts peering at us from a corner? Did their shades follow us, ghoul-like, from room to room?

(I see my little chaplain snigger. Oh, sitting at the centre of a maze in the glorious sunlight, the little curmudgeon can titter and giggle. Nevertheless, I have seen him tremble down at the edge of the marshes when the sun sets and the darkness creeps in from the forest! And yes, before he asks, I have seen ghosts. I have been along the great gallery at Hampton Court, just near the royal chapel where Catherine Howard, the Great Beast's fifth wife, ran screaming and shrieking, begging her base, syphilitic husband to spare her the headsman's axe. I have sat in a window-seat on the anniversary of her death. I have heard her terrible ghostly scream and the patter of high-heeled shoes which stops abruptly, just before the chapel door. Oh, I have seen ghosts! More than I like to recount. Indeed, my stories gave Will Shakespeare the idea of Brutus seeing Caesar's shade before the battle at Philippi.)

Now in that old hunting lodge I felt the ghosts throng round me. I was about to leave my master to his searches when I heard his triumphant cry. I found him in a small chamber, crouched beside a battered fireplace.

'Look, Roger!'

He held up two huge pots, put these on the floor and pointed to the hearth piled high with burnt rags and grey dust. I picked up a stick and sifted amongst the remains in the hearth.

'They're clothes,' I declared. 'Someone has burnt clothing here.'

'And look at this, Roger.'

Benjamin thrust one of the cracked bowls into my hand. The inside was stained black with a little liquid still in the bottom, like a piece of slime from a pool. I dabbed at it with my finger and sniffed.

'It's paint,' I declared, rubbing it between my fingers. I sniffed again. 'Though rather odourless.'

'Look at my hair, Roger!'

'Master,' I replied, 'are you witless?'

Benjamin grinned and pointed to his temple. The hair was usually a premature grey: now it was as black as night.

'It's dye,' he explained. 'Robert Sakker came here. I suspect Sakker killed a man in Maidstone and left evidence to make others think it was he who had been slain, then he came here. Perhaps to collect booty Master Pelleter and his bailiffs failed to unearth. He also changed his clothes and dyed his auburn hair dark.'

'Of course!' I breathed. 'And the cunning bastard had probably grown a beard and moustache to cover that scar on his chin.' I sat down, my back to the wall, desperately trying to recall all whom I had met in the Tower. 'Allardyce!' I exclaimed. 'Philip Allardyce, the clerk to the stores. Don't you remember, Master? Tall, deep-voiced, black-haired, with a luxuriant moustache and beard; that's the description we were given.'

'But he's dead,' Benjamin explained. 'Others saw him ill with the plague. The old woman felt for the life pulse in his throat. The bailiff who examined the corpse in the death-cart pronounced him dead as a stone.'

I recalled old Ragusa screeching at me earlier in the day: her numb, vein-streaked hands pressing into mine.

'Ragusa's an old mad crone,' I replied slowly. 'I'd wager if she felt my pulse or yours she'd pronounce us dead. I have suffered the sweating sickness, Master; it would be easy for a cunning man to simulate it. Sweat, fever, retching and choking. Allardyce wasn't tended by a physician, but by a mad old crone who doesn't want to be turned out because she is inept at what she does.'

'But the bailiff on the death-cart?' Benjamin asked.

'What happens if it was not Allardyce's corpse taken out? If he'd been alive, the soldiers would have suspected as much when they dragged the corpse down to the Lion Gate.'

'So you are saying that Allardyce was really Sakker? He gains employment in the Tower, simulates the sweating sickness and pretends to die?' Benjamin nodded. 'I can accept that. Few people would go near him. Moreover, once the body was sheeted, no one would care. But who could smuggle a corpse into the Tower as a substitute?'

'Why not ask one of our hangmen?' I replied. 'Aren't they responsible for the corpses of their victims?'

Benjamin agreed.

'And so, Master.' I continued, staring at the pot of black dye. 'Sakker is in the Tower, pretending to be Allardyce. I suspect the real Allardyce was the man our villain killed in Maidstone. Later, before the sweating sickness really takes hold in the city, Sakker slips out of the Tower. He is now free to deliver letters to Westminster, or post proclamations at St Paul's and St Mary's, Cheapside. He can lay a trail of gunpowder and seize that gold the King is now so furious at losing. Because we are not looking for him, he can wander the city at his will, baiting and taunting us. When he wishes, now under a new disguise, he slips back into the Tower to kill Horehound and Wormwood as he did Hellbane and Undershaft.'

'But who is his accomplice?' Benjamin asked.

'Ah, Master, there's the rub.' I put the pot down on the floor. 'How do we know he has one? What happens if he is the sole villain?'

'But how can he re-enter the Tower if he's a soldier or member of the garrison?' Benjamin asked. 'People would

201

remember a stranger. He must have an accomplice.'

I sat and thought for a while, closing my eyes as I remembered the Tower as I had seen it: the soldiers, their women, the children, the officers, old Ragusa, the hangmen.

'Don't forget, Roger, the day we returned to the Tower from St Paul's, everyone had been locked in and could account for their movements when old Horehound was crushed to death in the basement of the Beauchamp Tower. Everyone except—'

'Except the hangmen!' I cried. 'They had all been drinking that afternoon and gone their separate ways. One of them must be Sakker's accomplice.'

Benjamin wiped his fingers and sat back, rocking on his heels. 'If so, how does Sakker communicate with him?' He chewed his lip. 'And who told Sakker when the real Allardyce was travelling to London so he could be ambushed in Maidstone? One of the officers or hangmen? Any of them could easily find out when the real Allardyce was to be at the Tower—'

'Or there again, Master,' I interrupted, 'once Sakker knew Allardyce was to leave Dover Castle, he'd simply wait there and follow him to Maidstone.'

Benjamin nodded. 'Roger, the web begins to unravel.' He kicked the cracked bowl with his foot and clapped his hands. 'I was sure Sakker was at the root of it all. Our visit here was worth while.'

We hastened downstairs and told the under-sheriff what we had found. He became excited as us and vowed that a swift return to the city was essential. 'If Sakker knows that we are now hunting him and have some idea about his disguise, perhaps we can tighten the net around him,' he exclaimed.

Miranda clapped her hands, eyes shining with delight. She leaned on tiptoe and kissed Benjamin on both cheeks. He blushed and stammered, pointing to me. Of course, I received no kiss; nothing but her brilliant smile.

In the end we did not reach London that day. The sky became overcast; one of those summer black storms swept over the flat Kent countryside. We were forced to take shelter in one of the many great taverns which line the pilgrims' way. We ate and drank well. For a while we forgot Sakker whilst Benjamin regaled the Pelleters with stories of our earlier exploits at the manor outside Ipswich. Even a blind man could have realised that Benjamin and Miranda had fallen deeply in love. They only had eyes for each other, and it was not a friendship which Master Pelleter opposed. Oh, Benjamin was a gentleman. He bade her a gallant goodnight, but only after spending hours with her in the corner of a taproom chattering and whispering. I sat like a ghost at a banquet, engaging Miranda's father in desultory conversation about the city and the effects of the sweating sickness. I did not sleep that night. Instead I tossed and turned on my pallet-bed, not because of the fleas which infested the blankets or the rats which came out to nose at my boots: all I could do was gaze at Benjamin sleeping in his bed like a child, lost in golden dreams about a woman I loved but who barely recognised my existence. Only then did I realise why people murder! How the red fury can cloud the mind, kill the soul, and turn one's being into a single thrust of a dagger. Of all the men I have ever known, Benjamin is the only one I have loved; yet, that night, the thought of murder crossed my mind!

(Ah, I see my little clerk has stopped writing. Ever since I mentioned the name Miranda, he's had a look of puzzlement on his moon-like face. He sits, tapping the quill against his podgy nose, and squirming his fat little rump. He abruptly remembered the picture in my secret chamber, the letters in my coffers, and now he announces it. I can mouth the words for him: 'But Miranda was your wife, your first wife? I have seen her picture!' Oh, he looks at me, the little man, his head cocked to one side, a look of puzzlement in those

203

blackcurrant eyes of his. 'Explain! Explain!' His squat body throbs with curiosity. Well, the little turd will have to wait. He'll have to find out how this woman, so beloved of Benjamin, so deeply enamoured of my master, became my wife. But not now. Ah no! As the good book says, there is a time and a place under heaven for everything and my little clerk will just have to wait. Enough about love!)

The next morning we rose early. Our horses, now rested, took us swiftly back into London. As we crossed London Bridge, going on towards Catte Street, Pelleter explained that perhaps his bailiffs and spies may have found out something about Quicksilver, and invited us to join him at the Guildhall. Benjamin accepted. Anything to stay as long as possible with Miranda! They had been talking ever since we left the tavern, and continued to do so as we forced our way through the busy, smelling streets. The traders, taking advantage of the good weather and the disappearance of the sweating sickness, now shouted boisterously, drawing the crowds to throng around their stalls. The city had come back to life: the naps and foists, the rogues, the bawds, the apple-squires thronged the mouths of alleyways or the doors of taverns. The kennels and runnels stank as richly as ever. I gazed around, drinking it all in, and suddenly, in my bones, I knew Quicksilver would be back to float with the rest of the scum of London's underworld. At the Guildhall, Pelleter dismounted and told us to wait. He was gone a few minutes, barely giving me time to attempt a fruitless flirtation with Miranda, before he came trotting back, a burly, thick-set bailiff in tow.

'We can leave the horses here,' he exclaimed. 'My men have found Quicksilver.'

Oh, I grinned to hear the news! My heart leapt with joy! The blood sang in my body! I even forgot my disappointment over Miranda at the prospect of seeing my old friend and shaking him warmly by the neck! As we hurried through the streets up Aldersgate towards Charterhouse, I imagined what I would do to him. Fingernails or toenails first, I wondered? Now Pelleter had told Miranda to return to their house: of course he might as well have told the breeze. She wasn't disobedient: she just smiled prettily, blinked, and, like many women, acted as if she hadn't heard. Pelleter looked wryly at her, but all he received was a beaming smile – and so she came with us.

As we went, the bailiff told us in hushed tones how the clacking tongues amongst the rogues and villains had described Quicksilver's new haunt: a little house on Beech Lane, between Red Cross and White Cross Street, opposite the Ramsey inn.

'He's doing a roaring trade by the sound of it,' the fellow muttered. 'Believes he has found a concoction to cure the sweating sickness.'

'Of course,' I nodded. 'Now the bloody thing's gone, he's probably claiming the credit for it. You have not approached him, have you?'

The fellow grinned in a show of cracked yellow teeth. 'Master Shallot, we have more sense than you think. If Quicksilver suspects there's a trap set, he'll be in Dover by dusk.'

I congratulated the man on his wisdom, and slipped a coin into his hand. At last we reached the corner of Beech Lane. It was a clean thoroughfare; the houses on each side were screened by huge copper beeches, their branches spread out, intertwining together to form a natural arch. A sweet-smelling, restful place, where the houses were painted smartly in black and white, mullioned glass filled the bay windows, doors hung straight and the red-tiled roofs gleamed in the sun. The Ramsey inn was a prosperous-looking hostelry, its sign and woodwork freshly daubed. Inside the herb-scented taproom were the sheriff's men, a motley group of rogues busily drinking ale and beer whilst keeping an eye on the house opposite. Pelleter would have cursed them for wasting the city money, but Benjamin intervened. He understood my hatred for my old friend, and offered to pay the men even more if Dr Quicksilver proved to be at home.

'Well, we don't know,' one of them replied. 'He was there last night. This morning a fine, tall lady, her face veiled, came trotting along for an assignation.'

'Probably needed some mercury or cure for the pox!' another exclaimed.

I just stared across the street at the broad, black-painted door.

'Well, let's see,' I muttered, and before Benjamin or Pelleter could stop me, I was across the street, hammering on the door. I had my cowl above my head, so if there were any spy-holes, Quicksilver would not see it was me and try to flee over the back fence. I knocked again but there was no reply, so I pulled down the latch and the door swung back on its hinges. My first impression was that old Quicksilver must have made a merry pile: the passageways looked swept and clean, there were pots of herbs upon the table, whilst the hooks screwed into the wall were of pure brass, polished till they shone.

'Dr Quicksilver!' I called, disguising my voice to make me sound like some pompous merchant.

There was no reply. Now at first that did not disconcert me. Perhaps Quicksilver was involved in some assignation, or toasting his new-found wealth by lying in a drunken stupor. There would be no slatterns or servants. A man like Quicksilver does not like anyone around him who might see through his trickery and either blackmail him or proclaim him to be the charlatan he was. I went further along the passageway, past a small parlour. Staring through a crack in the door I could see no sign of life. I entered the kitchen: at first I smiled, I thought I had caught my victim napping.

Quicksilver sat on a chair with his back to me, head on his arm, resting on the kitchen table. I thought he had been drinking, and that the sticky red substance dripping on to the floor came from a spilled goblet of wine. Then my elation gave way to anger. Quicksilver was dead. Someone had come up behind him and slashed his throat from ear to ear. Behind me, Benjamin and Pelleter entered the house. They came crashing into the kitchen even as I pulled Quicksilver's head back by his greasy white hair. His eyes, sunk in their sockets, stared sightlessly up at me; those lips, so skilled in knavery, were now silenced for good. I took one look at the blood splashed on the front of his velvet jerkin and let the head go.

'Dead as a doornail,' I pronounced.

'Perhaps he tricked people once too often,' Pelleter declared.

Benjamin crouched down beside the corpse, studying it carefully.

'I don't think so.' He glanced up at me. 'Roger, we made a mistake in mentioning Dr Quicksilver in Kemble's chamber at the Tower.'

Of course I objected loudly, pointing out that I was not the only one after the old charlatan's blood. Yet in my heart I knew I had made a dreadful error. Of course, the assassin in Kemble's chamber would not want me to interrogate Quicksilver, and so had taken matters into his own hands. We went out and spoke to Pelleter's bailiffs who had been guarding both the back and front of the house.

'Oh yes,' their leader declared, 'Quicksilver had only one visitor: that was the tall, masked lady. Looked like a widow, she did. She must have been there for about an hour, and then left.'

Benjamin thanked the man, then quietly persuaded Miranda, standing in the passageway, that this was not the best place for her, and perhaps she had best return home. She did so and, as I turned away, she stood on tiptoe to kiss Benjamin tenderly on each cheek. She whispered something to him, and then allowed one of her father's men to escort her back to Catte Street. I stood, seething with fury and jealousy. However, though I am a rogue, I have no malice, and I quickly joined my master, Pelleter and the other officials in a thorough search of Quicksilver's house. Now you know what happens on such occasions: it's every man for himself. Pelleter was honest, but the rest... Well, you can't blame the lads. The city corporation paid them little and so, if it moved, they took it: candlesticks, pill-holders, whatever. I even saw one stuff a bolster-cover up his jerkin. Benjamin turned a blind eye to this, declaring that if Quicksilver conned the poor people, then everything in this house belonged to them. However, he gave strict instructions that any manuscripts or documents were to be brought to the kitchen. We went back there. Benjamin lay the blood-soaked corpse out on the floor and slit the thick, ornate cuff hiding Quicksilver's right wrist. The scar beneath was a broad, dark purple weal.

'It looks like a sword cut,' Benjamin declared.

I glanced at old Quicksilver's face. 'He was an ugly bugger in life,' I observed, 'and now he's dead.' I covered his face with a rag and glanced at my master. 'Do you really think he's Greene?' I asked. 'The man whom Sir Thomas More mentions as being responsible for the Princes' murder?'

'I think so,' Benjamin replied. 'And that scar proves it. Greene must have been a mere stripling, though ancient in knavery, some forty years ago. He must have had a hand in the death of the Princes.'

Benjamin got to his feet and walked away from the corpse, beckoning me to follow. He closed the door and we sat on the stools. Above us we could hear Pelleter's bailiffs crashing about.

'After 1485,' Benjamin began, 'when the Tudors came to the throne, Greene went into hiding.'

'Yes, yes, that's true,' I replied. 'Quicksilver once told me he had spent many years on the Welsh March.'

'Aye,' Benjamin replied. 'Then he returned to London as Dr Quicksilver. A born charlatan, he took up quackery. His only problem was that scar on his wrist.'

'Do you think he could have been involved in the blackmail?' I asked.

'I doubt it,' Benjamin replied. 'A born rogue, Quicksilver would not wish to excite attention. Which brings us to the intentions and true motives of the men we are hunting.' He ran the nail of his thumb round his lips. 'Sakker is definitely involved. An Oxford-trained clerk, he would know all about the Chancery and how to draft and publish a letter.' Benjamin tapped me on the knee. 'I'm sure your theory is correct. He probably worked in the Tower for a while as Philip Allardyce, clerk of the stores. Somehow he faked his own death, which left him free to run about the city issuing proclamations, killing Undershaft and the rest.'

Benjamin paused, staring into the cold ash in the fire hearth. 'A man like Sakker would love that, cocking a snoot at authority whilst carrying out his own private war against the hangmen who executed his family. But –' he held up a finger – 'the mystery still remains. Who is his accomplice?' Benjamin paused. 'We know Sakker must hate the hangmen, yet, out of fear or some other motive, one of them might be his accomplice.' He sighed. 'Whatever, Sakker seems to move in and out of the Tower as he pleases.' He stood up. 'But come, let's find out what our friends have discovered.'

So far, it transpired, very little, but then old Shallot became involved. One of the great virtues of being a rogue is that you know where people hide things. Oh, the bailiffs had found potion books, elixirs, even a grimoire of black magic, but nothing to prove that

Quicksilver was really Greene, or that he had a hand in any dark deeds at the Tower. Nevertheless, I soon corrected that. You see, people always hide things in the same place: they also believe that their bedchambers are, somehow, the safest place: the receptacle of all their great secrets. (Even my little chaplain here, I know he has been moving my great four-poster! He will find nothing there! I have, over the years, learnt never to hide anything in my bedchamber.)

Quicksilver was not so fortunate. His bedchamber had already been plundered, but I pulled the bed aside. I ignored the bailiffs' sniggers as I failed to find any loose board beneath, and I turned my attention to the bed itself. The headboard and posts proved solid, but I pulled the mattress off and beneath found a secret pocket cleverly sewn into its base. I rummaged about and drew out a sheaf of documents. My master cleared the chamber and took these over to the window to examine. The vellum had turned yellow and greasy with old age and the ink had faded. One was a love letter to Greene, probably from some long-dead doxy. Another was an indenture between Robert Brackenbury, constable of the Tower, and Edward Greene, yeoman; the date was January 1484. The third document was much more exciting: it was a plan of the Tower, or at least its walls, showing all the postern-gates and doors. Benjamin studied this closely and became excited.

'Look, Roger, here! In the wall near the Flint Tower, there's a small water-gate. I am sure this was not on Spurge's map.' He rolled it up. 'We are finished here,' he announced.

He called Pelleter and told him we were leaving, and fairly hustled me out of the house. We hurried down to East Watergate, where we hired a skiff to take us back to the Tower. Once we were there, Benjamin immediately called a council with Kemble, Vetch, Spurge, Mallow and the hangmen. We met in the constable's chamber. Benjamin demanded Spurge's map and spread it out on the table, alongside the faded, greasy one taken from Quicksilver's mattress.

'Study them!' Benjamin exclaimed.

Spurge leaned over the table and did so. 'Where did you get this from?' he asked.

'Never mind! Never mind!' Benjamin replied. 'Tell me, Master Spurge, can you see any difference?'

For a while we sat in silence. No one dared object: Benjamin's face and curt, clipped words being a stark reminder that he was the King's commissioner in this matter and had to be obeyed. We all waited whilst Spurge ran his finger round both maps; taking eye-glasses out of a velvet pouch, he put these on, whispering to himself. Now and again he would glance up anxiously at Benjamin who was sitting opposite.

'They are similar,' he muttered. 'Except—'

'Except what?' Benjamin snapped.

'Here, near the Flint Tower, there's a small water-gate I have never seen before.' He glanced anxiously up at the constable. 'Nor was it on the maps I saw when I came here.'

Kemble just shook his head. Benjamin cut any discussion short and we all accompanied him down to Tower Green. After a great deal of searching, we found the water-gate carefully concealed by long grass and bushes which sprouted along the wall on either side of Flint Tower. The gate, or small portal, was no more than three foot high, built in the base of the wall. Nevertheless, despite it being hidden, Benjamin could lift the latch easily, open it, and look down to where the green slime of the moat gently swirled backwards and forwards.

'The gate's been used,' Benjamin said. 'The hinges and lock are all greased and oiled to make no sound.' He crouched down and peered across the moat. 'Somewhere, in the reeds on the far side, I am sure we will find

211

a small, flat boat which could be poled across in the darkness.'

'That could be done very easily,' Vetch interrupted. 'There are few guards on the ramparts above; we did not believe there was any gate or entrance here to guard.'

'Nor can it be seen from the other side,' Snakeroot spoke up.

We all looked at him expectantly. 'Well,' he stammered, 'across the moat is a good place to take a doxy. I have never seen the gate.'

The others chorused their agreement. Benjamin listened, then opening the gates, slipped through. We waited a while, then heard a knock on the gate. We reopened it and Benjamin, his coat all covered with mud and slime, stood there grinning from ear to ear.

'If you go out,' he said, 'you'll find gorse and bushes growing along the muddy bank, on this side of the Tower. It's quite simple: when the person left or entered, they pulled the vegetation across, so from the far side of the moat, all you saw were bushes and gorse growing at the base of the wall. Whilst this side was hidden by the same device.' He straightened up, shaking the mud from his gown. 'Philip Allardyce was clerk to the stores?' he inquired.

His question was directed to the constable, who nodded quickly.

'And who hired him?' Benjamin continued.

'Why?' Kemble replied.

'Master Constable, the Allardyce who came here was really Robert Sakker!'

'Well, Master Daunbey, I did.' Kemble stuttered. 'I thought he was who he claimed to be.'

'But why him?'

Kemble's face broke into a grin. 'Because no less a person than your beloved uncle, Cardinal Wolsey, recommended him.'

212

Chapter 13

Now it was not often in my life I saw Benjamin lost for words, but he was as dumbstruck as myself. For a while he stood and gaped at Kemble before walking back on to the green. I followed, and Kemble caught up with us.

'It's true what I say,' he declared. 'Master Daunbey –' he stared round at the rest – 'come with me.'

We returned to his chamber. Benjamin slumped on to a stool at the huge oval table, whilst Kemble went to rummage amongst coffers and chests. Vetch, Spurge, Mallow and the other hangmen came in; they were fascinated by Benjamin's revelation.

'I would never have guessed,' Vetch whispered to me. 'He was an amiable soul but rather quiet, kept to himself.'

'He hardly spoke to us,' Mallow trumpeted. 'Really, Master Daunbey, are you saying this Philip Allardyce was really Robert Sakker?'

Benjamin nodded, his eyes never leaving Kemble.

At last the constable gave a cry and came back to the table, a small scroll in his hand. He tossed this to Benjamin who unrolled it. The seal and signature were immediately recognisable:

'Thomas Wolsey, Cardinal, Archbishop, Chancellor, to his faithful servant Sir Edward Kemble, Constable of the Tower, etc.'

The letter then went on to recommend Philip Allardyce, clerk of the stores of Dover Castle, to the vacant clerkship at the Tower. The letter described the fees, robes, etc, which would be his due: it had been sealed eight months earlier by Wolsey's own chancellor.

'It's no forgery,' Benjamin said.

'But if this Sakker could forge letters supposedly from Edward V, why not from Our Lord Cardinal?' Vetch cried.

Benjamin shook his head and tapped the letter. 'I know my own uncle's signature.' He looked up at Kemble, who sat down at the top of the table. 'So this Allardyce arrived eight months ago?'

'Yes, just after the Epiphany. I wasn't here when he arrived. I was away in my manor house, still celebrating Yuletide.'

'So to whom did he present this letter?' Benjamin asked.

'Why to me, sir,' Vetch replied. 'I am the constable's deputy, but I saw nothing amiss.' His smooth face became more worried. 'How was I to know?' His voice rose. 'A young man comes into the Tower armed with a letter from His Excellency the Cardinal, not to mention other documents. I remember it well. I accepted the letter and provided him with quarters.' He shrugged. 'To all intents and purposes, Allardyce was Allardyce, a quiet, industrious, most competent clerk.'

'He did good work.' Spurge spoke up. 'Cataloguing the goods in the stores, making sure that all was in order, never once was he found wanting.'

'Is this true, Sir Edward?' Benjamin asked.

Kemble nodded. 'I had few dealings with him myself. I can add nothing to what has been said. The man calling himself Allardyce was soberly dressed, loyal and obedient.'

'And didn't he talk to any of you?' Benjamin asked. 'Surely there were festivities? He ate and drank?'

'He was very reserved,' Mallow declared.

'What about the King's birthday party?' I asked.

'Don't forget, Master Shallot –' Mallow preened himself at being able to correct me – 'those festivities are intended for the Guild of Hangmen.'

'Bugger that!' I snorted. 'Did he come or didn't he?'

'Yes he did,' Snakeroot sneered, 'but he drank rather deeply early on in the evening, then disappeared.'

I could see Benjamin was bemused, so I whispered that we should withdraw. My master agreed, picking up the letter Kemble had thrown at him; he muttered that no one in the Tower should leave without his permission. We left and returned to our own quarters.

Once we were back in the chamber, Benjamin slammed the door behind him. He sat at the table, head in hands, refusing to answer my flow of questions. At last he sighed and sat back in his chair.

'Do you think, dear Roger, that this could be one of beloved Uncle's tricks?'

'You mean . . .?'

'I mean dear Uncle is not above frightening the King.' Benjamin shook his head. 'No, no, that's unworthy of me.' He drew a deep breath. 'We have constructed a hypothesis, Roger, that Philip Allardyce was really Robert Sakker who feigned his own death to remove him from any suspicion whilst he carried on his wickedness in the city. Now,' Benjamin paused and rubbed his chin, 'what happens if that hypothesis is incorrect? What if Allardyce was who he claimed to be? Died of the plague and his soul's gone to his Maker?' He gazed bleakly at me. 'Can't you see, Roger? I thought that Allardyce's appointment was the work of someone in the Tower but, if it was due to beloved Uncle—'

'It would be known to others,' I snapped. 'Your uncle's Chancery would inform the Tower about who was going to fill the vacancy.'

I recalled that old hunting lodge in the forest on the country road, the clothes burnt in the hearth.

'Master, I believe Sakker was also told this, and that

he trapped Allardyce at Maidstone. He killed him and fled, but not before he exchanged documents. He took your uncle's letter, and anything else Allardyce carried, disguised himself, and turned up at the Tower. And who would be suspicious? Dover's a good journey from London and, if inquiries are made, Sakker could always flee into the city.' I pulled a stool across and sat beside him. 'Master, your uncle's involved in no villainy here. This is too dangerous. The King would have his head. No, Sakker killed Allardyce, took his identity and came to the Tower. As I have said, who'd suspect? Moreover, Sakker's accomplice is also in the Tower and ready to protect him. Once we have unmasked him, we'll catch Sakker.'

'I don't think so,' Benjamin snapped. 'What happens, Roger, if you were Sakker's mysterious accomplice? You now realise that we suspect the truth: Sakker has been unmasked as a wanted felon, not only for the depredations he committed on the Canterbury road, but for the death of the real Allardyce, the murder of the hangmen, as well as treason and blackmail directed against the King.' Benjamin ticked the points off on his fingers.

'Sakker's an impudent rogue,' I interrupted, 'able to slip in and out of places like the mist. He's also a master of disguise. I am sure the veiled woman who turned up to see Master Quicksilver was no less a person than Master Sakker himself. I think he's got the impertinence to brazen this matter through.'

'In which case, Roger, I ask you again: what would you do if you were Sakker's accomplice?'

I paused, staring at the light streaming through the arrow-slit windows.

'He's different,' I said. 'He's safe as long as the mask drawn over his villainy is not torn away. He knows we are scuttling about like mice in the dark. You do realise that, Master? Never once have we found any evidence to lay against the people we've just left in Kemble's chamber.'

'So?' Benjamin persisted. 'Where's the weakness?'

'Well, we could stumble on something.' I smiled. 'Or we could catch Sakker!'

'Let's press the matter further, Roger,' Benjamin declared. 'What happens if this secret accomplice thinks likewise, that Sakker is more of a danger than an asset, and that he must be killed. But Sakker is a very dangerous man. What would you do?'

'I'd probably invite him to meet me, not in the city but somewhere near the Tower, perhaps a little further up-river on the wild wastes along the bank of the Thames.'

'And he'll do it tonight,' Benjamin cursed under his breath. 'I regret revealing that secret entrance.' He grabbed his cloak. 'We'd best go!'

We left the Wakefield Tower. Benjamin first decided to visit Ragusa. We found her sprawled out on a bed of rough sacking. At first I thought she was dead: Benjamin crouched down, wrinkled his nose at the smell of ale, and slapped her gently on the face. The old woman simply smacked her lips, moaning quietly in her sleep. I felt her hands, they were ice-cold, the fingers stiff and gnarled.

'It's what I thought,' Benjamin muttered, 'Ragusa couldn't feel the pulse of any man.' He got to his feet, shaking his head. 'I still think it's Spurge,' he remarked absentmindedly. 'He must have known about that secret postern-gate and, somehow, smuggled a corpse through to dupe this old woman.'

We left Ragusa in her drunken stupor and went down to the quayside to hire a wherry to take us further up-river. Ah well, I admit I've been on many a goose chase, and this was no different. The two boatmen were most reluctant, loudly complaining about where we wished to go. The north bank of the Thames west of the Tower is lonely and deserted, the reeds growing long and lush.

The only sound to be heard in that place are the cries of the many birds who came to nest and feed there. Benjamin paid them another coin, told them to stop complaining and row us along the riverbank. The wherry-men agreed and bent over their oars. In a short while I became aware of the stillness: how quickly the noise and stench of the city had faded. At last Benjamin told the boatmen to take us to a shabby, rough-hewn jetty. We clambered ashore, walked up, and stared out across the wild gorse. In the fading light I could see the occasional farmhouse and small copse of trees.

'We're mistaken, Master,' I whispered. 'There's no one here.'

Benjamin tapped the scabbard of his dagger. 'The assassin in the Tower is going to strike,' he declared. 'I know he is. He won't go into the city, he can't be seen. If it's Spurge, or one of the hangmen, he *must* silence Sakker. I thought he would do it here.'

'Would Sakker be so stupid?' I asked him. 'He's a quick-witted rogue. He'd realise the danger of being invited to come to a place like this.' I gestured at the barren wasteland. 'Even a poor labourer wouldn't come here to sleep!'

'Oh, Lord save us, Roger, I've made a mistake!' Benjamin cried suddenly, pulling me by the sleeve, and hurrying back along the jetty, almost throwing me into the wherry. 'I forgot about the workmen in the Tower. We might find Sakker amongst them.'

We arrived back just as the sun was beginning to set. The labourers and stonemasons were putting away their tools in battered canvas bags, shouting and joking with each other. Benjamin strode across, demanding to see the master mason whom he'd spoken to previously. He was indistinguishable from the rest, covered in a fine white dust. At first he was reluctant to stay, wiping dry lips on the back of his hand.

'Master,' he moaned, 'I've done my day's work. I like my ale as much as any man.'

'A moment,' Benjamin replied soothingly. He led the mason away from the rest. 'Who hired those labourers?' Benjamin asked.

'Well, I did, that's one of the duties of a master mason.'

'And you know them all?'

'No, I hired them at St Paul's. I know most of them, good workers.'

'Are any of them missing?' Benjamin asked.

The fellow was about to shake his head and move away, then he held up a dusty hand. 'Ah, Ealdred is!'

'Ealdred?' Benjamin asked.

'I don't know where he came from,' the fellow replied. 'We moved into the Tower, after the sweating sickness. We put up the scaffolding and began to work: one day this tall, hulking fellow appeared, dressed in rags, hair and beard covered in dust. We asked him where he came from. He said he worked as a labourer in the Tower all the time. Master Spurge the surveyor had ordered him to join us. He carried some writ.' The fellow shrugged. 'I didn't have to pay him, and he proved to be a good worker.'

'All the time?' I asked.

'Well, no, sometimes he'd disappear. Yet, when he was here, he worked like a stoat, up and down the scaffolding like a monkey.'

'Sakker!' Benjamin hissed.

'Who?' The master mason asked.

'I don't suppose the man Ealdred is here now?'

'No.' The master mason shook his head. 'Yesterday afternoon was the last time I saw him.'

Benjamin thanked him and hurried away, shouting for Vetch.

'I want the guard turned out!' my master explained. 'I want every able-bodied man in the garrison out here on the green.'

Vetch was about to protest. My master plucked the Cardinal's warrant from his wallet and shoved it in his face.

'What's this? What's this?' Kemble came hurrying out of the royal apartments, Spurge trailing behind him.

'I want a search of the Tower,' Benjamin declared. 'I want every rubbish and midden-heap, every nook and cranny scrutinised.' Benjamin gazed steadily at Spurge. 'We are looking for the corpse of Robert Sakker: a born actor, a master of disguise known to some people as the clerk in the stores Philip Allardyce, and to others as the labourer Ealdred.'

Spurge stared back, slack-jawed. Benjamin pointed across to where the labourers were standing, intrigued by the excitement my master was causing.

'Oh, for the Lord's sake!' Kemble snapped. 'Are you saying this Sakker, having left the Tower faking his own death, had the impudence to return as the labourer Ealdred? Surely he would be recognised?'

Benjamin stared up at the sky, where the great ravens were cawing raucously at being disturbed.

'This Tower,' Benjamin murmured, 'is a narrow, straight place, full of doors and entrances, secret gullies and dark alleyways. Master Constable, it would be easy for a man to slip in and out, particularly if he changed the colour of his hair, or the way he walks, or his voice.' Benjamin pointed across to where the masons were now shuffling down towards Lion Gate. 'Could you tell one from the other? Do you ever look, Sir Edward, at a labourer as you would a court lady? To see the colour of his eyes, or the shape of his mouth, the cut of his beard? Master Spurge!' Benjamin beckoned the surveyor over. 'Did you give a labourer, calling himself Ealdred, the right to work on the walls?'

Spurge nodded fearfully. 'He came here when the Tower opened, said he was a mason, ready to work for nothing except his victuals.'

'And you accepted that?'

'Of course,' Spurge stuttered. 'Skilled labour is scarce, the work is done faster. It's not the first time—'

'Aye,' Benjamin interrupted, 'but will your accounts show he was paid?'

Spurge blushed at being caught out in one of his trade's ancient vices; submitting bills for labourers who were not paid a penny.

'Well,' Benjamin glanced at an angry Kemble, 'he was really Sakker!'

And, spinning on his heel, my master walked across the green, which was now thronged with scullions, men-at-arms, even grooms from the stable. They stood, some of them sleepy-eyed, others moaning at being pulled away from their duties. Benjamin went up the steps leading to the great keep. He stopped half-way and, clapping his hands, indicated for them to draw near. He opened his wallet and drew out a pure gold coin. He immediately had everyone's attention.

'Pure gold!' Benjamin shouted. 'A pure gold crown for whoever finds the man I am looking for!'

'Who is?' Vetch shouted.

'A corpse,' Benjamin replied.

'Where could it be?' a soldier shouted.

'Anywhere,' Benjamin replied. 'I don't know what he looks like, how he is dressed, but he is a corpse, freshly killed. This gold crown for the man who finds him. And,' he raised his voice, 'for all those who assist, a shilling to be paid from His Grace the Cardinal's bounty, as well as a hogshead of wine to celebrate!'

I tell you this, if Kemble or Vetch had tried to stop them, a mutiny would have broken out. Everything in the Tower ceased, even old Ragusa came staggering out, recovered from her drunken stupor, to join in this search.

Daylight began to fade, torches were lit and the task continued. Kemble and his officers, snorting with annoyance, retreated to their own quarters. However, just as darkness fell, a soldier, enterprising enough to search amongst a midden-heap, found what we were looking for: a corpse of a man, a crossbow quarrel

221

through the side of his throat. The body had been hidden in the refuse, covered with manure and rotting straw from the stables. Benjamin congratulated the man, handing across the gold piece and distributing coins to others. It was dark in that small corner of the Tower, so Benjamin had the corpse brought out, carried like some ancient warrior, ringed by torchlight, on to the green. Water was brought from the well, the dirt and ordure washed off. Once this was done, Benjamin and I crouched down on either side, oblivious to the people pressing around us.

'Robert Sakker!' Benjamin exclaimed. 'I knew it was he.'

He touched the deep scar which showed clearly through the wet and matted beard. I stared down at the strong, clever face, so serene in death: this villain who had led us a merry dance. I pointed to the dust on his hands.

'Your hypothesis was correct, Master. He worked on the walls.'

'I saw him! I saw him there!' a voice called. A groom pushed his way to the front. 'I glimpsed him on the scaffolding, but why should someone kill a poor labourer?'

I examined the crossbow bolt which had torn a great hole in Sakker's neck, a feathered barb sticking out at one end, the cruel arrow-point on the other. The blood from the wound had now dried and caked around the collar of his fustian tunic.

'He must have been killed some hours ago,' Benjamin whispered. 'Probably earlier in the day, after he had taken care of Dr Quicksilver. We are fortunate,' Benjamin added. 'I'm sure if we hadn't ordered our search, this corpse would have disappeared through that secret postern-gate.' He drew his knife and ripped open the rough clothing. 'Ragusa!' he called.

The old crone came tottering through the crowd.

Benjamin whispered in her ear: she crouched down, pulling back the clothing.

'It's him,' Ragusa muttered, 'Allardyce. But he died of the plague!'

'You are sure?' I asked.

She turned her head, lips curling back like a dog. 'I'm not stupid, just slightly drunk,' she rasped. 'There's a mark on his side: I remember it well.'

'And you wrapped him in a canvas sheeting, did you?'

'Yes, I did, and left him there; then the guards came and collected the body.'

Ragusa wiped the dribble from her mouth and went back into the crowd, muttering and shaking her head. Benjamin distributed more largesse and ordered Sakker's corpse to be taken to the death-house. He and I then walked back to our chamber in Wakefield Tower. For a long time Benjamin just stood looking out through the window. If I asked him a question, he'd shake his head and go back to his meditations. He must have stood there for a good hour. I lay on my bed half asleep, trying to decide in my own mind who the villain could be and what evidence we had.

'You'll stay here.' Benjamin came over and pressed me on my shoulder. 'Stay in this chamber, Roger. It would be very dangerous to wander the Tower alone tonight.'

'And where are you going?' I asked, half propping myself up on one elbow. 'Are we going to arrest Spurge?' I continued. 'He must have known about the secret entrance. He brought the corpse through there so that Ragusa would think it was Allardyce's. He hired Sakker as a labourer. He would also have known when the real Allardyce would be coming here.'

Benjamin put a finger to his lips. 'I'm going to trap a murderer,' he murmured and, grabbing his cloak, was out of the door before I could object or stop him.

I admit I am not very good either at waiting or amusing myself. No doxy, no merry maid to dandle on my knee, no Benjamin to question, no roaring boy with whom to drink the hours away and hear the chimes at midnight. Outside, I heard the sounds of the garrison beginning to die away: doors being slammed, the call of sentries on the ramparts, the occasional song. I began to wonder where Benjamin had gone. I became restless. I decided I was hungry and needed more wine, so I went down to the kitchen. I managed to filch some bread, cheese, apples and a jug of coarse wine. The heavy-eyed cook did not object, and I wandered slowly back to my own chamber. The night sky was like some great dark blanket with small pinpricks of light. The Tower was silent, the peace broken now and again by the occasional barking of a dog or the faint call of the sentries along the ramparts. I knew I was being watched: the hairs on the nape of my neck curled and I thought of all the grim, bloody happenings in that place. Did the ghosts walk, I wondered? Including those of the two young Princes? I reached the Wakefield Tower, slammed the door behind me and climbed the dark, winding steps. I reached the top. My chamber door was closed; I pushed it open and went in. There was no one there, no one lurking behind the arras or under the bed. Yet my uneasiness grew. Like the good dog I am, I knew there was something wrong. Had anybody watched me leave, then come up here to plot some villainy? But what? I went across to the water jug, this was still empty. I checked the bed carefully for a dagger hidden there: some stale bread lay on a platter but, apart from signs that it had been nibbled by a rat, I could detect nothing amiss.

Now the chamber was circular, with arrow-slit windows every few paces. I went around and stared through these, my unease turning to terror.

'Someone came up here,' I whispered.

I had left the door half-open, yet when I had returned it had been firmly shut. Outside, a raven, disturbed from its sleep, suddenly soared up past the window, its black feathery wings flapping like those of the angel of death. I jumped, almost dropping the wine and bread I had brought. What was wrong? No poison, no hidden dagger, no secret assassin! I looked at my bed but couldn't tell whether it had been disturbed or not. I went across and looked at Benjamin's. It was neat and tidy, as it always was. The coverlet was drawn up, except where it had been disturbed by my feeling for some knife in the mattress. I looked at the bolsters and walked slowly backwards. Hadn't Benjamin been sitting on the bed? Weren't the bolsters up against the wall as if he had used them as a rest? And hadn't he thrown something there? I stared round the room. A quilted, tasselled cushion lay in a corner. Had it been there before I left? I took out my sword, a long, evil-looking blade with a wire-mesh guard. I went back to Benjamin's bed. Gingerly using the point of the weapon, I pulled back the coverlet, dragging off one bolster, then the other.

Lord, I screamed, as the viper moved its sleek head, tongue lashing its venom at the person who dared disturb his sleep. Now I have fought rats. I have been chased by wolves, leopards, dogs, and every kind of assassin under the sun. But snakes hold a particular horror for me. I just closed my eyes and lashed out with the sword, chopping down, time and time again. When I opened my eyes, the snake was severed in at least five places, and Benjamin's bed was completely destroyed. I admit I am a coward, and there's nothing like a coward who's narrowly escaped death. I went round that chamber cutting at everything, thrusting my sword through bolsters, blankets, counterpanes, cushions, the straw padding of the two chairs. When I had finished, my arms ached and my body was drenched in sweat. I grabbed the wine jug, sat by a stool near the door, and drank myself stupid. I had eaten little that day, my belly was empty, and within the hour I was as drunk as a bishop. I dimly recall Benjamin returning, his exclamations of surprise at what he found. I remember getting up, solemnly declaiming how Satan had visited me in the form of a snake, before falling into a dead swoon at his feet.

I woke the next morning safe and sound, Benjamin sitting next to me. My mouth was dry as sand, my head thudded like a drum and my stomach heaved. Benjamin asked me to sit up. He fed me water and a rather bitter-sweet gruel.

'I obtained this from Ragusa,' he explained. 'I don't know what's in it, but she claims it's a universal remedy against intoxication.' He fed me like a baby. 'I found the snake,' he grinned. 'Or what was left of it. I told you not to leave.'

'Where did that come from?' I pushed away the horn spoon.

'In the grasslands north of the Tower,' Benjamin replied. 'You could fill a barrel with vipers and adders.' He held up the spoon. 'Ragusa says it will work soon.'

I suddenly felt sick, and headed like a greyhound to the latrines. God knows what was in that potion, yet it proved to be an almost miraculous cure. My head eventually cleared, my stomach settled, even my mouth tasted sweet. I hastily washed, shaved, changed my clothes and, at Benjamin's urging, helped him clean up the chamber.

'There's no real hurry,' he remarked. 'Our meeting with all our acquaintances here in the Tower is not until four o'clock.'

'Four o'clock, Master!' I exclaimed. 'What time is it now?'

'I let you sleep until noon,' Benjamin rejoined.

I finished tidying the room. Benjamin refused to be drawn on where he had been the previous night, but he seemed very pleased with himself. He went back and sat at the table until a bell began to toll and we left for the royal quarters.

I remember the sky was overcast: it had been raining and the breeze was strong and fresh. I stretched till my limbs cracked, and watched as others made their way to the constable's chamber, including Ragusa, hobbling on a stick. Kemble, Vetch and Spurge were waiting for us, chairs had been placed round the table, torches and candles lit, giving the room a ghostly appearance. Mallow and his two hangmen sat at a distance from Ragusa, who squatted on a stool, swaying backwards and forwards. Benjamin and I sat on Kemble's left.

'Well, Master Daunbey –' Kemble drummed his fingers on the table – 'you have brought us here.'

'Yes, Constable, I have,' Benjamin replied quickly. 'I have asked all of you to be present to see the King's justice done.'

And, without a by-your-leave, my master rose and walked round the table. He gently laid his hand on Mallow's shoulder.

'John Mallow, formerly known as John Dighton, henchman of the usurper Richard of York, I arrest you for murder, horrible conspiracy, and treason against Your Sovereign Lord, King Henry the Eighth.'

Well, you could have heard a pin drop. Even old Ragusa seemed to have regained her wits and stared, open-mouthed, at Mallow. He just sat there, lips tight, swallowing quickly.

'You have proof, Master Daunbey?' Kemble asked, his eyes wide in surprise. 'Mallow, a traitor, a murderer!'

'Let me explain. Master Vetch, I would be grateful if you would sit on Mallow's right and hold this.' Benjamin quickly bent down and plucked out Mallow's dagger and threw it down the table.

Vetch hurried to obey.

'Master Mallow,' Spurge squeaked, 'I have known you for some years.' The little surveyor put out his hands. 'For the love of God, tell us this is not true!'

'My name is John Dighton,' Mallow admitted. He rubbed his face in his hands. 'Forty years ago, when I was a mere stripling, I was hired by one of Richard the Third's henchmen. I worked here in the Tower as the body squire to the two Princes.' He gazed across at Benjamin and, from a flicker in his eyes, I knew something was dreadfully wrong. 'After Richard was killed, I fled to the Isles of Scilly. I married, but my wife died. I became involved in a fight and fled back to London, where I became an apprentice hangman.'

'No, no,' Benjamin intervened, 'that's not the full story, Master Mallow. In the chaos following Bosworth, and before you fled the Tower, you found a leather pouch containing the seals of the young king, Edward the Fifth. You took these treasures, keeping them safe and fresh. On your return you became involved with the Sakker gang, particularly Robert, an able but villainous clerk. Whether you were involved with him before the rest of his family were hanged is neither here nor there.' Benjamin played with the ring on his finger. He refused to look at me. 'No one ever explained why Robert was not arrested by Master Pelleter the under-sheriff.' He straightened in his chair. 'Anyway, out of your friendship with Sakker came these horrible conspiracies. A new clerk of the stores had been appointed, a bachelor, a man with little family, Philip Allardyce. You knew when he was coming from Dover and what road he would be travelling. Sakker either followed or was waiting for him. Whatever, Sakker killed Allardyce and took his identity. He then disguised his appearance and came to work here as a competent, industrious clerk of stores.'

Benjamin paused. I stared round at the rest. They all sat, eyes intent on Benjamin, like his pupils back at our manor school outside Ipswich.

'You then developed your treasonable design,' Benjamin continued. 'However, on the night of the King's birthday, a party was held here. God knows what happened. I suspect you and Master Sakker were deep in conversation and your words were overheard.

However, in the poor light, and with all your colleagues being masked and cowled, you could not tell who it was.' Benjamin drew from his pouch the scrap of parchment Mistress Undershaft had given him. He held this up for all to see. 'This is a diagram drawn by one of the dead hangmen. I think it's of a gallery here in the Tower, and marks the room where you and Sakker had your treasonable conversation.'

I hid my own surprise at Benjamin's explanation, and glanced across at the chief hangman; he sat as if carved out of stone.

'Nevertheless,' Benjamin continued, 'this suited Master Sakker. He not only wanted to blackmail the King and become rich, but also to carry out revenge against those who had executed his family. You became his accomplice in this. Sakker was cunning. He knew he could not push Fortune's wheel too quickly. If the hangmen started dying, people might remember him, and inquiries might be made, so once again he faked his death, a victim of the sweating sickness.' Benjamin tapped my arm. 'Master Shallot here has had the same contagion and, with a few chosen herbs, it is easy to simulate.'

'But,' Snakeroot interrupted, 'Ragusa here, she looked after him . . .'

'No, no,' old Ragusa replied. 'You.' She pointed at Benjamin. 'With your narrow face and clever eyes, you have it right. All I did was mop his body.'

'But people visited him,' Spurge interrupted.

'A brief glance,' Benjamin replied. 'Everyone's terrified of the sweating sickness, so they kept their distance.'

'True, true,' Ragusa crooned. 'It's always the way.' She smiled shrewdly across at Benjamin and held up her hands. 'You knew I felt for a death pulse, but with these old, arthritic fingers I can feel very little. He lay sprawled there, eyes half open, so I wrapped him in a sheet and left him.'

229

'And that's where Mallow intervened,' Benjamin declared. 'Mistress Ragusa likes her drink. Sometimes she falls into a stupor, at others she goes wandering round the Tower. Mallow had another corpse ready which he'd brought through that hidden postern-gate. Sakker springs up full of life, this other corpse is wrapped and tied. The guards collect it and it is taken down to the Lion Gate. Sakker was now free. He washed the dye out of his hair and dressed in new clothes, and left the Tower by that secret postern-door. Now he was free to carry out revenge and other villainies. When the sickness was raging at its height, Undershaft was slain, stabbed, garrotted or his head staved in. At the dead of night, his corpse was pushed into the cage at Smithfield, and a blazing fire kindled beneath him.' Benjamin shrugged. 'Who'd care in a city when hundreds are dying every day?'

'But at the same time,' Vetch intervened, 'Sakker was running round the city leaving messages in St Paul's, Westminster or in Cheapside.'

'Precisely,' Benjamin agreed. 'The time was ripe: the city was ravaged by the sickness. His Grace the King was fearful that, if these letters were published abroad, people might see the sickness as God's vengeance on his family's seizure of the throne. At last the sweating sickness ended. The Tower was reopened, and Sakker could come and go as he wished. Sometimes he entered as he left, by that secret doorway overlooking the moat. Mallow would know about that: in his youth he had served here and would know every nook and cranny. At other times, Sakker – the master of disguise – came in as one of the labourers working for the masons on the wall. They never objected. They thought he had been sent by Spurge. And why should he or they object to more help?

'Sakker now has the run of the Tower,' Benjamin went on. 'He can come and go as he pleases, whilst Mallow keeps an eye on what is going on. Sakker followed my companion after he visited you, Mistress Ragusa, and pushed him into the wolf-pit. He'd already trapped Horehound and killed him, put him into a sack and cast him into the Thames. Hellbane, drunk as a sot, was an easy victim, whilst Wormwood, before he was put on the rack, was probably clubbed senseless.' Benjamin spread his hands. 'And that's the evil beauty of this design. Sakker is a labourer, his fair hair covered in dust, dressed in tattered clothes; no one would suspect he was once clerk of the stores. Once he's out of the Tower, Sakker can carry on his villainies in the city, posting proclamations, collecting gold, or baiting us. It was a subtle scheme: Sakker had his vengeance against the hangmen, committed gross impudence against the Crown, and was about to become very rich.' Benjamin pointed across the table. 'You, Master Mallow, as one of the former keepers of the young Princes, knew how our present King is most fearful of any rumours about their whereabouts.'

The chief hangman stirred. 'Where is the proof for all this, Master Daunbey? Some of it is true but—'

'Oh, the proof will come,' Benjamin whispered. 'Suffice it to say that eventually you knew we had discovered Sakker's involvement. You became fearful about your old acquaintance, Greene, now calling himself Dr Quicksilver. Sakker is warned. He visits him in disguise and cuts his throat. He then returns to the Tower. But by now you have decided that Sakker's usefulness is finished. The game is becoming too dangerous and, with the crossbow you keep in your room, you put a bolt through his neck.' Benjamin pushed back his chair. 'John Mallow, the King's torturers will elicit the full truth. I am finished with you. Master Vetch, call the guard! Have him taken away! These matters are finished!'

'You are wrong!' Mallow cried. 'Yes, my name is Dighton, but Sakker was no friend of mine. I found no

231

seals.' He swallowed hard. 'All I wanted was to hide from the past.'

'Enough!' Benjamin retorted. 'The King wanted the villain found and I have done it! Take him away!'

Chapter 14

For a while there was confusion and chaos. Vetch grabbed Mallow and hustled him to the door. The chief hangman protested his innocence even as he was bundled down the corridor. Benjamin went to the doorway.

'In the closest dungeon, Master Vetch!' he called out. 'You are to stay on guard personally and not leave him. Do you understand? He is to be fed and well looked after, and not hurt until the King's pleasure is known.'

The rest of the hangmen, Ragusa trailing behind, also left: the revelations about their master had clearly shaken them.

'Sir Edward, may I borrow some writing implements?' my master asked.

Kemble nodded. Benjamin went across to the desk and wrote two notes which he quickly sealed.

'Master Spurge!'

The surveyor, now eager to please, trotted across. 'You are to take this to the King at Windsor. Commandeer any barge or boat you wish!'

Spurge quickly agreed and, puffed up with his newly conferred importance, hurried from the room. Benjamin turned to the constable.

'Now, Sir Edward, please take this letter to the under-sheriff, Master Pelleter, in Catte Street. Tell him Sakker is dead and the murderer unmasked. I will meet him and his daughter Miranda for supper within the hour.'

Kemble took it without demur and, clasping Benjamin's hand, shook it firmly. 'Master Daunbey, the King will be pleased. You will mention my name?'

'Of course!'

Once Kemble had gone, Benjamin crossed the room and slammed the door behind him.

'Master, is it finished?' I asked.

Benjamin went across and filled two goblets of wine. 'No, Roger, it's only just beginning. Come with me!'

We went out into the deserted gallery. From below we could hear shouts and cries as the news began to spread. Benjamin took me further down the long gallery: we stopped half-way.

'Look at the wall!' my master ordered.

I did so: it was covered by wooden wainscoting or panelling, each square neatly carved in the linen fashion.

'I see a wall covered by wooden panelling,' I exclaimed.

'Now step back, Roger. The light is poor, but study the centre panels.'

I did so, recalling that secret room I had found at Windsor. I kept walking back.

'Do you see anything amiss?' Benjamin asked.

At first I didn't, but then I noticed how some of the panelling was more darkly stained. As I squinted through the gloom, Benjamin moved a torch up against the woodwork.

'Undershaft!' I exclaimed. 'The drawing his wife gave us.' I pointed. 'Look, Master, some of the panels are painted darker than the rest and form the letter "T". What's behind there?' I asked.

'I don't know,' Benjamin replied. 'But I have been outside, and there's a good stretch of masonry between that panelling and the end of the building.'

'A secret chamber?' I asked.

'Perhaps,' Benjamin replied. 'But, before you ask, why we don't break in? There's someone we have to meet.'

234

We went and sat on a window-seat.

Benjamin pointed to the panelling. 'That's what Undershaft saw,' he explained. 'Somewhere in there is a secret lever which releases a hidden door. On the night of the King's birthday party, I suspect Undershaft saw that door being opened. The perpetrator behind all this villainy realised his mistake, but in the gloom he couldn't decide which hangman it was.'

I stared back along the gallery. Benjamin was right. Daylight had faded, only a few torches were lit. It would be difficult to distinguish anyone's features if they were standing at the top of the stairs. At night, it would be nigh impossible, particularly if Undershaft had been dressed in his mask and hood. 'Now Undershaft,' Benjamin continued 'was probably intrigued.' He lowered his voice to a whisper. 'A carpenter by trade, he drew that picture and wondered where the secret lever was concealed. Of course, Undershaft himself had a great deal to hide. He did not want to be caught prying in other men's affairs, so he let the matter be.'

'But the story you told in there, about Sakker being Allardyce and then later disguised as a labourer?'

'Oh, that's true enough,' Benjamin replied. 'Don't forget, Roger, troops from the Tower were used by Pelleter to seize the Sakker gang. I suspect someone sent a warning to Robert and he escaped.' Benjamin rubbed his lips. 'And I wonder what happened to Allardyce's predecessor as clerk of stores? Did he meet with some unfortunate accident? I am sure that if we made inquiries, we would find Allardyce was a bachelor with few friends and no family.' He paused to collect his thoughts. 'Mind you, Allardyce was merely coincidental to the plot. Sooner or later, Sakker would have arrived at the Tower in some guise or other.' Benjamin glanced down the gallery. 'The rest was as I said. Sakker came here as Allardyce. A small mistake was made on the King's birthday, but Sakker didn't mind: he'd already sworn vengeance against the hangmen. Undershaft and the rest were going to die anyway.'

'And did Sakker fake his own death?'

'Oh yes, Ragusa is old, infirm and drunk as a sot. She wouldn't know if a man was alive or dead. Once the body was covered in a sheet, she'd trot off and the exchange was made. Sakker was now free to publish his letters at St Paul's Westminster or Cheapside. He also laid that trail of gunpowder in St Paul's when he seized the gold. He used that secret entrance into the Tower, and his disguise as a labourer, to slip back in to confer with his accomplice, as well as to launch that murderous attack on you, Hellbane and Wormwood. A man of shadows, Master Sakker. A good archer, he would know from his accomplice in the Tower where the real danger lay: that's why he pursued and tried to kill us.'

'But who,' I cried, 'was Sakker's real accomplice?'

'Well, Master Mallow lies under arrest.' Benjamin replied.

'But, we have no real proof against him! Not a shred of evidence. We haven't found the seals or the King's gold!'

'Precisely,' Benjamin replied. 'And that's why we are waiting here.' He heard a sound and tugged at my sleeve. 'And the real villain approaches.'

We tiptoed round a corner, past the panelling and down a passageway. We stood in the shadows, watching that piece of panelling still illuminated by a torch fixed above it. We, of course, were cloaked in darkness. I just prayed the person coming soft-footed along the gallery we'd just left was not some guard or servant. I saw a dark figure enter the pool of light thrown by the torch. The man turned, looking over his shoulder, and then quickly pressed a small button concealed in the woodwork. A panel opened like a small window. The figure put his hand inside and part of the wainscoting came away, swinging back quietly on oiled hinges. The

236

man then took a key out of his pocket, inserted it into the lock, and was pushing the secret door open when Benjamin raced quietly towards him. The man, however, stepped back and looked towards us. I glimpsed a podgy face, a hand going towards his belt, but Benjamin was already on to him, sending him crashing back to the floor.

'Roger, for the love of God help!' he called.

I shook myself from my reverie. I admit, I'd stood gaping there like some ploughboy. (Ah, I see my little chaplain snigger. I quickly rap him across the knuckles with my cane.) I hurried on down. Benjamin lay on top of Sir Edward Kemble, the wind fair knocked out of him. I helped Benjamin to his feet, and we both grasped the constable by the arms.

'I thought you'd return,' Benjamin gasped, trying to catch his breath.

Kemble stared back, his lips moving wordlessly.

'The guards outside are in my pay,' Benjamin explained. 'They were given explicit instructions to tell you that we'd left for the city.'

We bundled the constable through the doorway into the darkness. Benjamin, sword drawn, pushed Kemble away.

'Light the candles and torches, Master Constable. Let's see what this pit contains.'

As Kemble fumbled for his tinder, I became aware of the deathly quiet in that secret chamber. The air was stale and fetid, but something gripped my heart and chilled my soul, as if Death itself had swept into that chamber and was now watching us from the darkness. At first my eyes found it difficult to adjust to the flickering light, whilst the dancing shadows increased my fear. Kemble stood in a corner, arms crossed, staring fearfully at us. I shifted my gaze. Oh, horror upon horror! What a dreadful chamber that was! Now you know old Shallot, I have seen the terrors. I've been

237

pursued by the demon which stalks at midday; but even now, decades later, I still have nightmares about that sinister place. It was shaped in the form of a box, the walls made of brick: no window, no decoration, nothing to ease the eye. The floor was wooden; someone had laid down a very thick woollen carpet but this had begun to decay and rot. A huge beam stood upright in the centre of the room, with hooks driven into it: tattered, dusty, cobwebbed cloths hung there. There was a rickety table, stools and chairs, yet the real horror was the bed partly obscured by the beam. Only when I moved away did I understand my master's gasp of surprise. Oh, heaven forfend! Oh, Lord have pity! The bed was broad, standing on four stout wooden legs, the mattress was covered in dust and huge cobwebs stretched across the headboard. However, in the centre, lying side by side, were the pathetic remains of the two Princes: small skeletons lying together. I walked across and knelt beside the bed, holding the hilt of my sword before me like a cross.

'*O Jesus miserere!*' I muttered.

I have seen the destruction of princes, the end of noble lives at the gibbet or block. Men of power struck down by the assassin's dagger or the poisoner's cup. I have seen palaces in flames and the marble halls of Constantinople flowing in blood. But, nothing can compare to the silent horror of those two pathetic little skeletons still dressed in the tarnished remnants of their former glory. I glimpsed mother-of-pearl on one jerkin, a jewelled dagger beneath the yellowing robes of another. A silver cross hung awry between the ribs, a jewelled bonnet, mildewed and rotten, lay between the two skulls. I stood up and peered closer. Both the jaws slightly sagged. I noticed one had teeth all rotting along the top. God be my witness, I didn't know whether to scream, cry or pray. Instead I took my cloak off and covered them.

'You bastard!' Benjamin walked across to Kemble and

bringing his hand back, gave him a stinging slap across his face. 'You son of Satan! Had you no pity?' Again Benjamin's hand came back, drawing a trickle of blood from Kemble's lips.

The constable's face never changed. Benjamin pushed the constable against the wall and ran his hand over his doublet, looking for some concealed dagger or weapon. He then went across and, taking a stool, jammed it in the door to keep it open.

'Why blame me?' Kemble's voice was soft and slow. 'Did our noble King really want to find his precious Princes?'

'Had you no pity?' Benjamin retorted. 'Did you not think these little boys deserved decent burial?' Benjamin looked round the chamber. 'But now we have our proof: caught red-handed. You cannot disprove my accusations. Sir Edward Kemble, constable of the Tower, and once keeper of the King's royal palace at Woodstock, the same place where Robert Sakker, an Oxford clerk, also worked. Two dark souls who formed a friendship forged with the evil one.'

'Of course,' I interrupted, 'Pelleter told us how Sakker had been a clerk at a royal palace. They were born there?'

'The records will prove my guess,' Benjamin replied. 'And when Kemble came here, he was intrigued by the stories and did his own private search. He gathered all the maps and plans and discovered two things. First, the entrance to the postern-gate over the moat, and secondly his secret chamber. He then destroyed that map and gave Spurge others which did not betray his newly found secrets.' He paused to clear the dust from his throat. 'Spurge drew new maps up, certainly at our constable's behest, and this chamber and the postern-gate became Kemble's secret. He could not confess he'd come here and found a pouch made of the finest leather, fastened at the top, containing the Privy and Great Seal of

Edward the Fifth, who only reigned for a few months.'
Benjamin paused. 'You did find them here, didn't you,
Kemble? Kept in a pouch and probably placed in a
cedarwood casket, they would have stood the passage of
time and been in pristine condition.'

'But how?' I interrupted. 'Why were the seals and the
Princes left here so many years ago?'

'What I suspect,' Benjamin replied, still keeping his
eyes on Kemble, 'is that the Princes were not murdered
by Richard the Third. They were imprisoned here, but
in the summer of 1485, when the King's father landed
at Milford Haven, Richard the Third mustered to meet
him at Bosworth Field. The Princes were hurriedly
moved to this secret chamber, probably under the care
of his henchmen, Dighton and Greene. Now, as Kemble
knows, Richard was desperate for troops and Robert
Brackenbury, then constable of the Tower, took most of
the garrison to meet the King in Leicestershire, thinking
they would be victorious.' Benjamin leaned against the
wooden pillar. 'Of course all went wrong. Richard was
killed, as was Brackenbury, at Bosworth. Any Yorkist
left in the Tower would have fled at the Tudor's
approach, and that included Dighton and Greene.'

'And Mallow is Dighton?'

Benjamin shook his head. 'No, no, that was a little
mummery I concocted last night. I had glimpsed the
panelling before and, remembering Undershaft was a
carpenter, wondered if this had provoked his interest. Of
course, I couldn't break into it without alarming Kemble
here, whom I wished to trap. I went to Mallow and
persuaded him, in return for royal preferment, to act
out the nonsense you witnessed before.'

'So, where is Dighton?'

'Probably dead,' Benjamin replied. 'I suspect the
Princes here may have been poisoned by Greene, whom
we knew as Dr Quicksilver. The room was then locked
and sealed. Greene went into hiding until memory

240

faded and people had forgotten.' He pointed at Kemble. Until this villain appeared. He finds this secret chamber, takes the seals, and begins to plot how to become a very wealthy man. As keeper of the royal palace at Woodstock, he would know of the King's secret fears about anyone with Yorkist blood in them. The visitation of the sweating sickness provided him and Sakker with the ideal opportunity.' Benjamin walked towards the constable. 'You arranged Allardyce's murder at Maidstone: you saw it as a marvellous opportunity to bring Sakker into the Tower. If that hadn't presented itself, you would have found another way. You arranged Sakker's arrival during Yuletide – when you were absent – so no one would ever suspect.' Benjamin tapped Kemble on the chest. 'And where to then, eh? Sakker could not remain Allardyce for ever. Moreover, he wanted his revenge, whilst you desired the King's gold. I'm sure you had a plan, but then the sweating sickness arrived.'

'You must have been the only men in London to have welcomed the sweating sickness,' I scoffed. 'There was no need to close the Tower so completely, but you used your accomplice's so-called sickness to achieve that. It would not be hard for you and Sakker to bring a corpse, filched from somewhere, into the Tower. Your accomplice then walked free to carry on his villainy: you, however, could act the innocent and give the labourer, Ealdred every protection.'

'And what a mystery, eh?' Benjamin intervened. 'Where could the seals have been obtained from? Were the Princes really alive? How could the villain both be in the Tower to deliver the first letter, yet also in the city, issuing proclamations? Of course, you realised the King would intervene but, being constable, you knew exactly what was going to happen. You continued to use Sakker's disguise and that secret postern-gate to deepen the mystery: the attack on Shallot, the delivery of

241

blackmailing letters, the murders of the hangmen, the collection of the gold. On each occasion, you could account for your movements. How alarmed you must have been when we began to suspect that Sakker was involved. You used him for one last murder, the charlatan Quicksilver. After that, all you had to do was sit quiet and secure.'

Benjamin seized the unresisting Kemble by his jerkin, pushing him against the wall. 'How you must have chuckled when I arrested Mallow! What were you going to do, Sir Edward? Wait until the dust had settled, then taken up your new appointment as envoy to Brussels? You did tell us you were giving up your office to go there. But you intended only to slip away with your new-found wealth.'

Kemble opened his mouth to protest. Benjamin pushed him again.

'Now all that remains, Sir Edward, is the gold. Where is it?'

The constable, in some kind of stupor, licked his lips. I followed his quick glance and saw an old coffer peeping out of the shadows in a corner. I went across: the lock was new. I prised it loose with my dagger and drew back the lid. Inside was a roll of parchment, the best vellum money could buy, inkpots, quills, and a large sack which clinked as I moved it.

'The King's gold!' I exclaimed.

There was a second sack made of very thick leather, tied securely at the top. I cut this. Inside were two seals: one the size of a tennis ball, the Great Seal of King Edward V, the other his Privy Seal. I took these under the light and examined them. They were pristine, fresh, as if carved yesterday.

'Keep them, Roger.' Benjamin drew his dagger and pressed its point into the fleshy part of Kemble's neck. 'You killed Sakker in that lonely corner of the Tower: you placed that viper in our chamber. You are as evil as Satan, but you shall pay for your crimes and your mistakes.' He pushed Kemble out of the door.

I stopped to douse the candles and torchlights. I took one last, lingering look at that dreadful bed, and closed the secret door. I pushed the wainscoting back until it fell into place with a click, and followed my master along the gallery, down the stairs to the Tower Green.

Ah well, the rest is bits and pieces. Vetch was summoned. Benjamin ordered Mallow's release, the chief hangman joined us in the gatehouse where Benjamin was ordering astonished guards to place chains on Kemble's wrists and ankles. The chief hangman shuffled his feet with pleasure as Benjamin promised him more gold, as well as a letter of pardon for any offences he may have committed. Mallow was also instructed to inform the others, Benjamin promising that more silver would be left for them to celebrate. He turned to Vetch, who stood like a man pole-axed, and once again explained how he had trapped Kemble.

'The Tower is yours, Vetch. Master Shallot here needs ten good guards, the best you have. The prisoner is to be taken immediately to Windsor. I have other business in the city.'

I must admit I was surprised as anyone by that, and the old demon jealousy returned: I realised Benjamin was going to the Pelleters to celebrate with the marvellous Miranda. Oh well, that's old Shallot's luck! Night had fallen, but Benjamin insisted the prisoner be taken, so I had no choice. Whilst Benjamin went to bask in Miranda's golden smile, ten of the strongest rogues the Tower could muster rowed a silently weeping Kemble to his judgement at Windsor.

The night journey was long and cold, and by the time I arrived at Court, I was drunk from the wineskin I carried. The Great Beast and his familiar, the silk-garbed Cardinal, were waiting. With Kemble kneeling before me, I simply described what had happened and how we had trapped him. Oh yes, I was angry at Benjamin, so I emphasised my role even more. The King did not waste words on Kemble. He stepped down from his throne and kicked him in the face, and smiled as the guards took him away.

Within the week Kemble had been hanged, drawn and quartered. One part of his body was displayed on Windsor Castle, another at York, one quarter at Winchester, whilst the rest, with his head, were impaled above the Lion Gatehouse at the Tower. I spent days at Windsor being fawned on by Henry as if I were his pet dog. Purses of gold, silk jackets, velveteen boots, the swiftest horse in the stables, the right to draw rents from certain tenements in Suffolk. He patted my hair, and those piggy eyes would glare at me as he tweaked my cheek.

'Good dog, Shallot,' he growled. 'Sharp as a lurcher. Would you like to go hunting, Roger?'

Of course, I declined the offer, and the Great Beast bellowed with laughter. (Oh, by the way, he took the gold and destroyed the seals. As for that secret chamber and its grisly contents, he said it was the Princes' grave and so it should remain.) The Cardinal was more reserved. One night at supper I caught him watching me with those black, cunning eyes; it was then that he decided to become my friend and not just my patron. The following day he took me for a walk in the castle gardens, pointed out how the roses always reached full bloom in early autumn, whilst the small apple and pear trees, their branches now bowed, promised a succulent harvest. He talked about affairs of State and the death of Pope Adrian VI and, for the first time ever, I plotted as well as the rest. No one could hear. Dr Agrippa was God knows where, and I, Roger Shallot, the most base-born of rogues, became Wolsey's confidant. Two days later I left Windsor for London. I found Benjamin in the

Tower, busy studying a book on alchemy he'd found in the library. I told him about my reception at Windsor, the King's applause and munificence. Benjamin smiled and hugged me.

'And dearest Uncle?' he asked.

I drew from my doublet a sealed letter. 'What does it say, Roger?'

'Master,' I lied, 'I don't know, but His Excellency instructed me not to be present when you read it.'

I left him and went for a walk on Tower Green. Somehow, that dreadful fortress had lost its horror. Children played on the mangonel and catapults, soldiers' wives chattered and sang as they washed clothes over great open vats. Ragusa passed me, swaying like a leaf in the wind. Vetch and Spurge were sunning themselves on a bench, revelling in their new authority. Even the great ravens seemed more friendly, hopping towards me looking for morsels. I stared up at the sky, counted again to a hundred, then returned to our chamber.

Benjamin was sitting, beaming from ear to ear. My heart lurched. Had the Cardinal, I wondered, followed my advice?

'Good news, Master?'

'Roger, congratulate me.' He got up. 'Uncle wishes me a lead an embassy to Rome for the election of the new pope.'

'Oh, Master,' I cried, 'to see Italy again, the glories of Rome!'

Benjamin's face fell. 'Roger, I am sorry, dearest Uncle has said I must go alone: you are to remain in England for other duties.'

Well, even old Burbage could not have acted like I did. I slumped down on the bed, face in hands. Benjamin came and sat next to me, putting an arm round my shoulder. I looked up, the tears rolling down my cheeks.

'Doesn't he trust me, Master?' I cried. 'Doesn't he think I'm good enough to be his envoy?'

'Tush, tush, Roger! Dearest Uncle writes that he can spare one but not both of us. Someone has to look after the manor.' He touched me under the chin. 'And someone has to care for Miranda.'

I put my face in my hands: the trap had closed.

Ah well, what does old Macbeth say? 'Time is a fool and all our dusty yesterdays . . .' My little chaplain is looking at me expectantly. Aren't I going to tell him about Miranda, my beloved first wife? How could I marry the betrothed of my great friend? Well, he'll have to wait, won't he? That's another story. The sun is beginning to dip. The shadows are becoming longer. Old Shallot grows cold but, back in my bedchamber, Margot and Phoebe are heating the wine.

Author's Note

Once again, Shallot may not be telling such exotic tales. In Thomas More's *History of Richard III*, he claims that the Princes' corpses were buried under certain steps near the Great Keep. However, an account published by L. A. Du Maurier in 1680, from a manuscript translation of the Delaval, said that Prince Maurice of Naussau, Prince of Orange, had been told by Queen Elizabeth of a sealed, walled-up chamber in the Tower which contained the skeletons of the children of Edward IV. This story is repeated in Audrey Williamson's excellent book *The Mystery of the Princes*, published by Alan Sutton, 1990.

If you enjoyed this book here is a selection of other bestselling titles from Headline

THE DEMON ARCHER	Paul Doherty	£5.99	☐
JANE AND THE GENIUS OF THE PLACE	Stephanie Barron	£5.99	☐
PAST POISONS	Ed. Maxim Jakubowski	£5.99	☐
SQUIRE THROWLEIGH'S HEIR	Michael Jecks	£5.99	☐
THE COMPLAINT OF THE DOVE	Hannah March	£5.99	☐
THE FOXES OF WARWICK	Edward Marston	£5.99	☐
BEDFORD SQUARE	Anne Perry	£5.99	☐
THE GERMANICUS MOSAIC	Rosemary Rowe	£5.99	☐
THE CONCUBINE'S TATTOO	Laura Joh Rowland	£5.99	☐
THE WEAVER'S INHERITANCE	Kate Sedley	£5.99	☐
SEARCH THE DARK	Charles Todd	£5.99	☐
THE MONK WHO VANISHED	Peter Tremayne	£5.99	☐

Headline books are available at your local bookshop or newsagent. Alternatively, books can be ordered direct from the publisher. Just tick the titles you want and fill in the form below. Prices and availability subject to change without notice.

Buy four books from the selection above and get free postage and packaging and delivery within 48 hours. Just send a cheque or postal order made payable to Bookpoint Ltd to the value of the total cover price of the four books. Alternatively, if you wish to buy fewer than four books the following postage and packaging applies:

UK and BFPO £4.30 for one book; £6.30 for two books; £8.30 for three books.

Overseas and Eire: £4.80 for one book; £7.10 for 2 or 3 books (surface mail).

Please enclose a cheque or postal order made payable to *Bookpoint Limited*, and send to: Headline Publishing Ltd, 39 Milton Park, Abingdon, OXON OX14 4TD, UK.
Email Address: orders@bookpoint.co.uk

If you would prefer to pay by credit card, our call team would be delighted to take your order by telephone. Our direct line is 01235 400 414 (lines open 9.00 am–6.00 pm Monday to Saturday 24 hour message answering service). Alternatively you can send a fax on 01235 400 454.

Name ....

Address ....

....

....

If you would prefer to pay by credit card, please complete:
Please debit my Visa/Access/Diner's Card/American Express (delete as applicable) card number:

Signature .... Expiry Date..............